VENOM

PRODIGIUM ACADEMY BOOK THREE

KATIE MAY

EXPRESSO PUBLISHING, LLC

To everyone who has been told time and time again that you'll never be good enough. You are. Hang in there, and ignore the haters.

CONTENTS

FOREWORD

This is a paranormal academy reverse harem romance and is not suitable for anyone under the age of 18. There is strong language throughout the book, as well as sexual situations. This series also contains light MM themes. Put this book down if such material offends you. Of if you're related to me.

RECAP

Previously on Prodigium Academy...

Violet Dracula and her men compete to win the Roaring, a series of dangerous games that put monsters in life or death situations. During the second game, Violet is transported to a room with her father, Vladimir Dracula, and Dimitri Gray. She is told that she is actually the daughter of Lucifer Morningstar and Hera, but Hera begged Dracula to look after Violet when she was born in order to hide her from Lucifer, who believes her to be dead. The room explodes, Dracula is stabbed in the heart, and Medusa, Mason's mother, kidnaps Violet.

Elsewhere, Cal murders Alex's father, and Jack and Hux begin acting weird and disappear after the second game.

Characters:
Violet Dracula - Dracula's clumsy, eccentric daughter. She is revealed to be the mate of Frankie, Mason, Vin, Hux, and Jack. At the end of book two, you discover she's actually the biological daughter of Hera and Lucifer.

Vin - a Van Helsing, sworn to protect humanity from

monsters (particularly vampires) at all costs. He's originally rude and an asshole to Violet before he repents. His twin sister is Vanessa. He's one of Violet's mates.

Mason - the son of Medusa and a Fairy Blossom addict. He becomes Violet's first friend at the academy. He's one of Violet's mates.

Frankie - a cold man who is only passionate about his work...until he meets Violet. He is one of Frankenstein's experiments and also one of Violet's mates.

Hux - the alter-ego of Jack. He's slightly psychotic and already desperately in love with Violet. At the end of book two, he and Jack mysteriously disappear after attempting to blow up Violet and Cal with a grenade. He's one of Violet's mates.

Jack - the kinder alter-ego of Hux. He is more level-headed than his brother and refuses to use swear words or resort to violence. At the end of book two, he and Hux mysteriously disappear after attempting to blow up Violet and Cal with a grenade. He's one of Violet's mates.

Dimitri Gray - once a professor but now the headmaster of Prodigium Academy. He's a stone-cold assassin who has been looking after Violet since she first arrived at the academy. He knows the truth about her lineage.

Cal - otherwise known as Cupid. He's half-fairy and half-incubus. After helping supernaturals find their fated mates, the monster council forced him into detention, where he developed a relationship with Barret. At the end of book two, he turns dark and brutally murders Alex's father, believing the man to be responsible for Barret's death.

Barret - otherwise known as the Boogeyman. He's forced to remain in the upper levels of the school for a crime he committed. He's currently in a relationship with Cal and is close friends with Violet. Near the end of book two, he fakes his death with the help of Alex in order to save Violet's life. Because of that, Cal goes crazy and kills a man.

Cheryl - Vin's ex-girlfriend, who's desperate to win him back. She cheated on him with Mason, which broke off their relationship. She is the daughter of the Loch Ness Monster and also Violet's sworn enemy.

Vanessa - Vin's twin sister and a fellow hunter. She's Violet's best friend.

Cynthia - Violet's old roommate who found her fated mate, Pete the Pumpkin. She's a banshee and the Woman in White.

Dracula - Violet's father and the leader of all vampires. He is the most hated and feared monster in the entire world. At the end of book two, he was stabbed in the heart with a god-blessed dagger.

Alex - a transfer to the school and a necromancer. He hates vampires with a passion and seeks to make Violet's life a living hell.

Stefan Van Helsing - Vin's father and a feared monster hunter who targets vampires.

CHAPTER 1

VIN

I pace angrily, my stomach muscles clenching more intensely by the second.

Mason, beside me, releases a huff of agitation, his hands shaking by his sides. I have no idea if it's because of the stress of losing Violet or because he hasn't been able to have a hit in a few hours.

Probably a combination of both.

We stand in the living room of our shared house, Mason leaning against the far wall, me pacing, and Frankie sitting stoically in the armchair.

Round two of the Roaring completed less than an hour ago, but none of us can muster up even a shred of excitement or enthusiasm.

Violet Dracula, our fated mate, is...gone. Disappeared. The only saving grace is that we can sense through the innate bond that connects us that she's still alive, still breathing.

But what happened to her? One second, she was stepping

through the doorway designed to lead her to her own escape room, and the next…

"We need to find Dimitri," I snarl, spinning around to face the others. A lump the size of coal takes up residence in my chest when I realize that we're not only missing Violet, but Hux and Jack as well. But I can't focus on that—or how strange their behavior had been when they stepped out of their own portal. Not until I have Violet safe in my arms and I know with unwavering certainty that she's okay.

"Dimitri." Mason's brows furrow together as he peers up at me. I note that the skin under his eyes is violet with exhaustion and that he has nasty-looking cuts and burns on his arms. Still, I don't bother to suggest that he heads to the nurse station. I imagine his response to that would be the same as my own if the situations were reversed.

"He's the headmaster," Frankie reasons, sounding uncharacteristically tired. That's another thing that has changed since Violet came into our lives. While before, I would only consider Frankie an acquaintance and roommate, I now classify him as a close friend of mine. His aloof exterior is gradually melting away, revealing the vulnerable man underneath.

The man who, for all intents and purposes, is just as obsessed with Violet as we are.

"And he helped set up the games," I point out, crossing my arms over my chest to hide the way my hands tremble. Fuck, where is Violet? What might be happening to her right now?

My mind conjures up images from when she was attacked on her date with Frankie, the way those vampire haters carved horrible words into the flesh of her arm. My heart stutters and gets caught in my throat as a blinding rage crashes over me, drowning me in its intensity.

"We need to talk to Alex and Cheryl," I grit out, trying to ignore the dark and insidious entity that slithers through me like a ten-foot python. "Alex is the head of the Anti-Vampire Resistance."

The same cloying darkness I feel inside of myself materializes in Frankie's eyes as he sits up.

"You think they have something to do with this?" He scratches at his chin absently before focusing on me with laser-sharp eyes. "How could they have done that? Alex and Cheryl both competed in round two. They wouldn't have had time to do anything to Violet."

"That doesn't mean they don't know who did," Mason points out. His hand twitches once more, and rage burns through my chest.

"Are you going to be okay to help us look for Violet?" I snap. I know I'm being a jackass, but I'm honestly past the point of caring.

Something akin to hurt flashes in his eyes, there and gone faster than a shooting bullet. It's almost immediately replaced by rage. "Fuck off, Vin," he hisses. "At least I'm not embarrassed of her."

A growl rumbles through my body as I take a threatening step in his direction. "What the fuck is that supposed to mean?"

He pushes himself off the wall, his movements almost sluggish, and stalks forward until he's directly in front of me, his eyes white-hot. "I actually told my family about her." His words are like a garrote cutting into my neck until I'm dripping blood. I try to hide my involuntary flinch at his words. "Yet your entire family seems to think you're still dating Cheryl fucking Ness. Why is that, Vinny Poo?" His entire face twists with disgust when he says the nickname my ex had given me. "Are you embarrassed of your mate?"

"Fuck off," I seethe. Dark red dots distort my vision as I try my hardest not to grab the nearest knife and stab it into his neck. "You know it's not safe for my family to know."

As a Van Helsing, my sole focus is to kill any and all vampires, regardless of their crimes.

And to discover that my fated mate and the love of my existence is not just a vampire but Dracula's fucking daughter? That's a kick to the nuts if I ever felt one.

"For her or for you?" Mason taunts, and another growl is ripped from my throat. Before I can stop myself, I shove at his shoulders, watching with grim satisfaction when he staggers slightly, his customary gray beanie becoming askew.

"Guys," Frankie drawls from where he still sits on the armchair.

"I'll do anything to protect my mate!" I hiss. "Even if that means keeping her a secret."

"Oh, please. You're just using that as an excuse. Just admit you're embarrassed of her." Mason takes another step closer until we're toe to toe. This close, I can see that his pupils are dilated and red streaks bleed into the whites of his eyes. Fuck. He's going through goddamn withdrawals, today of all fucking days. "Or maybe you actually don't care about Violet. Maybe you want to be with Cheryl and—"

"Enough!"

Frankie's voice slashes at my skin like a leather whip, and the anger curling through my veins dissolves.

We're acting like fucking children when we need to get our shit together. Mason isn't the enemy. He's just…

He's my best friend, suffering from withdrawals and worrying about our mate. I can't fault him for that, not when I'm feeling the exact same way. Without Violet here to ground me, I fear my world will implode at any second and I'll be helpless to survive the blast.

Mason seems to be on the same wavelength as me, because he instantly settles back on his heels, his shoulders slumping downward as a pitiful, despondent expression clouds his face.

"Fuck, you're right. You're right." He scrubs a hand down his right cheek. "I'm sorry, man." He doesn't lift his head up to stare at me, but I know his words are sincere.

"Me too," I confess. "I'm just…"

"Freaking the fuck out?" he finishes for me, finally lifting his head to quirk an eyebrow. I try to smile, but it feels wrong on my face.

What is there to smile about when my mate is missing, enduring God knows what?

"That's an understatement."

I don't know if I'll even be able to breathe correctly until I have Violet Dracula in my arms. I'm so fucking dependent on her that it's almost surreal. What happened to me? I used to be a fierce monster hunter, the defender of the innocents, the police officer in charge of keeping unruly beasts in line. And now…

Now I revolve around a tiny slip of a girl with golden-blonde hair, a penchant for pink clothes, a broad smile on her face, and a laugh capable of turning even the fiercest of monsters into puddles of goo.

"We need a plan," Frankie continues curtly, rising to his feet and moving to stand beside us. He crosses his arms over his chest, one of the only indications that he's not as stoic and aloof as he would like us to believe. His black glasses slide down his nose, but for once, he doesn't lift a finger to push them back into place.

Oh shit.

Frankie's spiraling.

When have I ever seen the man with crooked glasses?

"Vin, go find Alex and Cheryl. See if you can get information out of them. If the vampire haters have Violet, they'll know," Frankie instructs, turning to pierce me with that ice-cold gaze of his. I nod once, feeling surprisingly better now that there's something I can do, someone I can maim. Or kill.

Or torture. Or all of the above. "Mason," Frankie turns to face Medusa's son, "I want you to look for Cal, Barret, Hux, and Jack. They care about Violet too, and the more people we have looking for her, the better we'll be." A muscle ticks in Mason's jaw, but otherwise, his face remains unreadable. He nods once.

"What will you do?" I ask Frankie, and the man slowly begins to smile.

It's not a nice one.

"I'm going to pay our headmaster a visit," he says darkly. "If anyone knows what happened to Violet, it'll be him."

WE SEPARATE IMMEDIATELY AFTER, MASON HEADING DOWN toward the stadium to see if he can find Barret, Cal, or Hux/Jack. Frankie turns in the direction of the academic building and headmaster's office. And I confront a far scarier monster than all of them combined.

My psychopathic ex-girlfriend.

Moving briskly through the crowd of irritable monsters, I search for the familiar shock of orange-red hair and blue skin. No surprise, I find the she-devil seconds later, her hand wrapped possessively around Alex's forearm.

The necromancer glances up first, his dark eyes appearing black in the setting sun, before looking away with a sneer distorting his features.

My hands ball into fists before I can stop myself, and it takes every inch of self-control I possess not to pound them into his face. The only thing that stops me is the appearance of my parents standing a little bit away from the others, chatting idly amongst themselves. Vanessa, my twin sister, is beside them, and when she sees me and the thunderous expression on my face, her brows knit together. I subtly shake my head to tell her that now isn't the time for her to ask.

"Vinny Poo." Cheryl's voice immediately scratches at my skin like rusty nails, and I wince instinctively. How did I ever find her attractive? Right now, she's so fucking abhorrent that I want to gouge my own eyes out. Maybe I'm only just now seeing her for who she truly is—a swamp monster who crawled out from beneath its bridge for its annual sacrifice of small children.

"We need to talk," I bark out as soon as I'm in front of them, gesturing for them to follow me. Alex gives me a dismissive once-over, his eyes jet-black, but doesn't make a move to come with me.

"What do you want to talk about, my love? Finally get sick of your vampire whore?" Cheryl asks coyly, fluttering her lashes as if she means to entice and entrap me. I just barely hold in my snort.

Not even Alex wants anything to do with her, and he's just as disgusting as she is.

"Oh, crawl back into the hole you came from, you disgusting cockroach," I hiss, and she gasps, placing one hand over her heart in horror.

"Vincent!" She stares at me as if I grew a second head, as if she's legitimately surprised that I had the balls to badmouth her. Well, I suppose you can say my balls have always been there, thank you very much. They're so freaking huge that—

Stop thinking about your balls, Vin.

"Alex," Cheryl whines, forcing my attention back onto her. "Are you going to let him talk to me like this?" She pushes her bottom lip out into a pout and once again places a manicured hand on his arm. With a grimace of disgust, Alex shakes her off of him and stealthily steps away. Cheryl's pout deepens, oddly resembling that of a constipated puppy, and I feel a flash of sympathy for her.

But only a flash.

The rest of me knows that Cheryl is a forked tongue snake.

"What do you want, Van Helsing?" Alex finally asks, spinning to face me fully.

Alex.

Fucking Alex.

He arrived at the school for the sole purpose of competing in the Roaring and immediately made Violet's life hell. He implemented restrictions on the feeding rooms in the cafeteria using brute force, and because of that, Violet can't drink blood there. He more than likely had a hand in the death of all of the human donors. He made Violet shit her fucking pants in the middle of the cafeteria. And now…

Now he's staring at me with a sly smirk on his lips, as if he hasn't got a care in the world. It makes me want to lunge forward and rip his head clear off his shoulders. I wonder if Cheryl would still find him attractive with his head smooshed beneath my foot like a fucking pumpkin.

"Where the fuck is Violet?" I lower my voice to a whisper so as to not be overheard by any of the monsters nearby. There's no one in the immediate vicinity, but that doesn't matter when it comes to creatures like us. Anyone could have enhanced hearing, and you'd be none the wiser.

Alex's brows pull low over glowering eyes, and I swear I see a flicker of surprise and worry in his gaze. "She didn't finish the second round?"

"Don't play dumb with me," I spit out. The hold on my rage is tenuous at best, and any second, it's going to shoot out of me like a motherfucking geyser. "If you had something to do with her disappearance—"

"I swear to you, I have no idea what you're talking about." Alex holds his hands up in the air placatingly as that same spark of worry I noted earlier makes a reappearance in his pitch-black gaze. "I don't know what happened to her. Do you think she…?" He swallows heavily, but I'm already shaking my head before he can even finish his ridiculous question.

"No. She's not dead." I thump at my chest, emotion coiling through my heart like barbed wire. "I would feel it."

"How the fuck would you feel it?" Cheryl demands. I nearly forgot she was there. Lurking. A demon in human flesh. I wonder who's guarding the gates of Hell if she's here?

I don't bother gifting her a response, keeping my gaze fixed on Alex's. The piercing in his right eyebrow glints in the waning sunlight as he scrunches his brows together and frowns.

"Do you think something happened to her?" he asks at last.

I stare at him intently, searching for any sign that he's being insincere or lying to my face. When I don't detect anything besides shock, I turn on my heel and stalk away.

"Vin!" he bellows after me. "Dammit, Vin! What the fuck happened?"

I don't answer him.

If he doesn't know where Violet is, then he's no help to me at all.

And if he does know…

A grim smile carves itself into my face as I move toward the academic building, hoping I'll be able to catch up with Frankie before he can confront Dimitri Gray.

If Alex does know what happened to Violet, I'll cut him into tiny pieces and feed him to the ravens. No one's allowed to harm a single hair on Violet's head without facing my wrath.

I may be human, but my soul is as dark as any monster's.

And this monster?

It's on the hunt for blood.

CHAPTER 2

"**J**ack! Come out, come out wherever you are!" I holler, cupping my mouth with my hands. When I receive no response, I switch up my approach. "Hux, your precious treasure is experiencing her Great Period. She needs chocolate, stat!"

Nothing. Dammit. I really thought that one would work.

I stand in the center of the cafeteria, surveying the sea of students and visiting monsters. I don't see Jack/Hux, Cal, or Barret anywhere.

Where in the world would three of the most terrifying monsters wander off to?

I squint my eyes, hoping that'll allow me to see better, as a violent tremor rushes through my body. Every muscle tightens, almost as if I'd been shot by a bolt of lightning, and my hands begin to shake by my sides.

Fuck. Fuck. Fuck.

I need a puff of Fairy Blossom before I explode. The need

claws at my chest, so keen and intense that it's impossible to ignore.

Unbidden, my eyes snap to Lyle the Scarecrow—the new dealer of Fairy Blossom now that Mikey has met his untimely demise. The man's sitting at a table with some of the other monsters, laughing at something Manny the Mannequin says.

It'll take me five seconds to go over there. Three seconds to ask for some Fairy Blossom. Maybe a minute to roll it up and smoke—

A shock of dark hair moves toward the feeding rooms the vampires use, down a hall connected to the cafeteria. I'd recognize that wicked scar anywhere.

Hux.

But when has Hux ever put his hair in a douchey-looking man bun?

Is he trying to be hip? Trying to get with the times? As soon as we find Violet, I'll have her tell him that douchey man buns are *not* in style. I'd tell him myself if I didn't truly believe that he'd rip off all my toenails, string me from the wall by my ankles, and slice methodically at my arms with a toothbrush to watch me bleed out.

Yup. Not today, Satan. Not today.

Now, where the fuck is he even going? Does he know something I don't about Violet's location? Is that why he's headed to the feeding rooms?

My curiosity piquing, I hurry in the direction Hux/Jack disappeared down.

I open doors at random, unsurprised to find monsters of all types fucking, before opening the very last door at the end of the hall.

"What the fuck?" I bellow when I set eyes upon the sight before me.

Hux/Jack stands on the opposite end of the room from

me, but he isn't alone. A pretty, blonde-haired monster leans against the wall in front of him, her face flushed and her lips parted. One of Hux/Jack's hands is placed directly beside her head as he whispers in her ear, too low for me to hear. As I watch, horrified and disgusted, he leans forward to nip at her earlobe. The girl gives a nervous giggle, her eyes flicking toward me. The lust in them is plain for anyone with eyes to see.

As quickly as the horror comes, it dissipates, replaced by white-hot, soul-crushing anger.

How fucking dare he?!?

"How could you?" I seethe, lunging forward. My hands ball into fists so tight, they almost conceal how shaky they are. Almost. "How could you do that to Violet?" I swing a punch at his smug, scarred face, but he merely moves to the side with a deceptively light laugh. The girl screams and stumbles to the side, her eyes wide with alarm.

"Mason, is it?" the man inquires, and I pause in my pursuit, tilting my head to the side. That voice…

It isn't Hux's or Jack's.

There's a distinct Irish lilt to it that neither of my friends possess. And that cadence…

I didn't think it was possible to hear such malice dripping from his tongue, poisoning his words.

One thing becomes painstakingly clear—this isn't Hux nor Jack.

"Who the fuck are you?" I demand as the intruder wearing my friend's face throws back his head in hearty laughter.

"You're smarter than you look," he taunts, a wicked grin pulling up lips that I now know with unwavering certainty do not belong to either Hux or Jack. It's too cruel, too cunning, and it looks odd on his face. "But I don't think my name matters."

Before I can respond, his arm bands around the girl's waist and he pulls her flush against his chest. A tiny mewl escapes her as he begins to finger the strap of her tank top.

I can't tell what type of monster she is, but from the fur coating both of her arms, I would guess some sort of were-wolf. Maybe a Chewbacca?

The man wearing Hux/Jack's face pulls down her strap enough for her tit to spill out, and he wastes no time cupping it in his hand, running his thumb over her nipple. He lowers his head so he can kiss up and down her neck, all the while maintaining eye contact with me.

Another surge of rage courses through me.

Logically, I know that the man touching the girl isn't one of Violet's mates, but it doesn't completely dampen the urge I have to rip his hand off for cheating on her.

"So you're not Hux or Jack," I continue, keeping my eyes on his despite the show he's attempting to put on. "But you're in their body."

"My body," he singsongs, lifting his head from the woman's neck. He pulls down her second strap to free her other tit, and I ignore the anger threatening to drown me. "Though I'm assuming Jack and Hux didn't tell anyone about me…" A wry, almost self-deprecating grin pulls up his lips. "The third brother."

"The third…" My mouth drops open. What the fuck? "You're their brother?"

"The one and only."

Before I can wrap my head around that—wrap my head around anything, really—the man brings his hands to the woman's throat and gives it a single twist. She falls to the ground, lifeless.

"What the fuck?" I bellow, dropping to my knees and feeling for her pulse. I already know she's dead—there's no way her head can be backward unless she has some poltergeist blood in her—but come the fuck on! We don't just murder other monsters here. The punishment for murder outside of the Roaring is death, and since this fucker is in the body of two of my best friends, I can't allow that to happen.

"Oh damn," the man laments in a droll voice. "My hands slipped."

I jump to my feet, trying to ignore how unsteady the motion makes me, and take a threatening step closer.

"You killed that woman."

"That monster," the man corrects, his lips curling away from his teeth. I can't quite tell if it's a smile or a grimace. Either way, it looks all sorts of wrong and fucked up. "Did you know she had vampire blood inside of her?"

"She had…" Horror submerges in a bucket of ice-cold water. All I can do is gape at this man with wide, unseeing eyes. "You killed her because she was part vampire?"

A strand of black hair falls free from his bun as he cocks his head to the side. His eyes—eyes that are usually always warm as Jack and confused as Hux—are now chips of granite. Hard, cold, and utterly unforgettable. The expression distorting his face isn't that of my two closest friends—it's the face of a stranger.

"Vampires are scum and deserve to be eradicated from this Earth," he hisses, his Irish accent making those hateful words sound almost amusing. Or that could be the withdrawals fucking with my head.

"How can you…? How…?" I struggle to articulate one of the many thoughts tangling together like knotted yarn in my brain. How can this man wear the face of Jack and Hux and want to kill vampires when the woman they love is one? How could Jack and Hux have allowed this to happen? Where are they?

"Close your mouth, mate." He gives my chin a condescending tap as he steps over the body and toward the door.

"Who the fuck are you?" I bellow, spinning to watch him retreat. He pauses at the door, looking like a high and mighty douche with that goddamn man bun, before smiling.

"You may call me Balor," he answers. And with that, he steps out the door and allows it to swing shut.

Leaving me behind with the half-naked, dead body, a mind that's struggling to piece itself together due to the withdrawals, and hands that shake way too much to be of any help.

Fuck.

CHAPTER 3

FRANKIE

I've always considered myself an impartial observer. I don't allow myself to get involved with the inner workings of Prodigium Academy, and I refuse to create emotional attachments. As a scientist, that impartiality is paramount. Fundamental even. If you allow pesky emotions to get in the way, then it's almost impossible to accomplish anything.

But with Violet?

I feel a shit ton of emotions, most of which I don't want to look at too closely. Observing them means accepting them, and while I decided I wanted to pursue a relationship with Violet—even acknowledged the fact that she's my mate —I don't want to think about what this means for me.

It's too terrifying to comprehend.

All of these thoughts reverberate through my head like my brain is some fucking rainmaker as I move through the academic building, toward Dimitri Gray's office. I have no idea if he's in there, but I'm willing to bet that he retired here after the game ended. Where else would the surly bastard be?

I don't bother knocking as I bypass the front desk, currently empty, and step into his office painted in cold, monochromatic shades. The curtains are drawn, giving the room a desolate feel, and besides a simple computer on his desk, it's empty.

I stand in the doorway, feeling uncharacteristically lost and confused. My entire plan hinged on being able to confront our headmaster about Violet's location, but to see his office empty…

He's probably somewhere else on campus, I tell myself curtly, already preparing to go classroom to classroom in order to find him. *You just need patience.*

Patience. I've been patient for years. The perfect experiment. The perfect son. The perfect being. My entire life revolved around that one insignificant word—patience. You needed to be patient if you wanted to be great. It's something my creator, Frankenstein, instilled in me from a young age.

I remember being a boy and creating a corrosive mixture in his lab. It was one of the first times he allowed me to experiment with him. As I tried to pour the ammonia into the beaker, my creator stopped me, placing a hand on my shoulder.

"Slowly, Frankie," he'd said, his red hair sticking out in all directions, embodying the look of a mad scientist. "Slow and patient."

His words had stuck with me, even to this day.

Isn't there even a saying about that?

Slow and steady wins the race.

But just now, I don't want to be patient or slow or even steady. I want the world to burn, because without Violet, it feels like my own is imploding.

Indecision wars within me as I hesitate in the doorway, my eyes scanning over every available surface.

I could potentially hack into Dimitri's computer and see what he has on his hard drive. I doubt the infamous assassin will have anything of value, but you can never be too sure. If I get caught, however, I'll face immediate expulsion.

I don't know who I am if I don't have my lab, if I don't have math books and homework assignments and science experiments. My world has revolved around my schooling for many, many years, and the prospect of losing all of it has me feeling oddly bereft and empty.

But then I think of Violet and her sheet of golden curls. The glimmer of defiance that always seems to spark in her eyes. The way her luscious lips curl upward into a smile, as if she's in the midst of telling a joke with no punchline. I'm pretty sure the entirety of Violet's life is a joke with no punchline.

A tiny smile dances on my face at the thought, and without preamble, I move around the desk and slide into Dimitri's leather chair. I quickly power up his computer, and immediately, a box materializes, demanding his password.

If I were a renowned serial killer, what would my password be?

I push my glasses up with the pad of my middle finger as I think through options. I don't know much about Dimitri Gray—no doubt his own doing—but I do know his father is Dorian Gray. And what is that legend concerning Dorian Gray? Something about paintings and mirrors?

I sift through my vague memories of his legend before typing in both words. 'Password failed' appears in bright red letters on the screen.

Think, Frankie. Think! Violet's depending on you. Use your big brain for something that actually matters.

Wait…

Chewing on my lower lip, I type in 'Violet.' Like before, 'password failed' flashes on the screen, and I just barely resist the urge to growl like a caveman.

My fingers tap against the top of his desk as I think through everything I know about Dimitri. The only thing I know with unwavering certainty is that he's as obsessed with Violet Dracula as I am.

I type in 'VioletDracula.'

This time, the computer flashes white, unveiling his home screen.

Bingo.

Footsteps just outside the office entrance draw my attention away from Dimitri's computer. I glance in both directions, desperate for a place to hide, before dropping out of the chair and onto my knees, crawling beneath the desk. Just in time, because a second later, the door to the office opens with an audible creak.

Is this Dimitri returning from the games? Someone else?

As an experiment with no blood, lungs, or heart, I don't need to breathe, but breathing has become so reflexive to me over the years that it's difficult to remain silent. My mechanical lungs quite literally burn in protest, which is impossible because they're nothing but machinery and parts.

Footsteps sound directly beside me, moving toward my hiding place. I hold myself perfectly still, my lips compressing into a thin line...

"What the fuck are you doing?" Vin exclaims from where he stands over me, his arms folded over his chest and a scowl plastered on his face.

"Um...preparing to give Dimitri oral?" I say in an expressionless voice, and his mouth actually pops open. Without another word, I crawl out of my hiding space and move to my feet, attempting to look graceful and dignified.

"Was that...?" Vin cocks his head to the side curiously. "Was that a joke?"

"Yes. Did it make you laugh?" I ask in a dead voice, once again reclaiming my seat in front of the computer.

A surprised bark of laughter escapes Vin before he can help himself. When he realizes what he just did, he quickly masks his amusement with a scowl.

"No."

"I've been told I can be quite tantalizing," I continue, sorting through Dimitri's files. Most of them concern the school's staff, but I don't rule them out as irrelevant immediately.

Vin makes a face as he moves toward the filing cabinet. He opens it up and begins sifting through the papers. "Don't say tantalizing. People these days don't say..." He trails off with a shudder. "They don't say 'tantalizing.'"

"We're not people," I point out as I begin to go through Dimitri's personal emails. "We're monsters."

"You are just full of jokes today," Vin deadpans as he grabs a manila file and rips it open. "Did someone upgrade your programming?"

"It's very rude to make an abnormality feel like an abnormality."

I pause when I find an email with the subject Dracula. Is this about Violet? I click on it immediately, my eyes scanning the words on the screen.

"Shit, man." Vin turns to face me, appearing stunned. "I didn't mean to offend you."

"I know." My eyes narrow on the email as I continue reading. "I was just joking."

"Errr..." Out of the corner of my vision, I watch Vin shake his head with a perplexed expression on his face. After a moment, he shoves the folder back into the filing cabinet, grabs another one, and scowls. "I take it you couldn't find Dimitri."

"And I take it that your meeting with Alex and Cheryl didn't go well?"

"Understatement." He blows out a breath. "I honestly don't think they have any idea where Violet is. Maybe…" His shoulders bunch up, practically reaching his ears. "I mean, is it possible that Violet just wasn't able to complete round two of the Roaring? Maybe there isn't some malevolent scheme. She could be just in another location with some of the other monsters who lost."

"I don't think so…" I trail off as I finish the email. "Look at this."

Vin sets down the file he's been holding and stalks behind me, placing one hand on the back of the chair. "What am I looking…? Oh my god." He hisses out a breath through his teeth as he reads through the same email I just found.

"Why would Dracula want to meet up with Dimitri Gray?" I query, more to myself than to the Van Helsing behind me. "How do they even know each other?"

"They both won the Roaring a few years back," Vin points out, though he doesn't sound convinced. "Maybe it has something to do with that."

"*Dimitri,*" I read, "*we need to meet. Urgent. About her. Vlad.*" I pause to place a finger under my chin in contemplation. "The 'her' obviously refers to Violet."

"Vladimir Dracula wouldn't be dumb enough to communicate through email about something that important." Vin shakes his head rapidly.

"No," I agree, "but the email also didn't state a time or a location. Maybe Dimitri called Vlad once he got the email?"

"But that doesn't help us," Vin says, sounding irritated. "We don't have Dimitri's phone. Can we see how many other emails have been sent between the two?"

I nod and begin to sort through all of the emails, marking any that might be of importance. "Here's one dated when Violet first arrived at the academy." I clear my throat once before reading. *"Waz up, homie. It's your homeboy Vlad. The fruit of my looms has made a nest in your sugar swamp. Woot. Woot."*

"Basically, Dracula is telling Dimitri that Violet's on campus," Vin translates, because apparently, I can't speak crazy, immortal vampire.

"But why would Dimitri care?" I counter. "Does this have something to do with the Roaring?"

"I don't know." Vin's jaw tenses as he grits his teeth together, a fierce and thunderous expression crossing his face. "But I swear to you, I'll find out. If Vladimir Dracula has secretly been working with Dimitri Gray..."

"It means that Violet's in way more shit than we initially suspected," I finish for him, swallowing. Curse emotions. I swear my artificial heart is pumping erratically, wanting to break free of my rib cage and crawl up my throat. What has this girl done to me? And why do I love it so damn much?

"We'll find her, Frankie." Vin gives my shoulder a quick, reassuring squeeze. "And when we do, we're never letting her out of our damn sight again."

CHAPTER 4

VIOLET

I've always wanted to see Mount Olympus. What little monster didn't? It was the land in the sky, where immense castles rested on fluffy white clouds. A world away from worlds. A place of ethereal beauty and elegance.

But as we step out of the portal, I feel nothing but icy numbness.

My father…

Is dead.

Vladimir Dracula, the fiercest monster of all creation, has been killed by a god-blessed dagger to his heart. And don't even get me started on Dimitri Gray, the headmaster of Prodigium Academy with a wicked tongue that does wonders to my pussy. The last time I saw him, he'd been unconscious, his chest rising and falling steadily as blood gushed from a wound on his head.

And then, I'd been taken.

Two guards dressed entirely in black hold my arms as we follow behind Medusa. Mason's mother.

She's exactly how I pictured the gorgon to be.

A silver dress, sparkling around her as if the stars had been plucked straight out of the sky and sewn together, cascades around her ankles with every step she takes. She's abnormally tall for a woman with a face I might've described as beautiful and elegant if it hadn't been twisted into a scowl. Her plush, ruby-red lips harden when she glances over her shoulder at me, the snakes on her head yipping and hissing.

I lower my head immediately to avoid making eye contact with any of those ferocious beasts. The legend about Medusa is true—if you stare too long into the snakes' eyes, you'll turn to stone.

My mind still reels with everything Dimitri and my father just told me.

I'm not Dracula's biological daughter. Hell, I'm not even a vampire. I'm…

Half goddess and half devil.

Literally.

My father is the king of Hell himself, Lucifer, and my mother is Hera. According to Dracula, Lucifer tried to kill my mother when he discovered she was pregnant with me. We both lived, but Lucifer became convinced that he terminated the pregnancy. Hera begged Dracula to watch over me and raise me as his own. He agreed, implanting false memories into my head of a mother who'd passed away due to a drug overdose.

Dracula is a strange man—he once went into the grocery store, stole all the shopping carts, and then organized a shopping cart race at his manor—but he's my father, blood or not, and I know he loves me unconditionally.

Well, *was* my father.

Pain consumes me when I think about his sightless eyes. That pain quickly distorts into white-hot anger directed at the woman currently gliding gracefully in front of me. Mason's mom or not, she has to pay for what she did.

Monsters aren't supposed to feel strong emotions. Don't ask me why—it's just the unspoken rule in the monster world. Pain, grief, love…it's immensely rare for any creature of the night to experience them.

Yet I've experienced all three in a span of hours. There's that soul-crushing pain I experienced as the world exploded in a kaleidoscope of bright colors, swatches of orange, red, and yellow. The pain I felt when I twisted my head and saw my father's dead, vacant eyes and the god-blessed dagger sticking out of his chest. Then, there's the grief. So much fucking grief, I'm afraid I'll drown in its torrent. My father's dead, murdered by my lover's mother.

And then…then there's the love. Love for my father, for my mates, for everyone who has remained beside me when shit hit the metaphorical fan—and the literal fan. A vampire hater once tried to throw extremely toxic basilisk crap at me, but he missed and it hit the ceiling fan instead.

"Why are you doing this?" I ask now, hurling daggers with my eyes at Medusa's long, slender neck. The snakes rise in agitation, their hisses growing in intensity, but I refuse to be cowed.

"We need to talk, young Violet," she says without turning back and meeting my eyes.

"Fuck you and your talks," I seethe, and the guard holding me on the right gives my arm a reprimanding shake. "Oh, knock it off." I whip my head around to level him with a vitriol-filled stare, my tone haughty and caustic. "You're nothing but a whipping boy for—holy shit."

My eyes practically pop out of my head as the wispy, pearlescent clouds transform into a fucking kingdom. A kingdom in the literal clouds.

In the middle of pink, glittering clouds, a mammoth cluster of walkways, spires, and turrets hover a few millimeters in the air. I can't tell what the buildings are constructed out of, but if I had to guess, I would say some sort of…holy brick. No, I'm not pulling your leg. I've never seen crystal stone that can shimmer before, the walls reflecting the bright, penetrating sunlight. At the front of the city, a long bridge—appearing to be hewn from pure gold—extends, stretching over thousands of miles of open air. If you fall over the bridge, I have no doubt you'll fall to your death on the ground below. The godlike power the entire city emits is insurmountable, and a trickle of appreciation and awe joins the unease already present.

"Welcome to the City of Olympus," the guard beside me says, the respect and wonder in his voice plain to hear.

The city is fucking gorgeous, unlike anything I've ever laid eyes on before.

Out loud, I murmur, "Eh, it's okay. My bathroom's prettier, especially after I take a nasty shit."

Point one—Violet.

Medusa releases a rather unladylike scoff as she begins to cross the bridge, one of her hands drifting over the gold railing. I follow behind her at a much slower pace, intentionally dragging my feet so the guards are forced to practically carry me.

Some might argue that this is a point for my monster-in-law. Wrong.

Ya home girl Violet doesn't feel like walking, thank you very much.

"Why did you murder my dad?" I call to Medusa as the guards lift me into the air, each of them grabbing an arm and hefting it upward so my legs kick helplessly behind me. "The monster world is going to make you pay for what you did,

Medusa." Venom coats my words, a promise of retribution and revenge for what she took from me.

We monsters are nothing if not predictable. And when someone harms us or a member of our family, we retaliate with guns blazing.

"Silence, child," Medusa barks dismissively, stepping off the bridge and into the heart of the city.

It's even more beautiful up close, the giant castle surrounded by pink, silvery huts, previously dwarfed by distance, and each with flat roofs. The streets are paved with the same shimmery material that the bridge was made out of, though the color appears to be white instead of gold.

We walk forward in absolute silence. Not even a bird caws.

There are no people, no monsters, no gods or goddesses. It's just...empty. Doors are hanging open, squeaking on their hinges, and I see an outdoor table with uneaten food on top of it. It almost reminds me of those apocalyptic movies where everything is left behind in the state of an evacuation.

"Where is everyone?" I whisper subduedly, barely breathing.

Predictably, Medusa doesn't answer, but I notice her back and shoulders stiffen almost imperceptibly. I have no idea if it's because of my question or because she too is bombarded by the same sense of danger and wrongness that I am, but either way, I don't speak again until we step through the bright, ten-foot-tall doors leading into the palace.

Everything is...sparkly. The interior of the palace appears as if a teenage girl's magazine vomited over the entire room. Shades of light pink and white permeate every available surface, all of them coated with an undefinable, sparkly glow.

Surprisingly enough, we don't have to walk through any hallways to enter the throne room. We literally step through the front door…and voila! A single throne rests against the far wall of the room, nearly twice the size of me in height. It, too, is colored in shades of silver, white, pink, and gold, giving it an oddly feminine flare, considering the man sitting on top of it.

I've never seen him in person before, but his harsh, chiseled features make him unmistakable. Thick black hair hangs in waves around his face, merging with the prominent beard on his chin. His eyes are sharp and keen, surveying me with an astute intensity. He tilts his head to the side, a vein in his neck bulging, but doesn't speak as I'm guided directly in front of his throne and forced to my knees. A ruby-red robe provides the only color in this monotonous room, a size too small for his bulging figure.

Zeus.

The Zeus.

Oh my god.

I'm dead.

Yup. It was nice knowing you, world. Adios, amigos. This is the last you'll see of Violet motherfucking Dracula. Zeus will whip me with a lightning bolt—and not in the way I might like—and then strangle me to death—again, not in the way I'd like.

I can already see my gravestone—*here lies Violet Dracula, the most perfect specimen who ever walked the Earth. She's so fucking perfect and beautiful, that all other monsters should be in awe of her. She'll be remembered by her many, many loved ones, because how could she not? She's so freaking awesome. And have you seen her tits? Best. Tits. Ever. Rest in peace.*

Yeah, it's a pretty big gravestone.

Zeus doesn't speak as he surveys me with cold, clinical intensity. Medusa moves to stand beside me, one of her claw-like talons digging into my shoulder. I bite my lip to contain the threats that want to bubble up.

The last thing I want them to know is that they rattled me. Destroyed me. If they understood what Dracula's death did to me, then they'll have leverage…and I can't allow that to happen.

Zeus leans forward slowly, resting his elbow on his knee, as I meet his stare with a defiant one of my own.

And then, he laughs.

Fucking guffaws as if I'm on stage at a comedy club and just told the funniest joke ever—spoiler alert, I'm not funny. I'm super freaking serious, and I want to stab him in the eye for murdering my father and hurting Dimitri.

Laugh it up, asshole. Laugh. It. Up.

"Does someone want to tell me what the fuck is going on?" I bark as he holds his stomach, tears rolling down his eyes.

Medusa's lips purse.

"She's a hoot!" Zeus says through his laughter, wiping at a wayward tear that has escaped. "Do you like video games, Violet?" His laughter stops as abruptly as it began, and he once more tilts his head to the side, regarding me with unwavering intensity.

"Um…" The fuck? "Yes?"

No. I haven't played a video game in my life. I tried to play a vampire game with Dracula once, but after my character got killed for the fiftieth time in the span of an hour, my father snapped my neck and stormed out of the room complaining I was "shit at life."

Thoughts of Dracula have my throat closing with emotion.

Fuck, is he truly dead? Is there a way he could've survived a god-blessed dagger to the heart? Why did Medusa do that to him?

And why am I here?

Do they know the truth about my heritage?

"Come." Zeus stands, towering over me in a blur of bright red. He has to be at least eight feet tall, his entire body hewn from pure muscle. "We will play video games and talk."

Um…okay?

CHAPTER 5

"They have, um, video games in the clouds? In Mount Olympus?" I query as I follow Zeus through a door near the back of the throne room. The two guards from earlier still flank me, and Medusa follows a short distance behind, huffing and puffing like the Big Bad Wolf... but with snakes on her head. The Big Bad Snake? Nah, that sounds too sexual.

The Big Bad Snake Girl?

Maybe?

The Big Bad—

"In here," Zeus instructs, opening up the door at the end of the hall.

When I don't immediately enter, fear making my feet immobile, the large god releases a heavy sigh and stares at me with barely veiled annoyance.

"Do you not trust me, little Dracula?"

"Errr..." My brain struggles to play catch up as my heart hammers a mile a minute. "I don't trust anyone, if you must know. I see a therapist about it though! Apparently, you can only be murdered so many times before you start to develop trust issues. Not that I've actually been murdered, mind you, because as you can see, I'm still here and alive. But people try to kill me all the time. Just the other day, Bloody Mary's son pretended to be my friend and then tried to assassinate me. It's a real issue."

When in doubt, ramble until the person's eyes roll into the back of their head and they tune you out. Lifehack number one.

"Yes, yes, I imagine that's an issue," Zeus says dismissively, opening up the door wider. Once again, I don't make a move to enter—for all I know, it could be the chamber of death and pain—and Medusa hisses behind me.

"For Pete's sake…" she snaps, shoving past me to enter the room. Biting on my lower lip, I venture a tentative step forward. Just one.

And then I think about the burning need for revenge, for vengeance, and I stalk the rest of the way into the room like a shark on the hunt for fresh blood.

When I catch a glimpse of my surroundings, I'm dumb-founded.

"It's…a game room." I blink rapidly.

"What did you expect?" Zeus huffs, shouldering past me to enter as well. The door slams shut behind him, leaving the two guards on the other side.

Okay, Zeus and Medusa in here.

At least two guards out there.

Escaping will be *such* a bitch.

"I told you I wanted to play video games," Zeus continues, sounding oddly petulant as he throws himself into a bean bag in front of a flat-screen TV. Yup, you heard me right. The head honcho of gods, the god of all gods, is casually reclining in a bean bag as if he isn't the most feared creature in the entire world.

The room itself reminds me of a bachelor pad back on Earth. A black leather couch rests in the center of the room, with two bean bags directly in front of it. They all face a sixty-inch flat screen that is hooked up to apparently every video game device.

I even see a motherfucking PlayStation. Not a PlayStation 2 or 3 or 4. Nope, a legit PlayStation from the prehistoric days. Who even has one anymore?

He grabs a controller for one of the devices and hands it to me before grabbing one for himself. He then fires up the game and reclines indolently in the bean bag.

"Can someone please tell me what the fuck is going on?" I move to perch on the sofa, the controller dangling from my fingertips as I struggle to wrap my head around…all of this. "You guys killed my father—"

"You have to choose an avatar," Zeus interrupts.

I blink at him. "…the fuck?"

"You have to choose an avatar." The large, domineering man nods toward the screen, where the game is requiring me to choose a character to play.

"Oh um." I click a person at random—a man with a bright red mohawk, leather pants, and a tattoo sleeve.

Zeus's lips purse as if he'd just swallowed a sour lemon. "You don't want to be him."

"Why the fuck not?" I'm about twenty seconds away from throwing my controller at his head, consequences be damned. I don't even care that I'd be pissing off one of the most powerful men alive. He murdered my dad, for fuck's sake, or at least had a hand in my father's death. Nothing he says now can change the fact.

"Because," Zeus sighs heavily as if my lack of knowledge is a burden to him, "he can't regenerate health fast enough.

Gimme." He crooks his finger in the come-hither gesture, and I all but throw the remote at him. He smiles, oblivious to my ire, and selects a new character for me—a woman with rainbow-colored hair, tan skin, and a bright pink dress. "There." Seemingly satisfied, he hands me back the remote.

"Crazy ass fucker," I murmur, too low for him to hear.

He almost reminds me of Dracula, what with their eccentricities and—

I shut that shit down before it can fester.

The second I start thinking about Dracula, and I mean truly thinking about him, I'll fall apart. My grief will cut me apart from the inside out until I'm simply a shell of a woman. No, not even a woman. A child, crying for her father.

But I can't allow that to happen. Not now. Not yet. I need to pretend I have my shit together for a few more Zeus-damn minutes. Maybe if I pretend it long enough, it'll actually come true.

"So I suppose you're wondering why we brought you here," Zeus begins conversationally as on the screen, our characters enter a sandy arena. My avatar appears to be carrying some sort of gun, though it's nearly three times the size of her and resting on her shoulder.

"I want to know why you killed—" *Don't fall apart, Violet.* I take a shuddering breath and try again. "I need to know why you killed my father."

Dozens of ninjas materialize on the screen, crawling out of holes in the dirt I hadn't noticed earlier. Two of them rush at me, but I move my character to the side and begin firing off random shots. Hopefully, I'll be able to hit…something.

"Has Mason ever told you about the prophecy?" Medusa begins from behind me, and the controller slips through suddenly numb fingers as I twist to stare at her.

"Prophecy?"

Her lips compress in a thin line. "I take it that he hasn't." Under her breath, she adds, "Foolish boy."

"What prophecy?" My voice comes out high and panicky, but come the fuck on. Can you blame me? I just discovered I'm some weird hybrid of two ruthless monsters and that my father isn't really my father. Not only that, but I watched him die before my very eyes.

I don't think I can handle any more of this shit. Not without a tub of ice cream first.

"There's been two prophecies in the last few months, both concerning you." Medusa sniffs, her eyes narrowing on my face. "And we can't allow them to come to fruition."

"What...what do they say?"

"FUCKING DAMMIT!" Zeus roars from beside me. He throws his controller across the room, causing the plastic to shatter into dozens of small pieces. He whips his head around to glare at me. "YOU NEED TO PAY FUCKING ATTENTION!"

"To the prophecies?" I swallow around the tennis-sized ball currently taking up residence in my throat. "I have been! This is the first time I heard—"

"Not the fucking prophecies," he snaps, seething. "But the MOTHERFUCKING GAME! WE JUST LOST BECAUSE OF YOU, YOU FILTHY BITCH!"

Oh. Um.

Okay then.

Zeus's chest heaves as he stares up at me, red splotches visible on his cheeks behind his beard. Anxiety and fear begin to poke through the numb barrier I resurrected around myself, because to be completely honest, Zeus appears mere seconds from murdering me.

I watch as he exaggeratedly breathes in and then exhales, the tension seeming to drain out of his shoulders. I can't help but think that his breathing is too...modulated, as if he's consciously remembering that he needs to breathe in and breathe out, breathe in, breathe out.

Maybe if I sit really still and pretend I'm not here…

"It's all right," Zeus says after a full minute of complete silence. "You didn't know." With a wave of his hand, the controller flies off the floor, reassembles itself, and lands in his hand. My mouth practically drops open at the sheer power he exudes—power I've never felt before in one single entity.

"Now, can we continue with the conversation?" Medusa demands, irritated.

"Yes, yes." Zeus waves his hand in the air dismissively, and the strangest thought occurs to me.

This man…

This god is technically my step-father. I mean, he *is* married to Hera, my bio mom.

Well…shit. I don't know if that's absolutely terrifying or pretty damn cool.

Then I remember that he had a hand to play in my true father's death, and any awe is eclipsed by murderous rage. Yup. Definitely not 'cool.'

"Why did you murder my father?" I demand as I refocus on the game. Once again, I have no idea what I'm doing. Once again, I run around in circles and pray I don't die—a parallel to my own life, if I'm being honest. Once again, I shoot my big ass gun at random, praying I hit the bad guys.

"We didn't murder your father."

Medusa's words don't penetrate the numbness in my brain at first. They're not even a blip on my radar. And then…

And then I get fucking mad.

I drop the controller onto the couch and swivel around to glare at the bitch.

"I saw it with my own eyes! I saw you—"

"Your father's still alive," she snaps, and her words detonate something inside of me.

For the longest moment, I simply stare at her, at a loss for what to say. I saw my dad die. I saw the life bleed from his eyes as steadily as the wound on his chest. Vampires can't survive being stabbed with god-blessed daggers. It's one of the few things in the world that can kill us.

How…?

What…?

"You're lying," I whisper. I don't dare believe even for a second that she's telling the truth. Because if I believe her, then this will mean I have hope. And if I have hope and it turns out not to be true…

The world will see what happens when a monster goes insane.

"I'm not." Medusa shakes her head rapidly, her snakes coiling tight. "Five minutes ago, both your father and Dimitri Gray were brought to the local monster hospital, where they're being treated for their wounds. We never wanted to actually kill them, Violet, but we needed to stop them from taking you away."

"Because you want to talk to me about the prophecies." It's not a question.

I can barely breathe through the sluicing of blood in my head. My heart pounds erratically, gaining speed with every second I stare at her. Her eyes are sincere, but is it a trick? A trap?

Is she trying to save her own ass?

"MOTHERFUCKER!" Zeus bellows in rage. "YOU NEED TO PAY ATTENTION! WE JUST DIED! AGAIN!" He turns to face me, his eyes planning murder. My murder.

And I rather like being un-murdered.

Quickly, I pick the remote back up and offer the god a sheepish smile. "Sorry, I—"

"One more fucking time," he interrupts, whipping his head around to face the screen as he reloads the game. I have no idea what the fuck will happen when that 'one more fucking time' ends. Will he kill me with lightning? Eat me? I imagine he needs a lot of sustenance to maintain his eight-foot frame, and unfortunately for me, a vampire is scarily nutritional. Like, we're a cannibal's wet dream because of our high protein level. No idea why. Maybe it's because of all the blood we drink?

As I play the game—read as, run into every wall that exists, despite being in the desert—Medusa talks.

"There are two prophecies the oracles have been raving about," Medusa begins from behind me. I can't see her face with my attention on the screen, but from the distinct lilt to her tone, I can tell she's not happy. With me? With the prophecy? With my existence? My guess? A mixture of all three. "The first one is something about ending the world." She scoffs, almost as if she's dismissing those words as unimportant.

But I think ending the world is very, very important.

"Say what now?" I ask, shooting at a ninja that attempts to grab me from behind. Not today, fucker. Not today.

"Something about a woman named Violet rising from the ashes and reclaiming her throne." Another scoff. "We took it to mean you taking over your father's…business." I can practically hear her lips curl away from her teeth.

Reclaiming my throne?

Dracula doesn't have a throne, not after the *incident*. I'm legally not allowed to talk about it because of a nondisclosure I signed, but it has to do with a throne, super glue, and a bleached ass.

No comment.

Does she mean…?

Does she mean Hera's throne? Lucifer's?

Are my birth parents somehow involved in this prophecy? How does Medusa even know I'm the Violet this prophecy speaks of?

"But the one I'm the most concerned with is the second prophecy," Medusa continues, and her words cause a cold chill to cascade across my arms.

"Which is?"

"That you'll kill my son," she snaps out, pain lacing her voice. "The second prophecy is that Dracula's daughter will be responsible for my son, my Mason's, death."

CHAPTER 6

DIMITRI

"I'm looking for Violet Dracula," I hiss at the orderly behind the counter. "Violet Dracula. Is she a patient here?"

"No, I'm sorry." She glances up from her computer screen to shake her head sadly. "We've had no one with that name be admitted here today." She offers me a grandmotherly smile, but I simply bare my teeth at her.

"You're hopeless." Pushing myself off the counter, I stalk down the hospital hallway, where monsters of all shapes and sizes scurry out of my way like their asses are on fire.

I woke up less than an hour ago on a scratchy hospital bed, my clothes removed and lying on the seat beside me. Despite the doctor's urging to remain in bed, I dressed in my customary suit and smoothed back my white-blond hair.

And now, I'm on the hunt.

Who the fuck exploded the room? Where's Violet?

I found her father almost immediately, having been sent to surgery as soon as he arrived. But Violet? I can't find her anywhere, and fear presses down on my heart like a heavy weight.

The last thing I remember is telling her the truth about her heritage, and then the room exploded. I threw myself on top of her to shield her from the blast, but unconsciousness claimed me before I could take her to safety.

Who has her? Those vampire haters?

I suppose there's someone I can ask…

I think about the prisoners in my dungeon, the despicable men who mutilated Violet by carving words into her perfect skin. Grim, almost insidious, satisfaction rolls through me as I remember the way they screamed, begged, cried.

But they're still alive.

For now.

It becomes painfully apparent to me that when I was knocked unconscious, Violet was taken, but by whom?

I suppose the "who" doesn't matter. The person is going to pay regardless. Brutally. Bloodily. Painfully.

Skirting past a nurse with a long, lizard-like tail thumping behind her, I duck inside one of the spare rooms. It consists of nothing but a cot, a white curtain that can be pulled around the bed, and a connecting bathroom.

It's the bathroom I venture toward, casting furtive glances over my shoulder to ensure I'm not being followed. Nobody will be stupid enough to stalk me, but you can never be too certain, especially with the Roaring in full swing.

I shut the bathroom door gently behind me and then move toward the stark white faucet, gripping it tightly and taking a deep breath. My stomach swirls rapidly as I slowly, almost painfully so, lift my head to stare at my reflection in the mirror.

It's the first time I've done so in almost five years. Normally, I travel through mirrors with my eyes closed, but I can't afford to make any mistakes this time. Not when Violet's life is on the line.

The legend of Dorian Gray is true, to an extent, but the stories fail to mention that certain traits passed on to his only son.

Every Gray has a painting of themselves that they keep locked away. It doesn't show our true faces, but the faces of our monsters, our beasts, our sins. Every mistake we make and every life we take chips away some of our beauty until our portraits reflect the darkness in our souls.

What the legend fails to note is that these reflections of us extend to mirrors as well, which is why I broke every single one in my apartment and office.

The last time I saw my face in the mirror, five years ago, after I committed my first murder, my skin had been hollow and a pale, blotchy pink color interwoven with streaks of red. It almost appeared as if my skin had been peeled away and only the muscle beneath remained. The sight was so horrifying, so grotesque, that I cried.

I haven't cried since that day.

With bated breath, I lift my head, prepared to see an even more disgusting version of myself. Will my eyes be black as pitch? Will my hair fall out in clumps?

I don't see any of that, however.

My skin is bright and unblemished, my hair a luminescent shade of white. Not a lick of pink or red is to be seen.

I bring my hands to my cheeks in wonder, but I don't have time to marvel at the change. Not now. Later, I'll analyze what happened to create such a drastic difference in my soul.

But for now, I need to find Violet.

I shove my fist through the mirror, squeezing my eyes to fight off the rising nausea. It's a sickening sensation, almost reminiscent of shoving your entire body into a pit of tar and trying to wade through it. I can feel the darkness of the mirror clinging to my body, shrouding it in its tepid, unassuming heat. The rest of my body quickly follows, and I find myself trudging forward, darkness devouring me from all sides. Normally, I relish the darkness, the sin it personifies, but today, I want nothing more than to claw at it until it dissipates.

Pockets of light flash intermittently in the darkness, and I pay keen attention to each of them until I find the one a little brighter than the others. Moving briskly, my hands pressed in the pockets of my dress pants, I step through the portal and into an elegantly furnished living room.

The beige carpeting, white walls, and dark furniture are immediately recognizable, as is the intricate woodworking around the fireplace.

My father's mansion.

Dorian Gray doesn't bother to look up from where he's resting on the couch, a notebook sitting on his knee as he writes in it. His free hand holds a mug of either tea or coffee, and I watch him take a dainty sip, his pinky finger extended.

"Dorian," he greets warmly, still not removing his eyes from his journal.

I bite the inside of my cheek. "It's Dimitri," I respond gruffly. "Dorian's your name."

"And it's the best name I've ever heard." Dorian's eyes—the same shade of blue as mine—sparkle as he finally glances up from his notebook. "What can I do for you, Dorian?"

"Dimitri," I correct through gritted teeth, though I don't know why I bother.

Dorian Gray is many, many things, most of them vain and self-serving, but a doting father isn't one of them.

Striding into the room, I stare down at my father's arresting face, noting the similarities with a sickening interest. I hate the fact that I look like him, that I inherited the curse of being beautiful with an ugly soul. The same white-blond hair, though his is cut short while mine is nearly to my shoulders. Same ice-blue eyes, such a striking shade that people are able to see the color from blocks away. Same broad shoulders and tapered waists. Looking at the two of us together, you'd think we were brothers, not father and son.

Which is exactly how my father prefers it.

"We need to talk about Violet Dracula," I begin curtly, not bothering with pleasantries.

Dorian's eyebrows rise to his hairline in surprise.

"The baby we saved from Hera?" he asks, genuine bemusement lacing his tone.

I don't bother to correct him that we saved Violet *for* Hera.

"Yes. What other Violet Dracula would there be?"

I remind myself repeatedly that it's not my father's fault, that it's his curse that makes him so vain and oblivious to the world as a whole. But fuck, I want to stab my knife in his eye more often than not, which I'm sure is not appropriate father-son bonding.

"I'm sorry, Dorian—"

"Dimitri." Why the fuck do I even bother?

"—but I don't understand what the issue is."

"The issue," my teeth grit together, "is that she's missing."

For the first time in all the years I've known him, something akin to fear and shock flash in his blue gaze. He straightens on the couch, his journal slipping out of his fingers and landing beside him with a heavy thud.

"What?"

"During the second round of the Roaring, she went missing. Dracula was critically injured."

The fear in my father's gaze causes my heart to crawl up my throat, becoming lodged there. Swallowing is nearly impossible, though outwardly, my mask remains in place, not a single crack for anyone to see. It's as immaculate as always…and just as impenetrable.

"And Violet?" Dorian clumsily gets to his feet, the hand holding the tiny mug shaking slightly.

"Missing," I repeat.

"You don't think Lucifer…?" Horror infuses those four words as he gapes at me. A part of me knows that he only cares about what will happen to him if Lucifer discovers his betrayal, but another part of me hopes it's because he's a decent man who gives a shit about the fate of the world.

And we both know what will happen to this world if Lucifer discovers the truth—not only that his daughter's alive, but about the power she can wield.

"You need to help me find her," I tell him briskly. "Now."

CHAPTER 7

JACK

There's not a lot to do in the darkness.

Sure, some people believe that monsters flourish in the absence of light, but not me. Never me.

Maybe there was a point in my life when I preferred the solitary only pure, absolute darkness could provide, but that all changed when I met Violet Dracula.

My mate. My love. My life.

My light.

Hux, beside me, begins to move even faster, his shadowy profile barely visible as my eyes continue to adjust to such oppressive darkness.

"I need to get to my precious treasure," he growls, charging forward. His spine straightens with resilience.

"Hux..." I begin cautiously. I'm always unsure how to behave with my psychotic brother. The last thing I want to do is risk offending him and facing the brunt of his wrath. I know innately that he'll never hurt me—that in his own, sadistic way, he loves me—but I can never be too cautious. He's a ticking time bomb desperate to get to the woman he loves, and he won't let anyone stand in his way…not even me.

"She could be hurt," he grits out, his hand clasping around my wrist as he pulls me forward.

"We need to think things through," I point out calmly, trying to ignore how erratically my heart hammers in my ears. It's the only sound I can hear in this barren wasteland. That, and the sluicing of blood as it pumps through my veins.

"What do we need to think through? There is some fucker in our body, and for all we know, he could've hurt my precious treasure." His words are a rumbling growl, and panic lights my heart on fire.

The thought of this stranger doing anything to Violet…

I push the horrible thought away and focus on calming down my brother. He's a raging storm—nothing but bloated storm clouds, crackling thunder, and flashes of white lightning. Metaphorical rain pelts us both, but while it slows me down, it doesn't deter Hux in the slightest.

"Please, Hux," I beg, giving my wrist a tug to stop him. "We need to be smart about this."

He whirls to face me, and though I can't distinguish his features—so similar yet so different to my own—I know his teeth will be bared in a fierce scowl. "Don't fucking test me, Jack."

Ignoring the threat in his words, I speak slowly, calmly, not allowing him to see how much he's getting to me. "We know that there's a third soul inhabiting our body," I begin, connecting the puzzle pieces together in my head. "And we suspect he has been with us for a while, unbeknownst to either of us."

It's the only thing that makes sense. Before Violet, Hux and I couldn't communicate outside of letters written to whoever wasn't inhabiting our shared body at the time. I'd thought my brother was a deranged serial killer, and come to find out, he thought the same about me.

So if it wasn't one of us who murdered all of those people, then that means our interloper is the killer.

Whoever the hell that may be.

"We need to talk to Jekyll and Hyde," Hux growls out, referring to our immortal father.

"We haven't seen or talked to either of them in over fifty years," I point out. At one point, that knowledge would've cut me deep, striking at my skin until I bled. I'd be the first to admit that I'm more sensitive than other monsters, a fact that my mating bond with Violet has only amplified. I don't like to curse, I prefer fighting with my words over my fists, and I have the desperate, irresistible need to be loved and love someone in return. I once searched for that love in my fathers before eventually directing it toward any woman who would give me the time of day.

But that 'love,' if you can even call it that, was superficial at best, toxic at worst. None of it lasted, and now, I know the reason why.

I'm not fundamentally broken like I initially believed. I couldn't find love in my hundreds of years of existence because the only one capable of evoking such a strong emotion out of me hadn't been born yet. I think that's why I struggle to venture through the darkness—because now that I've seen the light, I crave it with an intensity and passion I didn't know I was capable of. Violet has somehow found a way to carve a pathway straight to my soul, and now that she has embedded herself inside of it, I never want to be free of her.

"Maybe there's a way to remove this…intruder from the inside," I muse in contemplation, regarding our shared mind with interest. I don't quite know how to explain it.

I'm alive…but I'm not. Technically, I'm nothing but a soul wandering inside the darkness of our body, unable to climb into the proverbial driver's seat. But maybe…

"Maybe if we work together to take control of our body, we can push the intruder out," I tell Hux.

"How in the bloody hell would we do that?" he asks.

"Maybe if we push at the same time?" I suggest, but I don't sound confident even to my own ears.

He releases an exasperated grunt but doesn't argue. At this point, he's just as desperate as I am.

Without preamble, we both drop to our knees, prepared to push on the only solid surface we can find in this abyss of darkness—the ground.

"Brother." Hux's voice is softer than I've ever heard it before, a tone he usually only reserves for Violet.

"Yes?" I lift my head up and twist in his general direction. I can dimly make out his silhouette—all broad shoulders and muscular arms. I swear the man is ten times larger than me, despite the fact we share the same body. How is that even possible?

"No matter what happens," he clears his throat, "I'm happy I got to officially meet you. And I'm happy we share the same mate."

My heart swells with love for him, and if I didn't fear he'd stab me, I would've thrown myself into his arms. I've never hugged my brother before, but right then and there, I want to desperately.

Be cool, man. Be cool.

I try to think of an articulate reply, one that won't make me seem like a total baby in front of him. I open my mouth to say, "I'm glad I got to meet you too, even though you are a butt at times. And I'm happy you love Violet as much as I do."

What comes out is, "My Violet has a butt, and I'm glad."

My cheeks instantly warm as Hux stares at me in

complete silence. After a long—*long*—moment, he places his hand on my shoulder and gives it a squeeze.

"Yes," he says seriously. "Our Violet has a very, very exceptional butt. I like to squeeze it."

For the love of…

I pinch the bridge of my nose. "I don't need to hear about—"

"Can you imagine how she would look riding me?" he continues, oblivious to my unease. "One direction, we see that delectable ass bouncing, and the other, her perfect titties—"

"Don't say titties," I interrupt, fighting off a headache. Can I even get headaches in this non-corporeal form? I'm gonna have to go with a resounding yes.

"Titties is in the urban dictionary," Hux points out. "Along with double penetration. Who shall I double penetrate Violet with?"

"Why the heck are you looking up titties and double penetration?" I feel my brows climb up my forehead before I shake my head with a disgruntled sigh. "You know what? Don't answer that. I really don't want to know. Was it the same day you looked up menstrual cramps?"

Why the frick did I ask that?

"I need to know everything about my precious treasure," Hux responds stoutly, and I just know he's lifting his chin indignantly. "Including her body's inner workings. And outer workings. Did you know that to pleasure a female, you need to—"

"Let's see if we can get out of here and back to Violet," I interrupt, and as I expect, my words sharpen Hux's focus on the matter at hand.

"Yes. For my precious treasure."

"On the count of three," I begin, hovering my hands just above the dark ground. "One. T—"

"Three!" Hux exclaims, anxious as ever.

With a roll of my eyes, I stick my hands to the ground and push.

Push.

Push.

Push.

My arm muscles strain as I apply all the pressure I'm capable of, desperate to break through the dark prison I found myself trapped in. When I want to give up, I think about Violet the last time I saw her—her gorgeous locks of golden hair highlighted with strands of pure white—and I push even harder. I'm sure my mate would have a million dirty jokes to retort with right about now, and it's that thought that gives me an extra boost of strength.

"It's working!" I gasp as bright lights sprinkle from the floorboard like oozing magma, illuminating Hux's clenched jaw and scar. More and more cracks begin to appear across the pitch-black flooring, each one filled with vibrant white light.

Using all of my arm muscles, I push down on the floor one more time…

And fall directly into my body.

Hux? I question as I blink my eyes rapidly, attempting to orient myself to my surroundings.

I'm here, Brother, he responds instantly. And then, *Where's my precious treasure?!?*

I don't know, I respond truthfully as I reach a hand up toward my head, where a splitting migraine has erupted behind my eyebrows. Why the heck is my hair in a man bun?

I remove the ponytail and allow the thick, black strands to fall forward, obscuring my features from view. I don't have my glasses, but at the moment, that's the least of my worries.

"Oh my gosh," I breathe, staring at my surroundings in abject horror.

I appear to be in a classroom on campus, though I can't tell immediately which class it is.

Kind of hard to, when there's blood on every available surface.

Jack... Hux's voice rumbles through my head, his own horror intermingling with mine.

Bodies lay strewn across every available surface, their eyes sightless and their necks sliced open. I count at least a dozen, if not more. Some are werewolves; others are vampires. I can't recognize all the different types, but one thing remains clear—someone killed them all, painting the room red in their blood.

"Did he do this?" I ask out loud, referring to our mysterious intruder.

And if we're here...where the fuck did he go?

I didn't go anywhere, Jack. The voice is cold and malicious, causing goosebumps to skitter down my arms like an army of angry fire ants. *I'm right here.*

Who the fuck are you? Hux roars, battling against my defenses in an attempt to get free, to find Violet.

I'm you, the impostor snarks in a distinct Irish accent. *And you're me.*

Did you kill these people? I ask, horror inflating my heart.

Not people... he laments, his tone decidedly casual. *Monsters. Vampires.*

The voices in my head dim, eclipsed by the sound of the front door of the classroom being thrown open. Before I can even open my mouth, something wickedly sharp hits the side of my neck. Hux bellows in horror, and the stranger in our head simply laughs.

I glance sideways, surprised to see a dart protruding from my skin.

A dark, cloying fog evades my mind as I topple precariously to the side, just barely catching myself on the desk before I fall over completely. When I pull my hands away, they're stained red with blood.

Blood of the victims my body killed.

"What?" I slur as I come face to face with Stefan Van Helsing. Behind him, King Tut, a mummy and one of our instructors, stands with his wrapped arms folded over his chest.

Their words float to me as if I'm hearing them on the opposite end of an expansive tunnel. They enter one ear and immediately slip through the other.

"…murdered dozens of monsters," Stefan hisses. "The punishment for that is death."

"But since he's at our academy, under our watch, we'll decide on his punishment," King Tut insists. His eyes flick toward me, barely visible through his wrappings.

"The Van Helsings are in charge of distributing punishment," Stefan protests.

"Not at the academy."

I fall to my knees as in my head, the voices go completely silent. My eyelids flutter shut before immediately reopening.

"Violet…" I moan. I need to find her, need to go to her, need to hold her in my arms.

"Jack." King Tut leans over me, his eyes crinkling with something I would almost describe as sympathy. "For the murder of thirteen monsters, you and your brother are hereby sentenced to detention for the next six hundred and sixty-six years, set to be served starting right now."

No.

No.

No!

Darkness consumes me once more.

CHAPTER 8

MASON

"Vin!" I bellow, barreling into our shared house less than an hour after my confrontation with Balor, the slimy fucker inside of Jack and Hux's body. My hand shakes as I run it across my beanie, causing the hat to become askew. I hurry to right it as my gaze lands on Frankie and Vin, the former poring over a computer in the living room as the latter paces, his head bent.

Vin glances up first. "Did you find Hux and Jack?" he demands without preamble.

I blow out a breath. "That's what I needed to discuss with you." I move to sit in the chair opposite them, my legs wobbling erratically. If I don't sit down soon, I'm going to collapse. Vin's brows knit together as he watches me, but wisely, he doesn't comment. "Something happened. Something bad," I continue.

"Something worse than our mate going missing?" Frankie asks dryly, not pulling his gaze away from the computer screen.

When I raise a brow, silently asking what he's doing, Vin rushes to explain, "He's going through all of the emails Dimitri has exchanged in the last week. We started doing it in his office, but Frankie worried that we'd be caught."

"Have you found anything?" I ask desperately, my concern over Hux and Jack momentarily forgotten.

Frankie's jaw clenches as he slowly shakes his head. "Nothing yet. Dimitri loves to speak in code, apparently."

"Fuck…" I drop my head back, bringing my arm over my eyes. Everything's too bright, too intense, and I want nothing more than to retreat to the darkness of my room.

"What did you have to tell us?" Frankie asks, drawing my attention back to him. "You know, when you burst into the room screaming like a banshee from Hell."

"Shit, man. It's bad." How do I even begin to explain the clusterfuck that is Jack/Hux/Balor? I already spent thirty minutes disposing of that poor woman's body so her death won't be traced back to us. What else will Balor get up to before we're able to stop him? Does he know what happened to Violet?

The thought that he played a part in her disappearance sends a cold stab of fear straight to my heart. I can't imagine how Hux and Jack will react when they eventually return. Because trust me, I won't rest until Balor is gone and Hux and Jack are where they rightfully belong—in their shared body.

"It's Hux and Jack," I confess, bringing a shaky hand to my mouth. Black dots race across my vision, and I blink ten times to clear them away. Sweat beads on my forehead, dripping down my cheeks, and I know I'm spiraling, my body shutting down.

"What about them?" Vin barks, and I can see he's seconds from losing his shit. He's always been high-strung, but losing Violet has destroyed something inside of him. I imagine he won't rest—won't even fucking sleep—until we have her back safe and sound.

"Well, it's not just the two of them anymore."

Frankie whips his head up to stare at me, his brows furrowed. Vin simply blinks at me.

"What?" Frankie snaps out, his tone caustic and almost annoyed.

Why is it so hot in here?

As I speak, I begin to unbutton my flannel shirt, sliding it over my shoulders so I'm only in my gray tank top and jeans.

Though I'm seriously considering the merits of just sitting here naked. It wouldn't be weird, right? We're bros who live together, fight together, and get naked tog—

Oh. I see how it'll be weird.

"Mason!" Vin snaps his fingers in front of my face, his expression thunderous. "Focus."

"Focus." I nod once, forcing my mind to concentrate. When has the room started spinning? "I found their…body… vessel…whatever you want to call it in a room with another girl. He was…touching her." Bile swarms in my stomach at just the thought, mainly because I know my two friends— Hux especially—will freak the fuck out when they discover their body has been used to touch someone who isn't Violet. That's a violation to the greatest extent.

"Touching her?" Frankie parrots darkly. Slowly, he closes the laptop, giving me his complete and undivided attention.

To be completely honest, I don't remember Frankie being such a terrifying motherfucker. Sure, he's a little strange, what with his secret lab and experiments, but I never thought of him as downright scary before today. He looks at me as if I'm a fish he plucked from the ocean, watched flop around on dry land, and then gutted with a sinister grin on his face.

I don't want to be a fish stick, dammit.

"Mason…" Vin growls, once again snapping his fingers in front of my face.

"And then he snapped her neck," I finish, blinking rapidly to focus on Vin's face. "He said it was because she had vampire blood inside of her. He spoke with a strange Irish accent and claimed his name was Balor."

There. That's all the information they need to know.

Fuck, I'm burning up in here! I really need to tell Vin to turn the temperature down.

"You look like shit, man," Vin hisses, though I can't help but notice that his eyes flash with concern. "You need to lie down or something."

"No." I shake my head vehemently. "Not until we find her."

"You're no help to us when you're like this," Frankie muses dispassionately, already typing away on his computer.

"I can be of use!" I argue immediately, though I can't help but think my words sound like a lie. "What are you even looking up?"

"Balor," he answers vaguely, not peeling his gaze away from the computer screen. "I could've sworn I heard that name before…"

"Do we think he has something to do with Violet's disappearance?" Vin demands, shakily running a hand through his short dark hair.

"Wait." The familiar voice has us all spinning around on high alert, focusing on the intruder. We were so preoccupied with our conversation that we hadn't even heard the man enter our house. "Violet's missing?"

Barret—otherwise known as the Boogeyman—stands in the doorway of our living room, his green hair blowing in an invisible wind. His wide, guileless eyes focus on Vin first before moving to me.

"What happened to my cheese curd?" He moves farther

into the room until he's standing directly in front of me. "And why do you look ugly?"

"Apparently our house has an open-door policy," Frankie mumbles under his breath with a derisive shake of his head.

"Um…I don't look ugly," I protest as another bead of sweat cascades down my cheek.

"If we put you in an ugly dog contest, you'd win first place," Barret replies seriously.

Damn, man. Way to kick a guy while he's already down.

Why not just cut off my dick while you're at it?

"I'm not ugly," I grumble stubbornly, pouting.

Barret whirls around to face Vin, giving me his broad back.

He's easily the largest of all the monsters who have become so obsessed with Violet. Every inch of him is covered in solid muscle, and I imagine it's because he doesn't have much to do upstairs in detention besides work out. Maybe he bench presses Cal?

Is that a thing?

At one point, I might've been terrified of the tall and arresting man, with his dark skin, green hair, and muscular build, but I see the way he is with Violet. He's all bite, no bark. Or is it all bark, no bite? All doggy-style, no cowboy? Cowgirl? All cowgirl? No cowgirl?

Who the fuck is a cowgirl?

"Violet hasn't returned from the second game," Vin responds. He sounds tired. Wary. Lines of fatigue make him look years older than his actual age. "And we haven't been able to locate her since."

"What?" Barret's voice is shrill, and all around us, the furniture begins to shake.

Or maybe I'm just shaking?

Fuck if I know anymore.

"We'll find her," Frankie says determinedly, his eyes still

glued to the computer. I can see the reflection of the screen in his glasses as his fingers type rapidly away.

Click. Click. Click.

"You better fucking find her," Barret thunders, his hands clenching into fists and his chest heaving. He looks seconds away from pounding said fists into someone's head—hopefully Vin's, because he's the closest.

Maybe my 'ugliness' will deter him from killing me.

"We're doing everything we can," Vin says, his voice subdued. He places a hand on Barret's shoulder and gives it a squeeze. "Which is why we were looking for you and Cal—"

"No." Barret shakes his head rapidly and takes a step backward, forcing Vin's hand to fall to his side. "Cal can't know about this."

Fuck, it's cold in here. When did Vin turn on the air conditioning?

I grab the blanket from over the back of the chair and curl into it, my teeth chattering.

"W-w-why can't Cal k-know ab-bout this?" I grit out, my entire body convulsing. "D-d-doesn't he care about her?"

"He does," Barret confesses, "which is the problem."

"How is that a problem?" Vin demands, incredulous.

"I can't explain it." Barret shakes his head once more. "But trust me. The less Cal knows for now about Violet's disappearance, the better."

"Dimitri Gray knows where she is," Frankie interjects. "If we can find him, we can find her."

"W-w-where do w-w-we even begin to look—"

"No need to look," a glacial, indolent voice states from behind me, cutting me off. "I'm here."

I tilt my head backward, my eyes latching on Dimitri's graceful, panther-like form as he glides into the room. As always, he's dressed entirely in black, his white-blond hair a stark contrast. A sword is strapped to his back, making him look even more terrifying than usual. His ice-blue eyes, as cold as a snowy tundra, gives me a dismissive once-over before focusing on Vin.

Something tightens in my chest at that, though I can't say for certain why.

It's almost like…

It's almost like Dimitri Gray thinks I'm incapable of looking after my mate, and the thought cuts me deep.

"Where the fuck is Violet?" Vin demands without haste, pulling his own sword off his back and holding it at the ready.

Dimitri eyes the weapon with barely veiled distaste before heaving out a breath. "You should be thanking me, boy, for finding her in the first place. I used every mirror at my disposal to track down her location."

Every mirror?

My brain struggles to play catch up to his words. All I can hear is the rapid *thump-thump-thump* of my heart battering my rib cage and the chattering of my teeth.

"What did you do to her?" Vin hisses, baring his teeth.

Dimitri's expression doesn't change, not even a flicker of interest in his eyes. "Not a thing." He pauses, allowing those three words to sink in, before adding, "But I do know where she is."

"Where is she?" Barret asks eagerly, hopping from foot to foot.

"Mount Olympus," Dimitri answers, his brows drawing low over those glacial eyes of his. "She's with Medusa and Zeus. Though I don't know what Medusa wants with her…" He trails off with a pointed look in my direction, and I feel everything inside of me grow cold. Well, cold*er*. I'm already freezing my snakes off.

Oh…fuck.

Fuck. Fuck. Fuck.

Shit on a dick.

Shit on *my* dick.

Shit on—

"Mason!" Vin grips my shoulders, giving me a shake. "What the fuck does your mom want with Violet?"

"The prophecy." My voice is nothing but a whisper, barely audible over the pounding of my heart. Or maybe I'm screaming at this point. My throat does feel raw.

Burning.

I'm burning. My skin is on fire, every vein alit with flames.

But how can I be on fire, yet so cold at the same time?

"What prophecy?" Barret questions, sounding confused.

"The only one my mom cares about is the one that concerns me," I whisper.

No. No. No. No.

My mom wouldn't hurt Violet, would she? She knows how much the crazy vampire means to me. Surely, she wouldn't do something stupid like kill her.

Right?

Right?!

"Mason…" Vin grits out, his fingernails digging into my skin hard enough to bruise.

"I don't know everything, just what I've been told." My voice shakes as something cold slides through my veins like a single cube of ice. I force my gaze to meet my best friend's, the panic and fear in his eyes no doubt mirroring my own. "Dracula's daughter…" My chest feels uncomfortably tight. "She's going to be the one who kills me."

CHAPTER 9

VIOLET

I swallow around the sudden lump of coal that has taken up residence in my throat.

Mason? Dying? Because of Dracula's daughter?

Cue—nervous and slightly hysterical laughter that sounds like a chicken getting anal fisted. Not that I know what it sounds like, but I can't imagine it's pleasant.

The mere thought of anything happening to Mason sends cold sweat cascading down my spine.

"And you're sure the prophecy meant *your* Mason?" I ask, needing that clarification desperately. Since I'm unable to meet her eyes directly, I settle for staring at a speckle on her shoulder. She has rather nice shoulders for a woman with snakes for hair. They're not too bony, if that's even a thing.

But I swear some women have shoulders that look as if they can be registered as lethal weapons. Have you seen how sharp some of them are? I'm surprised they don't take someone's eye out. When those women shrug, do they stab their ears? Is that a thing? Death by shoulder stabbing?

Note to self—look up how many deaths occur worldwide because of shoulders.

And also note to self—freak the fuck out, because your boyfriend is fated to die.

"Yes," Medusa hisses, drawing my attention back to her. "Which is why we have…problems."

"No problems!" I blurt out, my voice abnormally loud and high-pitched. I work to lower it marginally, but that only serves to give me a masculine, husky voice instead as if I'm attempting to impersonate Morgan Freeman. "No problem."

"Do we have to talk about this now?" Zeus grumbles as he moves from the bean bag and toward the giant television. He bends down, unveiling a hairy ballsack that has vomit churning in my stomach, before straightening to his full, impressive height. Immediately, the television screen changes to a dance video game instead of a shooting one.

"Yes!" Medusa's face twists into a hideous sneer. "Because this little bitch is prophesied to kill my son!"

I tentatively raise a hand in the air. "Okay, first, calling me a bitch is rude. I'll take annoying cumstain, asswipe, mouth breather, dummy dummy toot-toot, walking disaster, brain-fried Barbie, ugly duckling, ugly step-sister, ugly fucker…I'll take all of those nicknames over bitch." I can feel her eyes narrowing on me, and it takes every ounce of self-control not to meet her gaze just to see what will happen.

It's like a motherfucking button that reads, 'Push here to destroy the world.' You know you shouldn't…but you really, really want to. Like, why did they have to make the button so red and vibrant? Why does it have to look so damn appealing?

"Is there a point to your little monologue?" she bites out, and one of her snakes hisses, alarmingly close to my face.

Music blares through the room as Zeus begins to dance in front of the couch, his hips swaying in a way that makes me question my birth mother's sanity. How does she find that attractive?

When he begins to moonwalk, his arms flailing in front of him, I decide that my mom has a few screws loose if she willingly slept with both him and the devil.

"Watch this," Zeus instructs, dropping to the ground and attempting to breakdance. He doesn't really know what he's doing, so his legs just kind of kick the air while his hands caress the floor like he's making carpet snow angels. His robe falls open, his erect dick—*now I know why my birth momma tapped that ass. Damn. That's the biggest cock I've ever seen*—hitting his stomach.

"Looking good." I give him an enthusiastic thumbs-up, and he beams.

Is this really the head honcho of Mount Olympus? Obviously, these Greek Gods didn't have the pick of the barrel when they were assigning leadership roles, if you know what I mean.

"Violet!" Medusa's shrill voice drags my attention back to her. I wince instinctively, attempting to make myself even smaller.

"Okay, well, I just wanted to say…" I take a deep, shuddering breath. Why not try for honesty? "I love your son. A lot. And if your reaction is any indication, you do too. I will never, ever hurt him. I can promise you, Medusa. Dracula has hundreds and hundreds of kids scattered throughout the world. I don't know which one will come for him, but I swear on my life that I'll do everything within my power to stop it from happening. I…" Emotions bombard me, tangling together until it's impossible to differentiate one from the next. "I can't lose him."

Medusa regards me in silence, those damn snakes of hers writhing and coiling around her head. I don't know what's going through her cunning brain, but I pray that it's not my murder. Or my stoning.

I don't want to be stoned.

"Violet," Zeus exclaims, but I keep my attention locked on Medusa, awaiting her response with bated breath. Fuck, does it make me pathetic to want her approval? I know Mason's relationship with his mom is rocky, but I desperately want her to flash me a smile and tell me…something. I don't know. Maybe something like, 'I'm happy my son has you.'

Medusa's ruby-red lips curl downward.

"Violet!" Zeus repeats, his voice almost a whine. "Viiiiiolet. Violet. Violet. Violet!"

For the love of…

"What?" I snap, spinning around to see the God of Gods attempting to do the worm. His entire face falls, and he freezes in mid-worm, his pasty ass cheeks visible.

"You didn't have to yell at me," he mumbles, and I take another deep breath, pinching the bridge of my nose.

"I'm sorry," I grit out. "Please. Let me see your worm."

The smile materializes on his face as if it never left in the first place. He immediately begins wiggling across the floor, gyrating his hips like he's trying to hump the fucking carpet.

Wait…

Maybe he is trying to fuck the carpet.

What the fuck am I watching?

My eyes widen in alarm when he grunts out, "Yes, you thirsty bitch. Rub that fiber on me."

"Ignore him." Medusa snaps her fingers in front of my face to regain my attention. "My god, you're like a fucking puppy. Can I keep your attention for longer than a second?"

"You can try." I shrug my shoulders helplessly. "But the second I see something shiny, you can bet your ass I'll—ohhh! What's that on your wrist? Is that a bracelet? Did Zeus get it for you? Mason? He hasn't ever gotten me a gift, though I'm not sure if he's just waiting for our anniversary." Her eyes narrow, and I awkwardly shift from foot to foot. "Just kiiiidding."

And to make matters worse, I give my kidnapper finger guns.

Finger. Guns.

I'm getting murdered tonight, aren't I?

"You know," Medusa begins, pacing the length of the room. Her silvery dress cascades behind her like water—an ocean with the moon reflected off its surface. She clasps her hands behind her back and tilts her chin up imperiously, radiating a confidence I can only attempt to emulate. Poorly, I might add. "I had every intention of killing you after this meet and greet with Zeus was over."

She speaks the words plainly, without a hint of emotion whatsoever.

Do I pee myself a little bit? Yes, yes I do.

"Oh…" I rock back on my heels. "And are you still feeling, um, stabby today? Because I can offer some amazing therapists who can help you with this problem. Or you can just stab them, if you want. They're probably more fun to stab than little ole me. I'm not fun to stab at all. I bleed probably more than your average monster. Not a surprise, considering I drink blood to survive. All that blood needs to go some-where." A nervous laugh escapes me. "But that blood doesn't need to go outside of my body. I rather like it *inside* my body. Though…" A horrifying thought occurs to me. "Though you probably wouldn't stab me, would you? You'd turn me into stone. Ha. Joke's on you. I'll pull my pants down and moon you, so you're forced to stare at my ass the rest of your life. Unless you shove me in a closet and hide me away from the world. Don't do that. Please."

"Calm down." Medusa waves a hand in the air, her nose scrunched in disgust. "I'm not going to kill you."

"You're not?" Disbelief is evident in my tone, but can you blame me? The crazy lady just confessed to my face that she plans to end my existence—not her exact words, but you get the gist.

"No." A cunning smile pulls up her lips, changing her from gorgeous to downright stunning. I can definitely see where Mason gets his good looks from…though I'll never in a million years confess that I think his mother is a hot piece of ass.

Too weird, even for me.

"I have another purpose in mind for you, my sweet girl," Medusa practically coos, moving to stand directly in front of me. One of her perfectly manicured hands rests on my cheek, though I keep my attention off her face. Unfortunately, that means I'm staring intently at her breasts, which is just another thing I don't want to have to explain to Mason.

Oh, hey! Just wanted to let you know that I mentally called your mom hot today and then stared at her boobs a second later. It's cool, though. She didn't kill me like she threatened. We totally bonded.

Medusa's words slap me across the face like a wet fish. "Wait. What? What's this ominous 'purpose' you have in store for me?"

She opens her mouth to answer, and I honestly think she's going to confess the truth to me, when the door to the game room creaks and a beautiful woman steps inside.

To say she's beautiful is like saying the sun is simply warm—an understatement. The vision who glides forward is downright stunning.

Golden curls frame an angelic face that artists throughout time have used as their muse. Her blue eyes, the exact shade as my own, are large and guileless with dark lashes framing them. Her petite body is covered in a flowy, white dress, one that cinches at her waist before flaring outward. She's beauty personified, and I know innately who this woman is before she even opens her mouth.

Hera.

My mother.

"Zeus," she greets cordially, turning toward her husband who is doing the robot. Her lips pull away in a sneer as she faces Medusa next, the woman who the world knows to be fucking her husband. Talk about awkward. "Medusa."

"Hera," Medusa responds, her voice clipped. Her entire face seems to twist and distort until she looks like the monster the world accuses her of being.

Finally, Hera's gaze slides to mine.

Surprise registers in her pretty features as her eyes widen and her mouth parts. This close, the similarities between us are uncanny, though I'm not sure if it's simply because I'm searching desperately for things that connect me to my mother or if it's because we truly look alike. I just pray that Medusa and Zeus don't see them as well. The last thing we need is the most powerful man in the universe—and the most conniving woman in the universe—discovering the truth about my birth parents.

Hera recovers faster than me, a pleasant smile tilting up her lips. "And who might this be?"

Is it just me that notices the way her voice trembles?

"Violet Dracula," Medusa introduces before I can. "And she was just leaving."

"Oh." Hera blinks once, smoothing a hand down her pale white dress. "Through the portal?"

"Noooo." Medusa rolls her eyes in exasperation. "We're pushing her through the clouds and praying she doesn't go splat," she finishes sarcastically.

Hera's right eye begins to twitch. "She's joking," I assure her. To Medusa, I ask, "You are joking, right?"

"I will escort the girl back to the academy," Hera interjects, her tone leaving no room for argument. Medusa's frown deepens, but she doesn't protest as Hera steps forward, grabs my arm, and all but drags me from the room.

"Ow," I deadpan, resisting the urge to ask her if she's giving me a timeout.

One, because that sounds a little too kinky for a grown-ass woman to ask her biological mother.

And two, I'm not sure if she knows who I am. Sure, she probably spotted the similarities, but that doesn't mean she knows I'm truly her daughter. Dracula has a bunch of kids, and I could be just another one of them for all she knows.

"You shouldn't be here." Hera's voice is curt and almost cold, but her blue eyes are wide with worry.

"So…"

How do I ask if she's truly my biological mother? If the story Dimitri and my father told me is true?

"You need to leave. Now." Her pace quickens as her fingers tighten around my arm.

Damn. She's speedy for someone shorter than me.

We move in silence, the only sound the click of her heels against the polished floors. When we reach a door at the end of the hall, opposite the throne room, she pauses and spins to face me. For a moment, we simply stare at each other, blue eyes locked on blue eyes.

She places her hands on my cheeks gingerly.

"Go, my sweet child. Your mates are looking for you."

And then she opens up the door behind me and pushes me through the portal inside of it.

CHAPTER 10

VIOLET

Do I scream like my pants are on fire and I'm a liar, liar as I fall through the portal?

Yup.

And do I say, "MOTHERFUCKING DUCK FACE, MOTHER! THIS IS NOT A TIMEOUT!"

Yup.

My stomach lurches, and it takes every ounce of willpower I possess not to vomit. But considering the fact I'm falling through darkness, spinning around and around in a circle, there's a highly probable chance that the vomit will land on my face.

Not gonna risk it, thank you very much. I prefer my face without vomit sticking to—

I do a backflip through the darkness and have to compress my lips together to stop myself from throwing up.

Fucking hell.

When I eventually land, there's nothing graceful about it. My knees hit the floor first, followed by my arms and head. I roll a few times until I'm sprawled on my back, every muscle in my body radiating pain.

"Ow…" I moan as I blink my eyes desperately, attempting to adjust them to the too-bright light above me. I don't know how long I fell through the darkness—probably only a few minutes—but it felt like hours. My eyes physically hurt from staring too long at the light bulb above me.

Another helpless grunt escapes me as I become aware of pounding footsteps.

"Violet?!" Frankie's voice is incredulous, rife with disbelief, and all I can do is lift my thumb in the air to tell him I'm okay. It hurts too much to speak, almost as if the wind has been knocked out of me.

"Violet!" A second later, Vin is on his knees beside me, his hands hovering over my body but not daring to touch me anywhere. His dark eyes are frantic, keen on my face. "Are you okay? Where the fuck were you?"

"Give my cheese curd some space," a familiar voice says diplomatically. Barret.

"I'm just peachy," I manage to get out. "But why is the ceiling moving? Are those stars? Preeetyyyy."

"She must've hit her head," a cold, clinical voice declares, and though I recognize it, it takes me a moment to figure out who it belongs to.

Why would Dimitri Gray be in the guys' house?

"It's Violet," Frankie says drolly from somewhere behind me. "She always talks like this."

"Fair point," Vin agrees.

A second later, I'm lifted into strong, muscular arms and held against a similarly sculpted chest. I breathe in his scent, half expecting it to be the pine and leather aroma I've come to associate with Vin. Instead, it's…

Dimitri?

You can't blame me for what I do next. I mean, this man is

way too sexy for his own good, exuding a danger and predatorial intensity that will have most girls running for the hills.

But I've never been like most girls.

"You gonna give me a spanking, Headmaster?" I mumble sleepily. "I've been bbbbbbad." And of course, because I'm a dumbass, I emphasize the 'b' like I'm a sheep.

"She might be concussed," Frankie says. "We should take her to my lab. I have some things that can help—"

"I'll handle her," Dimitri declares sagely, already turning toward the door with me in his arms.

"What the fuck do you think you're doing?" Vin rages. He places a hand on Dimitri's shoulder and spins the headmaster around to face him. "Our mate just disappeared, returned with a head injury, and you think you're going to—"

"You forget who you're speaking to, Vin Van Helsing." Dimitri's voice is low and threatening, nothing but a hiss of air that seems to reverberate through his chest. His chest, might I add, that I'm petting. It's a rather soft chest. Or maybe the white shirt he wears is just soft.

Soooo. Soft.

Like a sheep.

Ohhhh. Maybe he's the sheep.

Dimitri Graaayyyyy—but you need to pronounce the 'ay' like 'ayeeeeeeeeeee.'

God, maybe I did hit my head.

Almost absently, I bring my fingers to the back of my scalp, and when I pull them away, I see that they're red with blood.

My blood.

Oh. Pretty blood.

I wanna lick it.

"Why the fuck is she licking the blood from her fingers like it's a cock or some shit?" Vin demands.

At first, I think he's talking about a different 'she' and my mind goes literally red with rage at the prospect of some other ho licking her fingers like a cock.

But then I realize…

I'm the ho.

And I'm licking the fuck out of my fingers.

"My head's bleeding," I say with an enthusiastic and completely inappropriate—or very appropriate, depending on how you want to look at it—whoop. "And now I'm eating myself like a cannibal."

"Violet's behavior is a common side effect of long-distance portal travel, especially for her first time," Dimitri tells us, his voice grave.

"Is portal traveling some type of sex position? Because I call being the bottom," I slur, and his arms tighten around me almost imperceptibly.

"Dimitri," Vin growls, and out of my periphery, I watch as he advances a single step. "You can't just take our mate. We just found her and—"

"She will be taken care of," Dimitri announces simply. Before Vin, Frankie, or Barret can say anything else, Dimitri spins on his heel and walks straight into a mirror.

This sensation is different from the portal my mother pushed me into. I want to describe it as sticky—almost as if I'm wading through buckets of maple syrup—but the darkness doesn't tighten around me like it did in the other portal. I have no idea why that is, but I suspect the man holding me in his arms has a part to play in it.

When we finally exit the portal, my head is still spinning wildly, my thoughts painfully sluggish. I'm not able to even tell you what two plus two equals at the moment.

Dimitri doesn't immediately put me down. Instead, he moves us both a few steps to the side, fiddles with something on a tiny table, and then holds a vial up to my mouth.

"Here." His icy voice caresses my skin, rippling through

my veins with a confusing type of heat. "Drink this."

"Are you trying to have your way with me, Mr. Headmaster Sir?" I slur as he tilts my head back and pours the liquid into my mouth.

"It's a healing potion. But more than that, it's supposed to help with the effects of portal traveling. I needed to use dozens of them before I got used to it myself."

For some reason, I can't help but snort. The thought of Dimitri acting erratic and loopy is too surreal to even imagine. He's grace and stealth personified—a lethal vessel of pure destruction and masculinity. A lethal vessel I wanna bang, I might add.

I wanna bang that man good.

The effect of the potion is almost immediate.

One second, I'm thinking about licking his neck to taste the sin on him—and wondering if it'll be similar to chocolate—and the next, I realize that I'm sitting in his arms, my fingers coated in blood, and my tongue hanging out of my mouth like a demented tree frog.

Oh god.

Memories bombard me.

Dracula and Dimitri.

Medusa and Zeus.

Hera.

The prophecy.

"Oh my god," I whisper as Dimitri sets me on my feet. I wobble, my legs still slightly unsteady, but his hands are on my shoulders a second later to stabilize me.

"I see that you have your wits together once more," Dimitri says haughtily, stepping backward once I've reclaimed my balance.

"Sorry for, you know, licking and caressing you. Won't happen again. Scout's honor." I give him an awkward two-fingered salute as he simply quirks a blond brow at me.

As always, Dimitri Gray is a vision of darkness come to life. It's almost as if someone plucked the moon from the night sky and personified it to create this dangerous man. His pale skin and snow-white hair are a striking contrast to the black clothes he wears. Those blue eyes of his—a brilliant shade of cerulean speckled with lighter streaks—ensnare my own almost instantly.

"Vin and the others are going to be furious that you took me," I tell him, my heart racing madly inside my chest. I'm grateful I was able to see Vin, Frankie, and Barret, but what about Hux and Jack? Mason? Cal? Worry for them begins to penetrate the numb barrier I've attempted to erect around myself since I was first kidnapped by Medusa and saw my father stabbed.

Oh god.

Dad.

"I'll return you to them shortly," Dimitri says, finally tearing his eyes from mine and moving into a kitchen.

We appear to have landed in an apartment of some kind. Everything is sleek, expensive, and modern. Black leather furniture decorates the room, providing the area with a harsh, masculine look in contrast to the white walls and flooring. Even the kitchen cabinets are a strange combination of black and silver, almost giving me the impression of a futuristic space station.

The entire room would've felt empty and unwelcoming if it hadn't been for the dirty dishes left in the sink. It gives the room a homey feel to it that would've been missing if it had been immaculately clean.

"Is this…is this your apartment?" I query, spinning in a circle. The kitchen bleeds into a living room with a similar color scheme of white and black. From there, I can see two separate hallways branching out in different directions. A floor-to-ceiling window rests against the back wall, and moonlight filters through, illuminating everything in pastel shades.

"One of them," Dimitri answers as he moves toward the coffee maker and turns it on. "I have a couple of dozen around the world."

"A couple of dozen…" I trail off in wonder as I pad forward, stopping at his bar. I almost don't dare sit on one of the black stools, as if my dirtiness will tarnish the cleanliness of the room. Besides the dishes in the sink, I don't see a single speck of dust or anything out of place. Even the counter is polished so meticulously that I can see my reflection in it.

And my reflection?

Errr.

I've had better days.

"So you were with Medusa and Zeus," Dimitri says as he spins around to face me, crossing his arms over his chest. All I can hear is the whirl of the coffee maker as it works. There's no traffic, no conversation, no bugs chirping outside. Nothing.

Where the fuck does Dimitri live?

An abandoned island?

"I was," I agree, finally caving and sitting on the barstool in front of him. "When we were attacked," I swallow down the lump that has materialized in my throat, "Medusa took me with her to the City of Olympus. Or Mount Olympus. Or Olympus. I honestly don't know the official title." Sniffling, I attempt to get my thoughts in order. This entire day has been really freaking overwhelming, and I want nothing more than to find all my guys, kiss them senseless, and then kick them the fuck out of my room so I can soak in a bathtub while listening to Halloween songs and sipping glasses of red wine. You know, things a normal woman does when she's sad.

"Did they hurt you?" With his arms still crossed over his

chest, I almost miss the way his hands tighten into fists, as if the thought of any harm coming to me fills him with white-hot rage.

"No." I shake my head. "Zeus was...preoccupied," I confess, "and Medusa just wanted to talk."

"About the prophecy?" He cocks a blond brow.

Gritting my teeth together, I nod once. "You heard about it?"

"Which one are you referring to?" The coffee maker beeps, and Dimitri reaches behind him to grab two mugs out of the cupboard. I would've expected a man like him to have dozens of mugs the same color, but instead, the right one reads 'Spank That Booty' in gold cursive and the other has a picture of a book with a superhero cape on it. You can learn a lot about a man based on the type of mugs he has, and Dimitri's are interesting, to say the least. "The one about you rising from the ashes and reclaiming your father's throne? Or the one about Dracula's daughter killing Mason?"

I swear there's a tightness in my throat that hasn't been there prior. Is it just me, or is it suddenly hard to breathe?

"Both?" I begin tentatively, watching as Dimitri opens up his fridge and grabs a bottle of coffee creamer. Chocolate. My favorite. He pours it into the mug with the book on it, stirs the coffee with a spoon, and then brings the steaming mug of liquid gold over to me. I glance from the coffee to his piercing blue eyes and then back to the coffee.

He watches me in silence, sipping from his own mug as smoke wafts around his face.

"Aren't you going to put the chocolate cream in yours?" I ask, nodding toward his pitch-black coffee.

His brows knit together. "No. I prefer my coffee black."

"But why would you have chocolate creamer in your fridge then?" I point out, confusion dancing within me. He wouldn't have bought it just because it's my favorite, now would he? I mean, he ate my pussy out pretty nicely in his office the other day, but we're definitely not at the 'live together and share food' stage.

Or are we?

Dimitri ignores my question as he leans against the counter opposite me, adopting a pose I would almost describe as casual if I hadn't noted the tension thrumming through his muscles.

"So the prophecies…" he presses.

"I'm assuming the 'reclaiming her father's throne' has to do with me," I say, focusing on what truly matters. Though I refuse to let this creamer conversation drop. I'll bring it up again at a different time. "And I'm also assuming that the father the prophecy is referring to isn't Dracula." My hands shake as I take a tiny sip of coffee, nearly moaning at the chocolatey taste.

"If we are to believe the oracles, then you, my dear girl, are going to take over Hell," Dimitri tells me.

I choke on the sip of coffee I've been drinking and cough wildly. Not my most attractive moment.

"What?!" I gasp out as Dimitri frowns.

"I assumed you came to the same conclusion." Lines tug at his eyes, and I have the irresistible urge to rub them away with the pad of my thumb.

"I mean, I came to a conclusion, but the conclusion wasn't 'I'm going to be the next Queen of Hell.' It was more of a 'Dracula isn't my biological father, so obviously the prophecy isn't talking about him.' I'm not the top brass here, Dimitri. It takes my brain a second longer than most people's to catch up," I ramble as fear twists up my insides.

Fuck!

Queen of Hell?

Me?

Surely, there's someone more suited for the job. Literally

anyone. I'll even let Cheryl take the crown. After all, I'm ninety-nine percent sure she crawled out of there in the first place with a pitch-fork in hand and a forked tongue.

"The prophecy definitely can't mean that," I continue, a tiny bead of sweat cascading between my breasts. "Maybe they're talking about a different Violet and a different father. Or maybe they got the name wrong and it's actually Violetta. That's a real name, you know."

"Violet," he interrupts, his frown deepening.

"Fuck, I can't believe this is happening. I'm not truly the daughter of Hera and Lucifer, am I? I can't be. I'm just...me." I throw my hands in the air helplessly as a deranged, semi-hysterical giggle escapes me. "I guess some good news came out of all of this—I'm not going to be the one who kills Mason. The prophecy said Dracula's daughter, and as we discovered, I'm not truly his. Biologically, of course. That old man is still my father in all the ways that count. But...but I'm not going to murder Mason, so I suppose that's a plus." A thought occurs to me, and I feel my face drain of color. "But someone is still going to kill Mason. Oh god. What if we can't stop her in time? Who's that bitch who's going to murder my—"

"Violet," Dimitri repeats, a note of impatience in his voice.

"I'll stab her. Don't test me, Dimitri. I'll stab her titty hard. You should see me when I get angry. I don't just stab the underboob...I stab the whole boob. I'm not making any sense, am I? Oh god. I ramble when I get nervous. I want to go back to my mates now, please. I want to—"

In three long strides, Dimitri is around the bar and has his hands on my waist, lifting me onto the countertop in front of him. At first, I think he's going to say something, his eyes intense on mine, but then he leans in and devours my mouth with his own.

I suppose this is one way to shut a girl up.

CHAPTER 11

VIOLET

Dimitri doesn't just kiss me. He inhales me like I'm the air he needs to breathe. Licks of fire dance across my skin with every sweep of his tongue inside my mouth, every murmured praise against my lips, every touch of his hands on my bare skin.

The kiss turns frenzied as he all but tears my tank top apart. My sports bra comes off next, my tits springing free.

Well.

This is escalating fast.

He lowers his head to my right nipple and begins to suck on it, his other hand inching up my bare stomach to knead the sensitive flesh of my other breast. I've just placed my hands in his white-blond hair, determined to mess up that immaculate ponytail of his, when he captures my wrists and pulls them back toward my sides. His lips continue to suck and nibble on my nipples, one after the other, as I surrender helplessly.

"Dimitri," I moan as I jerk my hips upward.

Wanting him.

Needing him.

There's a monster inside of me, and that monster craves his darkness.

I attempt to free my hands, desperate to touch him, but he only tightens his grip on me as he trails open-mouthed kisses up my neck, his tongue flicking out to taste my skin.

When he reaches my ear, he growls out, "*This* is what you do to me." He brings one of my hands to his erection straining against his pants. I've only just cupped his cock when he forces my hand back to my side once more.

"I want to touch you," I all but cry. I want to run my fingers over the planes of his chest, through his shoulder-length hair, across his broad shoulders. I want to stroke his hard cock and marvel at the silky skin over solid steel.

Dimitri doesn't respond as he grabs something over my shoulder. A second later, my wrists are placed above my head, tied together by a kitchen towel.

"I never thought of using a towel this way. I mean, I can definitely see where the idea came from. You're in the kitchen, cooking some pancakes or whatever assassins eat, and you all of a sudden get a craving for dessert, if you know what I mean. And what can you do about ropes in a kitchen?" I ramble as Dimitri places a hand in the center of my chest, forcing me to lie back on the counter with my legs dangling over the edge.

He wastes absolutely no time tearing my shorts from my body, and my panties soon follow.

I'm bare for this man, and that aspect both terrifies and arouses me in equal measure.

He trails kisses down my body, stopping to give attention to each breast, before dropping to his knees before me. His callused hands brush over my thighs, sending electricity through my veins, before he grabs them and throws my legs over his shoulders.

Putting his mouth directly in front of my core.

Everything about Dimitri is cold, posh, and almost clinical.

But when he kisses me down there…he's fire. I swear I burn for him with every sensual kiss against my slit.

"You're not allowed to just leave me, Miss Dracula," he purrs in a deceptively nonchalant tone as he kisses my right inner thigh and then my left. I resist the urge to squeeze my legs around his head.

Because one, I might suffocate him.

Two, we're not at the 'squeeze his head against your pussy until he gives in and licks it' stage of our relationship yet.

And three, because I'm weak as fuck right now, his touch turning me into nothing but a puddle of goo.

"It wasn't…" I begin. He sucks down on my skin, and I gasp, the words tapering off. "It wasn't intentional."

"No matter." His fingers brush a slow, languid pathway up my stomach, stopping when they reach my breasts. He strokes the underside of them as I pant. "You'll be punished accordingly."

"Dimitri…"

He slaps my right breast hard enough to sway.

"You may address me as sir," he growls as he continues to kiss me everywhere but where I want him to.

Sir.

Goosebumps pebble on my skin at his domineering tone. I've experimented with the dom/sub relationship with Vin once before, but not like this. With the two of us, it felt experimental, something we'd both willingly give up if we wanted to. Our sex was a way for Vin to surrender a tiny piece of himself to me, a way for him to relinquish that rigid control he possesses.

But I get the innate sense that with Dimitri, my compliance is more than just a sex game. He needs it more than anything—my complete and utter submission.

I can give that to him, right?

"Yes…sir," I breathe out, and I can feel his grin against my thighs.

"Good girl." His lips finally travel to my aching pussy, and he licks me with an expertise that has my head spinning. Some guys lick pussies like they're trying to get all of the brownie batter out of the bowl, but Dimitri devours me like it's a goddamn Olympic sport. He probably has a dozen gold medals in the pussy licking sport—though in my imagination, he's only licking plastic dummies, not real women. He's not allowed to lick real women.

His tongue makes figure-eights inside of me, and all I can do is thrash and cry, mindless with pleasure. His nose brushes against my clit, amplifying my desire, and I scream his name as my orgasm builds and builds and builds—

He removes his lips from my core and stares up at me with ice-blue eyes.

"This is your first punishment," he declares in that nonplussed, glacial voice of his. I might've thought he actually didn't give a shit about me and what we were doing…if his eyes didn't betray his want for me. They burn with something I can't quite name, an emotion that has my throat closing and heart racing.

"Punishment?" I whimper as he runs a hand through my juices. Using my own wetness as lubrication, he brings a single finger to my ass and inserts it. "Oh, fuck."

"I told you," he says as thrusts his finger in and out of my back hole. "You must be punished for leaving me."

"Again—" I break off with a gasp as he uses his other hand to thrum my clit. "Not. In—" He kisses my belly. "—tentional."

I want to demand answers from the aloof headmaster—why does he care? What does he want from me? Why does my heart beat for him when my brain knows it shouldn't?—but not one of them manages to leave my too-tight throat.

And as he pistons his fingers in and out of my two holes, I come to the conclusion...

I'm ruined for this man.

Fuck.

My orgasm hits me like a freight train, but Dimitri doesn't let up as he makes my crescendo sharpen and heighten. I swear I have an out-of-body experience where I legitimately die, become a ghost, and come back to haunt the sexy fucker who killed me. Death by orgasm. What a way to go.

Desperation consumes me, and before I realize what I'm doing, I rip free of the towel and sit upright. With a burst of vampire speed—or maybe devil speed, because I'm not technically a vampire—I pull Dimitri to me and kiss him passionately, running my hands over his shoulders and down his arms.

He holds me tight against him and kisses me back, and I feel as if something clicks in my soul. Fuck, it sounds insane, but it's as if I've been living in darkness my entire life and his touch provides the color I need. It's similar to how I felt when I was with Vin, when I kissed Mason, when I got Hux off.

Completeness.

Unity.

Mine.

My hands fumble with the waistband of his pants, cries of pleasure escaping my lips, when he pulls away from me as if my touch physically burned him.

For once, his expression isn't impassive or icy or even cold.

It's...angry. Furious, even. Something akin to disgust swirls in his bright blue gaze, and emotion presses down on my rib cage until breathing is impossible.

"No," Dimitri bites out, a V forming between his eyes. "This isn't how it works."

"What?" Pain pinches at my heart as I struggle to keep my expression placid and unaffected. I want him to believe that I'm okay, that his words aren't knives slicing at my chest, making me bleed.

But...what. The. Fuck?

He straightens, smoothing out the crease in his black shirt. "You don't get to touch me, Violet. Not if we're going to do this."

Hurt slides through my veins like poison as I hold his stare.

"If we do what exactly?" I ask, and his upper lip pulls away from his teeth.

"Have sex," he states plainly, without a hint of emotion in his tone.

"Have sex?" I scoff and push at his chest, forcing him back another step. "Is that all this is to you? A booty call?"

His brow pinches as he opens, shuts, and then re-opens his mouth. "I'm not good for you, Violet. I live and breathe violence. You don't want that."

"Don't tell me what I want," I snap, searching for my clothes. Of course, they've all been completely destroyed thanks to Dimitri, so *yayyy*. I growl at my ripped shirt, wishing I had superpowers or something to put it back together.

Like Zeus.

Great. Now you're thinking about your kind of step-dad while you're naked in front of your headmaster. Your headmaster who, might I add, rejected you. Good for you, Violet. Good. For. You.

"There's nothing wrong with having sex without having

emotions cloud your judgment," Dimitri tells me, but I don't look in his direction. I *can't* look in his direction.

"Then go find another girl to have sex with, because this one is *out*."

"Violet…" he says in a low voice. I've just jumped off the counter when his next words stop me. "I don't want you to touch me. Because if you touch me, I'll bleed for you, and I can't bleed for anyone, Violet. I *can't*." There's something near pleading in his voice, something that urges me to turn around and meet his gaze.

Will it be as icy as it had been when he stopped me from touching him? As cold and cruel?

Or will it burn for me the way I do for him?

I don't turn around to find out.

"I'm taking a shower, Dimitri," I tell him, walking aimlessly in the direction I hope a bathroom is. It'll be real fucking embarrassing if I step into the wrong room, let me tell you. And I've already met my quota for embarrassment today.

"Violet," he snaps out.

"You know what's sad?" I pause, still not bothering to turn around and face him. I know if I do, he'll see the way that *I* bleed for *him*. "You believe you're only good for death and violence, so you push everyone away. But maybe if you opened yourself up, you'd realize that you're not the only one who lives in sin."

CHAPTER 12

Violet fucking Dracula is going to be the death of me.

With an enraged growl, I whip all of the items off my dresser and watch them drop to the floor.

Fuck her. And fuck the way she makes me feel, as if my heart is too fucking large for my rib cage to contain.

I've lived my entire life following a strict motto—don't let people in. And now, that has all gone to shit. The icy fortress I've attempted to erect around myself is melting with every impish smirk she directs my way. Every heated glance that licks at my soul like fire.

I wasn't lying to her when I said I lived and breathed violence. I'm not a good man. My soul has been tainted black long before Violet ever traipsed into my life. Does that make me the worst type of monster? To recognize the evil inside of me and refuse to change? My hands are painted red with blood, and it's the sweetest fucking sight in the world.

But to have Violet lick the blood off of me…

My cock, which is in a perpetual state of hardness around Violet, twitches, and I have to ball my hands into fists to stop myself from stroking it.

Control. You need to regain control, Dimitri.

But how can I regain control when my world is characterized by chaos in the form of a five-foot-tall vampire?

In the bathroom down the hall, I hear the sound of the shower running, and a groan tears from my throat at the thought of Violet in my personal space. Wet and soapy. Her hands caressing her gorgeous, naked body…

Focus, Dimitri. Figure out what Zeus and Medusa wanted from Violet and how much she told them. And then try to convince her to keep the truth of her parentage from her mates.

I work to center myself, to retreat to the place inside of me where the monsters come out to play. Where they flourish and thrive in the darkness, because the light is too fucking terrified of them to make itself known. At least in the darkness, I know who I am and what I stand for. And what I am is a vessel of death, intent on destruction and pain.

I'm no good for Violet.

I hear the shower shut off and the patter of tiny footsteps as Violet rifles through my bathroom. Will she be looking through my medicine cabinet, just as desperate to uncover the mystery of me as I am of her? Will she smell my towel and inhale my scent? Fuck, the thought of her wrapped in the towel I used just this morning, surrounded by my body wash, makes me hard as hell.

The bathroom door opens and shuts, and I hear the sound of Violet moving back into the kitchen.

I yearn to see her, put my arms around her, and resume what we started.

But terror keeps my feet planted firmly to the ground. I've never felt for a female what I feel for Violet Dracula, and the mere concept has me blinded by it. My entire world is shifting on its axis, changing the north to the south and the east to the west.

I take a deep breath, attempting to calm myself, and smooth out a wrinkle in my dark shirt. I'm painfully underdressed in the safety of my apartment. In my haste to find Violet, I didn't bother with my usual suit and tie combination. Instead, my black T-shirt is rumpled and my dark jeans look as if they belong in a thrift store for homeless people.

What must Violet think of me?

I shove the absurd thought away, telling myself that I don't care about one vampire's insignificant opinion. I'm her headmaster and teacher, nothing more, and I only agreed to look after her because of my father's promise to Dracula and Hera.

But when has this started feeling less like a job and obligation and more like an exciting adventure? When has the line blurred between a need and an innate want?

And when have I started looking at Violet as more than a nuisance?

She's a treasure I yearn to covet but know I can't have. Maybe I simply want a taste of the forbidden fruit? If I fuck her, will this need waging a war inside of me go away? Or will it strengthen?

Growling at the ridiculousness of my thoughts, I throw open my bedroom door and stomp straight to the kitchen, determined more than ever to focus on the topic at hand. I refuse to allow this slip of a girl to distract me a moment longer, not with the fate of the universe as a whole on the line. If the prophecy is true, if she's truly slated to become the new Queen of Hell, I need to know.

And I need to stop her.

The thought has my insides tightening, pain rushing through my bloodstream like magma, but I force the uncomfortable reaction away and push inside my kitchen.

"Violet…" My words taper off as a groan tears from deep within my chest. "Why the fuck are you naked?"

"Who? Me?" Violet asks innocently, batting her eyelashes. Water cascades down her body from her wet hair as she sashays forward. "I don't know what you mean."

"Violet," I growl out as my eyes devour her supple skin. It takes every ounce of willpower I possess—years in the making—to force my gaze back to hers. Instead of seeming impressed by my restraint, a crease forms between her eyebrows as those blue orbs of hers glint mischievously. "Is this your way of torturing me?"

"Not at all," she states as she begins to jog in place. "Just drying myself off. I didn't feel comfortable using one of your towels."

I don't believe her for a fucking second.

She wants me to see everything I'll never be able to have. I think she might actually kill me this time around.

Unbidden, my eyes drop to her tits as they bounce up and down, and all I can imagine is her riding on my cock, her head thrown back in ecstasy as I take one of her nipples into my mouth. She really does have an exceptional pair, each mound easily a handful and those pink nipples just begging for attention.

"What the fuck are you doing?" I ask, keeping my expression perfectly impassive even as my cock turns to stone in my pants.

"Just getting some exercise in," she answers as she brings both her hands up to her tits and fondles them. "Never know when I'm going to need to run for my life again."

"I know what you're doing," I grit out, once again willing my eyes to stay on her face.

"I don't know what you mean," she responds coquettishly as she pinches her nipples between her thumbs and forefingers and tugs at them. When she releases them, her breasts bounce enticingly as she hisses in pain. "Fucking sensitive titties," she murmurs, glaring at her breasts as if they offended her.

At least she stopped goddamn running.

"We need to talk about what happened today. What did Zeus and Medusa—oh for fuck's sake!"

"What?" Violet turns to stare at me over her shoulder where she bends at the waist, her perfectly sculpted ass and pussy lips on full display. "I'm just practicing my yoga positions. Never know when I'm gonna need to be bendy." She curls her body forward until her hands are around her ankles and her breasts are now staring me straight in the eye between her legs.

Ass. Pussy. Boobs.

She's definitely going to kill me.

A strangled noise escapes me as she slowly straightens, still keeping her back to me.

"What did Zeus and Medusa want?" I manage to snap out.

She finally spins around to face me…

With her finger inside of her pussy.

"Oops." She brings her other hand to her mouth in feigned horror. "How embarrassing. My finger slipped and happened to land in my pussy."

My right eye begins to twitch. "Violet, this is serious."

"I'm taking this very seriously," she tells me, moving to perch on the counter once more.

"I eat there," I tell her in a cold voice, but she simply flashes me a wicked grin, one that has even more blood rushing straight to my cock.

"Yes," she agrees, spreading her legs to give me an unrestricted view of her pussy, glistening with arousal. "*Me.*"

"A lot of girls, actually," I lie, though she'll never be able to tell. I've perfected the art of infusing sincerity into every word I say…even when I'm full of shit. I've never brought another person to this apartment before—hell, to any of my apartments—and I don't plan to.

But I can tell the lie meets its mark when her face falls, surprise and hurt giving way to unreadability.

"Is that so?" Slowly, she presses her legs together, and I finally feel as if I can breathe normally again.

"And I'll probably do it again tonight after I return you to the academy," I tell her, wanting her to hurt. Wanting her to suffer.

A part of me hates myself for it, but the rest of me recognizes my words for what they are—a way to survive.

And I can't fucking survive if I'm stuck feeling anything for Violet Dracula besides careful indifference and a little bit of lust.

Once again, hurt flashes in Violet's eyes, so deep and pronounced that I feel as if it cuts *me* open. The fact only reinforces what I have to do.

You can't afford to get attached to her, Dimitri. You can't afford to feel anything for her besides the occasional lust.

"I see," she says curtly, her lips thinning.

"I told you," I tell her, twisting the knife I already shoved in her chest. "I don't do feelings or relationships. What we have is nothing but sex and lust. Do you understand?" My heart beats fiercely in my chest, and I half want to fall at her feet and promise her that I haven't touched a single female since she first arrived at the academy. Hell, I haven't even looked at a single female, my mind too consumed with her and the way she makes me feel.

But if I say that out loud, I'm giving away a piece of myself I'm not sure I'll ever get back. I imagine it's the equivalent of handing my balls to her on a silver fucking platter and praying she doesn't just throw them away. A man like me needs his balls to survive.

"I want to go back to the academy," she tells me, and I see

the exact moment when she hardens herself. When her mask slides back into place as if it never left in the first place. When her eyes turn hard and cruel and she stares at me like I'm the gum beneath her shoe. "I want to see my father."

"Naked?" I ask drolly, lifting a white brow as I give her a dismissive once-over. She doesn't need to know I'm harder than I've ever been in my life. That my heart is racing erratically in a way it has never done before. That my hands feel clammy, despite the sweat forming on the back of my neck.

Frankie may think he's nothing but a machine, but I know the truth. If any of us were formed from wires and computers, then that person would be me. I truly believe I'm incapable of feeling love for another person.

Well, I *thought* I was incapable.

"What do you want, Dimitri?" Violet asks, suddenly sounding tired. I have to give her some credit. Most girls would rush to hide herself, maybe ask for a robe or shirt in an attempt to not feel as vulnerable. But my girl? She simply owns her stunning body—as she should—and pushes her chest out as if she doesn't give a damn that her nipples are beaded and her pussy is on display.

"What happened with Medusa and Zeus?" I demand.

She blows out an irritated breath and flashes me a glare so full of hatred and vitriol, I want to bristle. And beg for her forgiveness.

The contradicting emotions confuse me.

"Why?" She cocks her head to the side, a strand of golden hair falling forward. "You want to hear all about how Zeus fucked me? How I rode his hard cock while screaming his name?"

Blinding jealousy crashes over me like a tsunami, and I have to bite down on the string of curses that wants to escape.

"That's not true," I hiss out. Because if it is, I might just march into Olympus and stab Zeus in the neck, consequences be damned. I'll be able to—I'm damn good at my job —but the gods won't be able to function without their fearless leader there to rule them.

"Why does it matter either way?" Violet huffs, crossing her arms under her chest and forcing her breasts up even further. And then, because she's an evil minx created to drag me straight to Hell, her tongue snakes out and she licks one of her nipples, all the while holding furious eye contact with me.

"It doesn't," I tell her coldly, wanting nothing more than to fill that naughty mouth with my cock. Maybe that would finally shut her up. "And stop doing that."

"Doing what?" She licks at her nipple again while holding my glare.

"You look like a fucking frog," I tell her.

"And you look like a major asshole," she retorts, reaching behind her to open up one of my drawers. I watch her with my arms crossed, waiting to see what she'll do next. When she grabs a metal mixer, my brow furrows.

"What are you doing?" I demand, but instead of answering, she places the mixer to her slick opening and begins to fuck herself with it.

Holy. Fuck.

"Yes, Zeus, yes," she praises, squeezing her eyelids shut as she fucks herself with the kitchen appliance. "I love your monster cock inside of me."

I growl in warning, taking a threatening step closer.

"You didn't fuck Zeus," I tell her, though my words are guttural as something dark and insidious comes to life inside of me.

"Zeus, you feel so good!" she screams as she bounces wildly.

With a roar, I launch myself across the room and all but

grab the mixer from her hands. She blinks at me in alarm, something impish and dark flashing to life in her eyes, and in a moment of complete helplessness, I begin to lick the mixer. I groan at the taste of her arousal exploding on my tongue, sending heat straight to my groin. She tastes like chocolate and sin combined. Like every naughty dream I've ever had, considering I'm her headmaster and she's my student.

Her eyes glaze over with lust as she watches me lick the mixer clean. She leans forward slightly, her tits brushing against my arm, and begins to lick as well, her eyes never leaving mine.

I want her.

I want her so damn much that feelings like these shouldn't be possible, especially for a monster like me. But even when my brain warns me against them, even when my heart attempts to harden, I still lean toward her, helpless to resist her magnetic pull.

She pulls away quickly with a look of disgust glimmering in her eyes.

Disgust aimed at me.

Fuck, why does that hurt me so badly?

"I didn't fuck Zeus," she tells me with a scowl. "He's technically my step-dad, so ew. Gross. He just wanted to…um… play video games."

My hands curl into fists. "Please don't tell me 'video games' is slang for something sexual."

"No. Not at all." Her brows dip. "Medusa was there too."

"And she told you about the two prophecies," I conclude, dropping the mixer back onto the counter and taking a step away. Every second I share her air, I feel myself falling further and further. It's terrifying.

"She did," Violet agrees. "But she doesn't know about Lucifer and Hera."

"Good. That's good." I run my hand down my cheek.

"Zeus and Medusa can never learn the truth about this. Zeus may seem harmless, but he's a jealous, sadistic asshole. He'll be furious when he discovers his wife cheated on him—despite the fact that he's been cheating on her his entire life. He might even harm you to teach your birth mother a point. And Medusa…"

"Is a power-hungry bitch?" Violet supplies with a quirked brow. "Yes, I understand. We can't let them know."

"I don't believe they'll be stupid enough to tell Lucifer, but it's still not safe," I agree, bracing myself for what I need to say next. Violet is definitely not going to like this. "Saying all of that, I don't think it'll be a good idea for you to tell your… mates what you know." My lip pulls away from my teeth at the thought of all of those other men pawing at her while I'm stuck…not pawing at her. Fuck my life.

Violet bristles as if I insulted her baby or some shit, her eyes widening and her spine straightening with steel. "I don't think that's your choice to make."

"I've been working to keep you safe my entire life," I hiss out, wanting nothing more than to grab her off the counter, wrap her in my arms, and—

"Don't worry," she snaps, giving me a frosty glare. "I don't want or need your help anymore." She jumps down from the counter and jabs a finger into my chest. "And you definitely don't get to control what I tell my guys."

"If word gets out—"

"My men are the most trustworthy people I've ever met," she hisses. "I trust them more than I trust you."

Her words are like a knife to the gut, though I know I deserve them. I deserve everything she throws at me and then some.

I keep my expression carefully blank as I tilt my chin down to stare into her eyes, allowing her to see a brief glimpse of myself I normally keep hidden—the man desperate to be loved. Even when I'm furious with her, she's able to tear past my defenses like no other. "I just want to keep you safe."

Her tiny pink tongue darts out to lick her upper lip as she holds my stare. When the silence between us grows excruciating, and I fear she won't respond, she manages to say, "So do they."

Just like that, the moment between us is over, and I have to wonder if I'd imagined the entire interaction. I take a step away from her, refusing to break her stare.

"Take me home, please," she whispers, wrapping her arms around her stomach. My heart lurches at hearing the word 'home' leave her lips.

She'll never consider me her 'home.'

Not after the things I said to her, the way I hurt her.

Steeling my heart one last time, I nod and extend my hand. "As you wish. But maybe…maybe you should consider putting some clothes on first."

CHAPTER 13

"Precious Treasure?" Her name is nothing but a whisper on my tongue as consciousness returns to me, slow and sluggish. My head pounds as if someone has taken a…what's the word?…dildo to it.

Yes, my head hurts as if someone had whacked me repeatedly with a dildo.

That's not the saying, Jack says in my head, his tone a mixture of impatience and fear. *It's 'sledgehammer.'*

Why would someone take a sledgehammer to my head? I ask as I attempt to get my bearings. We appear to be in some type of classroom, the desks perfectly spaced and facing a blank whiteboard near the front of the room. *It seems more probable that someone would take a dildo to the face, especially during an intense lovemaking session. Now…where the fuck are we?*

Detention, Jack responds, a sliver of fear in his voice. *In the upper levels of the academy.*

And where's my precious treasure? Genuine terror clamps down on my heart at the thought of my beloved being alone somewhere. Has she even completed the second game of the Roaring? What if something happened to her?

She's fine, Hux, Jack soothes. *We'd be able to sense if something happened to her, remember? Through the bond?*

I can't lose her, Jack. I can't.

You won't, he assures me.

I move slowly down the aisle, the darkness of the room permeating my system and leaving me cold after months in the light. It's almost reminiscent of the time I spent relegated to a corner of Jack's head, nothing but a dirty secret he wished to eradicate from his life. And maybe I deserved to be that dirty secret. After all, I was a monster with no purpose, wandering aimlessly through life.

Yes, I admittedly left a pile of bodies in my wake during that time, but I don't believe for one second that makes me a bad man, just a murderous one.

But now I have a purpose, and her name is Violet Dracula. My precious treasure.

We need to figure out how we're getting out of this mess, Jack tells me as I step into the hallway.

In every direction, the darkness is broken apart by the red glow from the exit sign, hanging tauntingly above the door at the end of the hall.

But there's no escape from this prison.

Anger coils through me like a python as I think about the reason why we were sent here in the first place.

The intruder in our head. The intruder in our head that I can't currently sense, almost as if he left the metaphorical building.

"Who the fuck is he?" I rage out loud, my anger unable to be contained by my measly human vessel. It demands an outlet, a way to be set free and wreak havoc on a world that seeks to destroy me.

I don't know, Jack responds, sounding despondent by the fact. *But whoever he is, we can't trust him.*

Obviously. I scoff at the ridiculous notion that I'd ever believe a word the murderous asshole in my head tells me.

At least he can't hurt Violet while we're in here, Jack continues, always the optimist, even in the worst possible situations.

Red distorts my vision at the thought of *my hand* being used to inflict any pain upon my precious treasure. If the stranger in my head can't see that she's a goddess sent straight from heaven for the mortals to worship and praise, then he's more stupid than he looks.

He looks like us, Hux, Jack reminds me, and I growl.

"I don't want to be compared to that…that monster," I bite out, my tone scathing and heated. I'm a lot of things—most of them I'll admit to without pause or hesitation—but I'm not like that…that *demon*. I kill people because they deserve it, not because they happen to be a particular supernatural.

Jack's response is interrupted by a low, carnal growl echoing from farther down the hall.

My spine straightens, a rush of irrational fear flowing through me, as I turn toward the noise. Every hair on my body rises to attention.

Is there someone in here with us? Jack whispers shakily, and I realize that his fear has intermingled with my own, exacerbating my emotions tenfold.

"Who's there?" I growl out, my hands curling into fists. "I'll fuck your ass up."

That's not how the saying goes, Jack tells me, his tone heady with exasperation. And fear. I hate that more than anything.

"I'll fuck your ass up so hard!" I continue. Mentally, I tell Jack, *Yes, I believe that is the saying. Mason taught me it, along* with, 'Your mom's a whore.' And, 'Chitty chitty bang bang, look at this wiener go.'

Another growl reverberates down the dark hallway, but this time, I'm prepared for it. You can never be too careful in the monster world. A snarl of my own escapes as I wait for the intruder to make himself known.

Wait... Jack breathes in shock as the figure slowly ambles forward. *Is that Cal?*

The cupid? I ask in disbelief as I see a shock of pink hair and deeply tan skin.

"Cal?" My brows furrow together. "Is that you?" When the figure only continues to move forward, strange gurgling noises escaping him, I bite out, "Answer me this damn instant!"

The red glow of the exit sign finally illuminates Violet's friend as he takes a single step closer and then pauses, canting his head to the side.

His eyes are completely red—the color of blood and hellfire. Wings extend on either side of his body, the feathers shaded in black.

Oh...frick, Jack laments, terror infusing his mental voice.

What? I demand.

I've read about this before, he tells me as Cal continues to advance, his back muscles hunched and his red eyes glimmering.

He doesn't look as friendly as he did the last time I saw him, I tell Jack, widening my stance and lifting my hands. I can feel Jack's desperate need to run away, but he should know by now that I'll never run away from a challenge. I'll—as Mason likes to say—deep dick the challenge in the ass. At least, I think that's how the saying goes.

This shouldn't be possible, Jack continues fearfully. *Not unless he's half fairy.*

What do you mean? I demand.

A fairy's eyes turn red and their wings start turning black when they transition from a light fairy to a dark fairy, he explains, and something cold settles in the pit of my stomach, squeezing at my organs until I fear I'll vomit.

Cal's an incubus, I tell him matter-of-factly.

I'm just telling you what I know, Jack says.

My eyes roam over the other male as my heart crawls up my throat. He's one of Violet's best friends, so I'd hate to have to kill him. However, I can't allow him to kill me either —which he seems inclined to.

It seems we're at a stalemate. Perhaps if I kill him, I can gift Violet his head as an offering of peace? She can stuff him then and use his body as a chair. I imagine he'll be a comfy chair.

We're not killing Cal and making him into a chair! Jack screams in my head, and I resist the urge to pout.

So we let him kill us? I roar in vehement denial.

No. We talk to him.

My upper lip peels away from my teeth. *I'm not very good at...talking. I like stabbing. And maiming. And beheading. And slaughtering. And—*

Violet cares about him, Jack reminds me. *So you can't do anything to him without upsetting her.*

Horror fills me at even the prospect of upsetting my precious treasure. That girl owned me from the minute she handed me a chocolate bar, not knowing how precious a gift like that was to a monster like me. For a man who's lived his entire life pushed into the shadows, it was an exhilarating experience to step out into the light. As a wise man once told me...

She grabbed me by the balls and never let me go.

And yes, Mason was that wise man.

She molded me into a monster that fought, bled, and died

in her name—and all she needs to do now is flash me one of her signature impish smirks.

I don't even care if that makes me "whipped" or however you say it. She owns me—heart, body, and soul.

She's my WAP—Woman I Adore and Protect.

Mason taught me that one as well. I'll have to bring it up to her sometime. Tell her she's my WAP.

After I deal with the deranged incubus—or dark fairy, if Jack's to be believed—intent on killing me, of course.

"I killed a man the other night." Cal's voice is guttural—low and deep and dripping with violence. Everything about him seems *wrong*. His eyes are a shade too red, his teeth are a little too sharp for his mouth, and his wings are slightly crooked, as if they've been broken and haphazardly knitted back together. "Alex's father, actually," he continues. "For touching Barret and Violet."

"Good," I grunt out, insidious satisfaction filling me. I want all men and women to pay in blood for laying their hands on my precious treasure. "Did you hide the body?"

Hux! Jack chastises. *Now is not the time.*

There's always time to talk about murder, I point out. *Especially murder on behalf of our perfect mate.*

I don't need to see my brother to know that his eyes would've rolled to the back of his head in exasperation. For some strange reason, Jack doesn't revel in violence as much as I do. He doesn't taste its sweet scent on his tongue or lose himself to the darkness in his soul. I crave violence and death like an addict needs his next fix. It drives my every waking moment—this thirst for blood that surpasses even what vampires feel.

Maybe that's why I was made for Violet.

We're both bloodthirsty.

"I was in the game with Violet when you threw that grenade," Cal continues in a low, predatory voice. He advances a step, his wings expanding in a move that feels almost threatening.

I bare my teeth in retaliation.

Grenade? What the bloody hell is he talking about? Did the third entity in our body throw a grenade at my PRECIOUS TREASURE?!?!

"No one," Cal hisses out, still advancing forward, "hurts my mate."

Mate?

I only have a second to think that one word when Cal lunges at me.

CHAPTER 14

VIOLET

I'm spit out of the mirror and into the living room of the guys' house.

Like before, I fall onto my hands and knees, only this time, I keep my wits about me. Thank Zeus. The last thing I need is to start petting my mates or trying to dry-hump their legs like a cat in heat. I may have a lady red rocket for them the size of Texas, but I need to maintain at least *some* level of dignity.

Even as I think that, I topple over, the bathrobe I threw on riding up and baring my flapper jack and squishy tushy to the world at large. I desperately try to fix the cotton robe, only to untangle it completely and have it fall to the ground at my feet.

Why am I always naked?

Honestly, I don't even care too much at this stage of my life—a mid-mid-life crisis, as in, halfway to fifty. I have a great pair of tits, and the fresh air feels good on my sausage taker and sausage maker.

"Violet!"

I'm jerked upright and into a pair of strong arms, Vin's distinct cinnamon and peppermint scent surrounding me and infusing my body with warmth.

"Where the fuck have you been?" he breathes against my head. "Are you hurt? Did they hurt you?"

I wound my arms around his waist, wanting to hold him just as tightly as he's currently holding me. Vin and I... we're fire and ice. On paper, the two of us should not work together—he's a fierce vampire hunter and part of the infamous Van Helsing family, while I'm a vampire and the daughter of Dracula. Well, at least I *thought* I was a vampire, but I refuse to think about the truth of my lineage right now. He's my mortal enemy, our names written together in blood, but he's also my mate. My love.

The world would balk at the prospect of us being together, but I can't imagine my life without him. Sure, he's combative, cantankerous, and a complete dick, but he's also fiercely passionate, protective, and sweet.

Sometimes. When he's not being a raging cock face.

"There's a lot we have to talk about," I tell him as I nuzzle against his neck. My fangs automatically extend, my eyes dipping to the vein pulsing in his neck, but I force myself to take a deep breath and push the thirst to a corner of my mind. Now isn't the time to lose myself to the bloodlust of my monster.

As I pull away from Vin, my gaze latches on a familiar pair of eyes over Vin's shoulder. My heart rate increases, desire rushing through my veins like magma, as Frankie takes a single step closer, moving to stand side by side with Vin.

Frankie's brown, wavy hair is tousled, almost as if he hasn't bothered to comb it today, which is strange because I can't remember a time it hasn't been immaculately brushed away from his face. His black glasses, the frame wider than Jack's, slide down his nose as he stares at me intently. While Vin is hewn from solid muscle, Frankie is rounder, alleviating some of the danger that exudes off of him in palpable waves.

But there's no denying he's a force to be reckoned with, especially when he's angry.

Vin, on the other hand, has tawny-brown skin, almost as if he spends the majority of his time outside tanning. Or staking vampires. His dark brown hair is longer at the top than the sides, appearing almost black in the artificial lighting of the kitchen. Tribal tattoos run up the length of his arm, disappearing into the dark T-shirt he wears.

Both of them are sexy as hell despite their differences and make my heart race.

"Where are the others?" I ask, suddenly desperate to see them and ensure they're okay.

When Frankie and Vin exchange anxious glances, my terror amplifies, sliding through my bloodstream like poison.

"Where are they?" I ask softly, my throat closing. My skin feels itchy all of a sudden. Why am I so itchy? And where did this tightness come from in my throat and chest? Why can't I breathe? Did I turn into a cat sometime in the last few minutes and am now choking up a hairball?

"Violet." Frankie takes a step closer and pulls me against his chest, comforting me the only way he knows how. "Take a deep breath for me. We'll explain everything."

"Are they…?" I don't dare voice the rest of my question. I'm spiraling, falling deeper and deeper down a black hole I don't think I'll ever be able to emerge from. Emotions claw at me, ripping me open and spilling my blood and guts. The feeling is unlike anything I've ever experienced before.

"They're alive," Frankie assures me, pushing me back

enough to press a tender kiss to my nose. "Let's go to the living room and chat."

"Living room. Yes. Living room." My mind is numb, absently focusing on one or two words at a time and repeating them over and over. I can't seem to comprehend anything else.

Frankie leads me to the couch in the center of the living room and sits down beside me, resting one hand on my still bare knee. Vin remains standing in the center of the room, his customary scowl firmly in place.

"Tell me what happened," he barks, all dogmatic and shit. Normally, I'd find his alpha attitude a total turn on, but it only fills me with blistering rage now. I'm too consumed with worry for my mates and friends to focus on anything else.

"You tell me what happened," I retort, glaring.

His frown deepens. "No, you tell me what happened first."

"No, you," I fire back.

"You."

"No, you."

"You, Violet!" he seethes, his teeth bared. "I'm not fucking around."

"I'm not either!" I cross my arms over my chest and narrow my eyes, just waiting for him to break.

I can stare at him *allllll* day. My eyes are fortresses, and I'll kill myself before I blink. Hell hath no fury like Violet fucking Dracula when she's competing in a staring contest.

Surprisingly, it's not Vin who caves.

It's Frankie.

"We finished round two of the Roaring and couldn't find you," he tells me, his hand tightening on my knee. When I glance in his direction, his face is creased with pain I can't quite understand. Or maybe I can understand—I imagine it's similar to the way I feel now, not knowing where my mates are or what happened to them. It's a keen type of pain that's almost reminiscent of loss and death. Grief.

Why does it feel like I'm missing a limb and am forced to relearn how to navigate the world without it? I can't lose my mates. I've finally come to terms with the fact they *are* my mates, something I knew innately for weeks but chose to deny until now. I can't lose them. I won't. I refuse—

Frankie's lips on mine stop my downward spiral in mid-spiral. So instead of a full-on fall and die type of spiral, it's a hover in the air and think about death type.

Why am I thinking so much about spirals?

I kiss him back instinctively, my lips moving against his even as my mind struggles to shut off. Vin murmurs something I can't quite hear, his tone laced with jealousy, and the annoyance I feel over that is enough to stop my rapidly swirling thoughts. I pull away from Frankie's lips to glare at the asshole.

"Something you need to say, Vin?" I ask scathingly, placing my head onto Frankie's shoulder as he wraps an arm around me. And though I know Frankie doesn't have a real heart, I can still hear the machine in his chest beat erratically, almost as if it's reacting to my presence.

Vin ignores my question and continues where Frankie left off. "We ran into Mason right away, and all three of us started looking for you. But Mason..." He rubs a hand through his dark hair as my heart takes a running nosedive off a cliff, splattering on the rocky shoreline far below. My breath escapes me in short, shallow spurts as terror digs into my throat like a garrote.

"Is he okay?"

"He's upstairs with Barret," Vin tells me with a nod. "But he's..."

"He's suffering from withdrawals," Frankie supplies in that no-nonsense way of his. At one point, I would've thought him to be impassive and maybe even cruel, but I now know that's just the way Frankie is. If the rest of us see the world in vibrant shades of color, he only recognizes and catalogs black and white. It gives him a unique view of life itself while still maintaining that innocence I've come to love about him. He's brash and to the point, and right now, I'm not in the mood to be coddled.

"Fuck," I curse, worry for Mason scratching at my heart. "I didn't know it had gotten so bad."

"I didn't either." Vin's jaw clenches as his eyes flicker toward the staircase leading to Mason's bedroom. In that one stare, I can see a lifetime of self-loathing and misdirected anger.

"It's not your fault," I tell Vin firmly, and his gaze snaps to me.

"How can you say that?" His voice is heady with disbelief. "I'm his best friend. Of course it's my fault. I should've realized something was wrong."

"And I'm his mate," I bite out. "If anyone should've noticed how far he'd fallen, it's me."

Both Frankie and Vin freeze at my strident words. I'm not even sure they're breathing.

This is probably the first time I've ever acknowledged out loud the truth of what these men are to me, and I to them. It's not as if we hide our feelings for one another, but all of us seem to believe that if we bury the truth, shove it in a steel box and never allow it to see the light of day, then it's not real.

But what we have is very, very real, and I'll be damned if I keep it silent for a second longer. Not after the day I had.

"Why is Barret with Mason?" I query. Barret is the sweetest monster known to mankind, but he's not exactly... how do I put this?...friendly with everyone. He's really only nice to Cal and me.

He has a teeny tiny little problem of eating people.

"His powers," Vin explains. When I continue to give him an 'I'm stupid, so explain in simple terms' look, he elaborates. "Barret, as the Boogeyman, is able to enter dreams. Since Mason was so distressed by your disappearance, he started having nightmares." I'm on my feet in seconds, but Vin moves in front of me, placing his hands on my shoulders to force me back down. "Don't go to him right now. He's resting, which is what he needs after the day he had."

"Fuck." I place a hand over my chest to stop my galloping heart, only to grab a handful of boob instead.

Oh.

I'm still naked.

I absently pluck at my nipple, rolling it between my fingers as I think. It's honestly quite soothing to give yourself a nipple massage. Very calming. "Is there anything we can do for him? Like, is there a facility we can send him to? A potion he can drink?"

Vin's eyes drop to where my fingers play with my breasts, his eyes flaring with heat. He curses and turns away from me. "There is, but he won't go. You know how he is. Stubborn to the core."

"He wouldn't want to leave you," Frankie adds. Unlike Vin, he doesn't pull his attention away from my breast, his eyes glued to my fingers and nipple. I should honestly write a book about how to hypnotize a guy with nothing but tits. Nipple-tize them. Tittie-tize. Ohhh I like that one.

Tittie-tize: The Official Guide to World Domination.

An autobiography by Violet Dracula.

"And Jack and Hux?" I ask, and once again, Frankie and Vin exchange one of those man-bro-dude glances. All of my hackles rise with alarm. "Where are they?"

"That's complicated," Vin responds, moving to sit on the armchair opposite us. He leans forward, clasping his hands together and placing them between his open legs. I suddenly realize how tired he looks, how vulnerable, and I know my disappearance had a big role to play in that.

"How is it complicated?"

"Because it's not just Jack and Hux anymore," Frankie responds, still staring at my boobs.

"What do you mean?" My brows furrow together as Vin releases a huff of air.

"There's a third entity inside of them, one that might've been there for centuries. He's...not a good man," Vin tells me, and everything inside of me tightens and rebels at the knowledge.

Hux and Jack...and a mysterious third entity?

Who the fuck is this whore shacking up with my mates?!?

"What's his name?" I growl out, anger pulsating through me.

"Balor," Frankie answers.

"Never heard that name before. He must be a stupid idiot with a tiny peen," I say.

I mentally give myself a high five for the insult.

"I haven't either," Vin admits with a shrug. "But, Violet... he murdered a female today just because she's part vampire."

"Oh...Oh fuck," I curse as realization settles in the pit of my stomach like a leaden weight.

Jack and Hux are apparently sharing the same headspace as a murderous asshole who hates vampires. And now, if I understand Vin and Frankie correctly, we have no idea where Jack and Hux are.

Or if the man we're looking for *is* even Jack or Hux.

Fuck.

Fuck.

Fuck!

"Okay, what else is going on? Lay it on me. I'm ready." I pull at my nipple hard enough to hurt as Vin's eyes turn glazed with wanton need. Frankie's hand on my knee inches upward, until his pinkie finger is caressing my inner leg. "How's Vanessa? Cal?"

"Vanessa's fine," Frankie assures me. "But she's been spending a lot of time with her parents, so you might need to maintain your distance until they leave."

Relief fills me. I really need to message her and see how she's doing, as well as assure her I'm okay.

"And we don't know where Cal is," Vin finishes. "But Barret assured us he's fine. Just…upset."

One of the last times I saw Cal, he murdered Alex's father in a fit of rage, believing the man to have killed Barret.

The three of us left the club quickly, but it doesn't change the fact that someone might've seen us. Or Alex's father's corpse. Fuck. Do the authorities already know that Alex's father is dead? Do they know who did it?

And what happened to Cal?

"This is a lot to take in," I confess as one of Frankie's fingers slowly enters me, swirling through my juices. I open my legs up wide, allowing him better access, and he thrusts his digit in and out of my wet heat. Somehow, someway, despite the horrendous circumstances…I find myself getting impossibly wetter for him. My skin feels flushed with heat.

I really am a filthy, insatiable ho, aren't I?

"Now it's your turn," Vin growls out, crossing his arms over his chest and watching me.

"My turn…for…orgasm?" I question dazedly, a moan tearing from my lips as Frankie works his magical fingers. When he begins to circle them inside of me, I swear my eyes roll into the back of my head.

Vin pinches the bridge of his nose. "Tell us what happened. Where have you been? Dimitri mentioned that you were in Mount Olympus with Mason's mom?" His voice pitches high in disbelief, turning the statement into a question. "And that she wanted to kill you? And that you disappeared with him?"

Thoughts of Dimitri have the fire in my core dissipating like a bucket of water being thrown over my pussy.

But then Frankie lowers his mouth to my neglected breast and swirls his tongue around my nipple, and…voila. Fire. Lots and lots of fire that eats away at my skin.

"For fuck's sake…" Vin grumbles, even as his hand moves to his crotch and he rubs himself through the denim of his jeans.

"So basically what happened…Oh fuck!" I curse as Frankie's hand pinches down on my clit at the same time his teeth graze my aching nipple. "The escape room for the second game of the Roaring? Not actually an escape room. I had a meeting with my dad and Dimitri." Thoughts of my dad cool any and all lust I might've felt from my mate's touch.

Fuck, I haven't checked in on him since I've been back. Is he still in the hospital? Is he okay?

Frankie, easily able to read that I'm no longer in the mood for the horizontal tango, pulls away from me. "What happened?"

"I learned some interesting things," I confess, my throat feeling uncomfortably tight.

"Like what?" Vin grits out, his frown deepening and emphasizing the lines in his face. He truly is sexy when he frowns like that—all scowly and growly.

"Like…" I duck my head and mumble the next words under my breath. "IamthedaughterofHeraandLucifer. AndthereisaprophecythatstatesIwillbecometherulerofhell."

There's a beat of silence, and then both Vin and Frankie exclaim, "What?"

"Apparently," I blow out a sigh, forcing myself to meet first Vin's eyes and then Frankie's, "I'm the daughter of Hera and Lucifer, and there's a prophecy that states I'll become the next ruler of Hell or whatever." I force a cheerful smile, though it feels odd on my face. I don't know what I'll do if they reject me now, if they push me away or claim I'm too much drama to deal with. Drama is my middle name. Pettiness is my surname.

Violet fucking Drama fucking Pettiness fucking Dracula.

Vin blinks at me, his face draining of all color and his eyes going wide in his handsome face. Frankie simply places his hand on my knee and tightens it once more, his fingers digging into my sensitive skin.

"What?" Vin manages to say.

I shrug helplessly. "Dimitri and Dad were in the process of telling me all of that when Medusa came for me," I continue, still speaking faster than an average human but at least being somewhat coherent. "Dad was staked by a god-blessed dagger, but according to Medusa and Dimitri, he's alive and in the hospital. I need to go visit him. Maybe send him flowers? Oh! I'll find him a nice child, give the child a lollipop, and then allow him to steal candy from a baby. He likes things like that." I nod once, set in my plan. "Maybe I'll even jump out at him and—"

"What the fuck happened when Medusa kidnapped you?" Vin demands, his voice a measly gasp of air. Panic underlies his words.

"She brought me back to Mount Olympus." I scratch absently at my boob, causing both men to dip their gazes to stare at the bouncing flesh. I blame it on the bra I wore earlier today. It irritated my skin, and now, I'm stuck with a boob rash.

"And then?" Frankie's voice is devoid of any inflection or emotion, but the heat in his gaze betrays his true intentions.

"It was kind of weird," I confess. "Mount Olympus was completely empty. Like, it looked like an evacuation zone or something. Is that normal? For the gods and goddesses to evacuate? Is there, like, a bunker or something for them? Anyway," I shake my head and focus on the conversation at hand, "I met Zeus. He's a strange man...god...creature... thing. He can't dance for shit, but he's super big. Like, he'll break me in half if he tried. So, so big."

"Why the fuck are you looking at Zeus's cock?" Vin rages, jumping to his feet and stalking toward me. His eyes burn with hellfire, and damn my hormones, but my pussy jumps up and down for joy at the sight.

"I wasn't talking about his cock, dumbass," I snap with an eye roll. *Though he did have a big one.* "I meant he was tall."

"Oh." Vin flushes, slowly moving backward to reclaim his chair. "Carry on."

"Medusa talked to me about the two prophecies—one stating that Dracula's daughter would kill Mason." My throat burns even saying that, and Vin's eyes harden, turning into chips of obsidian stone. Mason is his best friend, so I imagine he isn't pleased with that tidbit of information either, though I suspect he already knew about that particular prophecy. "And the one about me reclaiming my father's throne... which Dimitri took to mean Lucifer's. Daddy L. The big dad. Daddikins. Dad—"

"Where is Dimitri?" Frankie asks, canting his head backward as if he expects the assassin to be standing behind him with a sword. Knowing what I did of the aloof assassin-turned-teacher-turned-headmaster, it wouldn't surprise me.

"Who even cares?" I sniff haughtily, crossing my arms over my chest and unintentionally pushing my breasts up. "He's a sad, lonely man, with sad, lonely man problems. He can suck my tits for all I care." Heat blazes through me at the thought of Dimitri Gray sucking my tits, but I mentally chastise myself for being such a hussy.

As if the words "suck my tits" hold a power all their own,

Frankie leans his head forward to once again suck on my nipple, his hand moving back to my core.

"We're so happy you're okay, Vi," Vin breathes, focusing on where Frankie touches me. His words rush through me in a cascade of burning, tantalizing heat. The need in his eyes calls to me, and I'm helpless to resist it. Resist *him*. While one of my hands curls into Frankie's hair, the other beckons Vin forward. He swallows. "There's still a lot we need to talk about. Most of us made it to the third round of the Roaring, and we know—"

"I don't care about that right now," I whisper.

As if he's been tethered to me by an unbreakable cord, he slowly rises from the chair and ambles forward, stopping until he's able to kneel in front of me, ducking his head submissively. Frankie lifts his head, confusion swarming in his gaze, but doesn't question Vin's sudden change in demeanor. I place one finger underneath Vin's chin and force his eyes onto mine.

"Show me how much you missed me."

VIOLET

There's a tightness in my chest that hasn't been there prior as I volley my gaze between Frankie and Vin. So different from one another but united by one single thing—me.

"Look at you," I purr, brushing my fingers across Vin's chiseled jawline. "So submissive."

His eyes remain lowered, willingly playing my game with me.

Frankie watches us with barely veiled amusement and interest.

Turning toward him completely, and ignoring a still kneeling Vin, I pepper kisses along Frankie's jaw as my hand moves to his pants. I caress the bulge in his jeans once, a tantalizing promise of what's to come, before whispering, "Stand beside Vin."

His brows cinch together, confusion filling his face, but he doesn't hesitate to move from the couch and stand beside a still kneeling Vin. I gauge both of their reactions carefully, making absolutely certain that they want this, want me. When I only see lust reflected back at me, a smile curls up my lips. I'm not sure if they've ever shared a girl before—especially with each other—but a tiny part of me hopes that I'm their first.

And that I'll be their last.

Vin remains kneeling, but he stares up at me through his fringe of ebony lashes. Frankie glances between the two of us, but he doesn't make a move to grab me or ask what we're up to. He simply waits, the cogs turning in his mind as he considers us.

My heart thrashes in my rib cage at the control they're offering me. The power. It's a heady sensation, one that sets my body alight. God, I need this. I need this so damn much. I'm still revved up from my time with Dimitri, and my body's desperate for release.

To play these games, you need to have a certain level of trust in your partner—trust that you'll stop if they ask you to, trust that they enjoy the pleasure you inflict upon them…and the pain too. Trust.

"The safe word is supercalifragilisticexpialidocious," I tell them seriously as I move to my knees in front of Frankie and resume rubbing his crotch.

Vin snorts out a laugh but quickly stifles it when I turn to glare at him. I'm trying to be sexy, dammit. He doesn't get to laugh.

I suppose I'll have to punish him.

Maintaining eye contact with Vin, I unbutton Frankie's pants and pull the zipper down. Slowly.

When his pants are unbuttoned, I move my hand up and down his boxers, twisting my head to watch his cock harden with rapt fascination. I kiss his erection through the cotton fabric before grabbing the waistband of his boxers and allowing his dick to spring free.

It's already rock-hard for me, a tiny bead of precum on the tip. I wrap my right hand around the base as I guide it into my mouth. My other hand remains in the waistband of his boxers.

I work his cock in my mouth, taking it to the base before licking at the tip, as I pull his pants and boxers down a little bit farther.

When a strong hand wraps around my neck, forcing me to take Frankie even deeper down my throat, I don't question it. At first.

Vin guides my movements as I suck the other man's cock, his hand tightening in my hair to the point of pain.

When he releases me, and I hear the sound of his own zipper, I whirl toward him with blazing eyes, my fangs elongated.

"Get back on your knees," I hiss, watching his reaction carefully. Defiance and heat blaze in his gaze as he holds my stare, but he knows how this works with me. In the bedroom, and only the bedroom, he relinquishes a tiny bit of that stoic control.

Vin continues to stare at me, and I lift a brow, wondering if he's going to push the issue. If he wants to quit the game and take me, I'll more than happily comply. But I think he likes me domming him too much to end it this quickly.

As expected, he rips his eyes away from mine, drops his head, and kneels on the floor once more.

"I'm sorry, mistress," he murmurs reverently.

"Take off your pants and bend down. I'll deal with you in a second," I declare, my heart hammering at what I intend to do.

I turn back to Frankie and grab at his thighs as I resume sucking his cock once more.

"Violet…" He moans, fisting his hands in my hair to guide me. I'm sure my lips are swollen and covered in saliva, but he still stares down at me as if I'm the most beautiful girl he's ever set eyes upon. Goosebumps pebble on my skin, and my stomach flutters deliciously. A bolt of heat slashes through me as we maintain eye contact, his cock halfway down my throat.

I slowly pull away from his cock and begin to kiss up his stomach, shoulders, neck, and finally his lips. He hugs me to him, his cock brushing against my stomach, as he kisses me back just as fiercely.

"You're my fucking world, Violet," he murmurs, and my skin flushes with pleasure and some other emotion. An emotion that's so fucking terrifying, I don't even dare think it.

"Oh, Frankie," I whisper, my fangs grazing his upper lip hard enough to draw blood. If he could bleed, that is. He gasps, but I capture the noise with my mouth.

I turn away from my mate to face Vin Van Helsing, now sans pants and boxers. His black T-shirt is still on, conforming to his muscles, but his cock hits his stomach, leaving a smear of wetness from the precum on the tip.

"I said bend down," I tell Vin, swaying my hips as I step forward. I pray I don't faceplant or something like that. Talk about embarrassing.

Vin's brows furrow, but he does as instructed, his muscular, tan ass facing me.

I swear Frankie's breathing goes ragged as his eyes flicker from my body to Vin's chiseled ass, that analytical mind of his trying to figure out what my next play is.

I pull back my hand and spank Vin as hard as I can, leaving behind a red handprint.

He grunts out a curse, the noise quickly transforming into a moan of pleasure.

Frankie steps forward, fascinated. "I suppose I did read an article about how pain can amplify the pleasure of most humans and monsters—" He cuts off with a moan when I grab his cock and give it a squeeze.

"No thinking," I whisper, spinning back around to kiss him on the lips before pulling away. "Just feeling."

He opens his mouth as if to protest—I'm pretty sure Frankie hasn't gone a minute in his life without overthinking every interaction—but he shuts up when I begin to stroke his hard dick.

The power of an orgasm, my friends.

Dropping to my knees between them, I turn to face Vin, finding his cock hard and ready for me, mere inches from my face. I lick my lips in anticipation before dropping a kiss to the slit at the end. He groans, his hips jerking, but doesn't make a move to grab at my hair the way he did with Frankie. I watch his head fall back and his eyes close in utter bliss. Smug, feminine satisfaction rumbles through me at the knowledge that I put that dopey-eyed expression on his face. Me. Well, my lips around his dick, but you get the idea.

I open my mouth wide and swallow him all the way, keeping my hand around Frankie's cock and stroking him in tandem. Both men unconsciously thrust their hips forward, but we all know who has complete and utter control at the moment—*moi*.

My lips leave Vin's dick, allowing it to brush my cheek and leave behind a wet spot, as I tug on Frankie's cock gently, urging him even closer. The tips of their dicks touch, but they don't seem to mind as I put my lips around Frankie's and begin stroking Vin's. I alternate between the two, running the pad of my tongue along their sides, sucking on their balls, and deep-throating them like a motherfucking champ. Saliva drips down my chin, and if they didn't stare at me like I was a goddess reincarnated, I might've been self-conscious.

But it's impossible to feel even an ounce of that negative, toxic emotion when they're staring at me like I'm their entire world.

I lift my head from where I've been sucking Vin's dick and begin to stroke them both in unison.

"Get your clothes off," I tell them, my breath ragged and uneasy. I need this. After the day I had, I need this more than anything. I know I need to find Hux and Jack, check in on Mason, talk to Barret about Cal, catch up with Vanessa and Cynthia, and see how my father is doing, but I can't focus on any of that right now. I just want to be with my men—my mates. For so long, I've been afraid of admitting the truth to even myself. It was one of those things I refused to consider, refused to believe was even possible. Vampires didn't have fated mates because society didn't believe we had souls.

But now...

Now that's all changed.

After Vin and Frankie hurry to do what I instructed, I guide Vin down onto the ground.

"Fuck..." he curses, his face pained as I crouch over him, the tip of his cock brushing against my pussy but not quite entering me yet. He lifts his hips up, almost as if he means to impale me on his length, but I place a hand around his throat and tighten until he stares into my eyes. And then—only then —do I slowly slide down onto him, his length filling me to the brim. "Oh, fuck," he curses again his hands going to my waist.

"Frankie?" I growl out, glancing over my shoulder to see the other man standing behind us, his cock in hand.

"Yes, my love?"

Oh...belly flutters. He's never called me that before, and I find an entire circus performing inside of me, complete with acrobats, tromping elephants, and a creepy little clown who probably sells children on the black market. Fuck clowns.

"Can you grab Vin's belt and restrain his hands for me above his head?" I ask sweetly, fluttering my lashes.

Vin's cock jerks inside of me.

"Violet…" he warns, his eyes devouring my naked body.

I lean down, the movement making his dick hit a sweet spot inside of me, and brush my lips against his.

"Do you want me to stop?" I whisper, the words just for him.

I can hear Frankie shuffling around behind us, but I don't tear my gaze away from my vampire hunter.

Vin's always been so…alpha, so I don't know how he feels about being a sub in front of Frankie. At the moment, this is just something we're experimenting with. I'm completely fine with stopping the game at any time, and he knows that.

His jaw clenches, his eyes burning with heat, and he slowly shakes his head. "No," he grits out, obediently moving his arms above his head. His biceps strain, all of that gorgeous tan skin and tribal tattoos on display, and I grin, pushing myself backward and placing a hand in the center of his chest to steady myself.

I work to remain perfectly still as Frankie moves to secure Vin's hands to a table over his head, prohibiting him from touching me. Only when Frankie backs away do I begin to move, bouncing on his cock with mewls of pleasure escaping me. My breasts bounce in front of Vin's face, and I know it's taking all of his mental strength and resolve not to break free of his confines and grab at one.

Lips move to my neck a split second before Frankie grabs both my tits from behind, kneading them in his large fists. I can feel his cock brush against my ass as I twist my head, determined to kiss him. Devour him. I want to share the air he breathes and consume him in the way I know he's doing to me.

"Please…" I beg against his lips, my words a cry. "I want your cock in me."

He hesitates, his lips moving to my cheek and then to my ear. "Are you sure?"

"Yes."

He pulls his hands away from my breasts to gather the juices leaking from me. Neither man seems to care when Frankie's hand accidentally brushes against Vin's hard length, still pistoning in and out of me.

"I don't know how much longer I can last," Vin breathes, looking sexy as hell beneath me, completely at my mercy.

I pinch at my nipple with one hand and thrum my clit with the other. Behind me, I can feel Frankie using my juices to lather up my asshole. His right hand moves to my waist, digging into my skin, as he slowly, slowly pushes a few fingers of his left hand inside of me.

It hurts as he breaches the tight ring of muscles, almost enough for me to cry out, but that pain quickly transitions into pure pleasure at the sensation of being full. Complete.

"Move," I beg. "You need to move."

We find a natural rhythm easily as I'm forced to bend over Vin, my tongue tangling with his desperately. I can feel myself on the precipice, desperate to fall over the edge, and when Vin's cock expands inside of me, I know he's there as well.

"Oh fuck!" I scream as an orgasm tears through me, so intense that I nearly blackout. It rips me apart and sews me back together in the span of seconds. Vin roars my name as he comes inside of me, his face slick with sweat and his eyes blazing.

Before I can even catch my breath, I'm on the ground on my back beside Vin and Frankie's hovering over top of me.

His cock rubs against my pussy lips as he stares deeply into my eyes, an emotion burning there that has my heart racing and desire coursing through me.

"I love you, Violet," he whispers just as he plunges himself inside of me. I gasp, my hands moving to his shoulders, as his large cock thrusts in and out of me. I kiss him desperately, attempting to articulate everything I want to say out loud, and he groans against my mouth.

And then his cock begins to vibrate.

"What the fuck?" I ask, tearing my face away from his with wide eyes. Pleasure cascades through my veins in a fiery stream, and tears begin to run down my face at the pressure of holding my impending orgasm at bay.

What.

The.

Fuck?

Frankie flashes me a decidedly sheepish smile. "You like it? I got it modified just for you."

"Fuck. Yes. Fuck." A scream is torn from my lips as I experience the most discombobulating orgasm I've ever had in my life. My brain turns to goo, my head falls clear off my shoulders, my hands and arms begin to shake erratically, and my pussy itself waves a white flag in the air and declares defeat.

Frankie collapses on top of me, his forehead pressed against my shoulder. For a long minute, nobody moves, the silence as taut as a rubber band, until Vin chuckles warily.

"Never would've expected my day to end like this," he teases.

"With kidnapping, prophecies, and orgasms?"

"With sharing the love of my life with another man," he responds without preamble.

Oh, be still the flutters in my heart.

"I love you," I blurt out before I can lose my nerve. "I love you both."

"I know," Vin responds smugly.

"We love you too," adds Frankie.

And for the first time in days, there's peace.

Too bad all good things have to come to an end.

CHAPTER 16

BARRET

I can barely breathe, barely think, as I watch Violet collapse between Frankie and Vin on the ground, her gorgeous body flushed from her orgasm and her bare breasts heaving.

Desire floods my system, more potent than anything I ever felt before, as I allow my eyes to trail over my naked cheese curd. I know I should look away, should hide behind a plant or play dead like a possum on the side of a street, but I can't move. My cock strains against my pants as she stretches like a cat, pushing up her perky tits, and I have the irresistible urge to bite them.

Is that weird? Biting a girl's tits? Sucking on her pointed nipples? I wouldn't know, considering the fact I haven't been with a girl in hundreds of years.

Oh god.

Realization slams me in the face like Cal's dick always does with startling clarity. Accompanied by that newfound realization is soul-crushing terror.

I have a crush on Violet Dracula.

I have a crush on one of my best friends, my cheese curd, who's right now happily mated to other men.

Oh…

Oh no.

This can't be happening. I refuse to allow it to happen.

I glare down at my disobedient cock and shove a hand into my pants, fisting it to the point of pain.

You will be flaccid.

You will be flaccid.

You. Will. Be. FLACCID!

The traitorous little bastard remains hard as rock. Straining, poking, prodding.

Oh…oh no. Will it poke a hole through my pants? I can't allow that to happen. I have no doubt Violet will discover the truth about my crush if I walk into the room with a dick-sized hole in the front of my jeans.

Panicking, I glance in both directions, wondering what I can possibly do to fix this problem. When no solution immediately occurs to me, I unbuckle my jeans and shimmy them down my legs. Once they're off, I kick them to the side, praying that my dick hole issue will be rectified.

Well, shit. What do I do about my boxers now?

Stupid, Barret. You didn't think this one through.

My eyes latch on to the potted plant in the corner of the living room, and a metaphorical lightbulb switches on inside of my brain.

Moving stealthily, my eyes constantly flickering between a sated, happy Violet and her similarly contented two mates, I tiptoe toward the plant, grab it, and hold it in front of my raging hard on. Yes, this covers it.

She'll never know.

"Barret?" Her sleepy voice is laced with curiosity and

something akin to amusement, and I freeze the way my victims always do when I eat them. Not that I'm thinking about eating Violet in *that* way. I mean, I *am* thinking about prying her tan legs apart and sticking my face—

She stretches, pushing herself onto her elbows to meet my gaze, not at all ashamed by her nudity.

I've never really paid attention to the soft curves of a female before, but Violet's are delectable. The roundness of her tits, those suckable nipples, her fit stomach leading down to—

Bad, Barret! Do not think about your best friend's thingy majiggy.

I can tell Frankie and Vin aren't as comfortable as her with their nudity. And *her* nudity. Both immediately sit up in alarm and grab the nearest blankets. They throw them over her head at the exact same moment, resulting in her falling backward with a scream of surprise.

"TOO MANY BLANKETS!" she screeches. "I'M GONNA SUFFOCATE! I HAVE NOT PREPARED MYSELF FOR THIS!"

"Shit! Sorry!" Vin scrambles to remove his blanket from her head and wraps it around his waist instead, glaring at me. Frankie grabs his discarded shirt and subtly places it on his cock.

And Violet...

All I see is a human-sized lump tangled in a single blanket as she struggles to break free. An arm extends outward, pawing at the air, before finally, her head emerges from the top.

She pants, her cheeks bright red and her hair disheveled, before leveling incandescent glares at both Frankie and Vin.

"I almost suffocated, you monsters!" she hisses, struggling to sit upright and keep the blanket around her simultaneously. I wish it would fall, baring her perfect tits to me. I wish—

Plant. Think of the plant, Barret. Think of the plant protecting your cock and consequential cock hole.

"Barret, what are you doing?" Violet asks, ensnaring me in her bright gaze. She really does have pretty eyes. I can see my reflection in them. Would it be weird if I waved at myself? Maybe she'll think I'm waving at her and—

Plant. Cock.

Cock hole. Think of your cock hole.

"Why are you holding a plant like that, man?" Vin demands, his scowl deepening. He really needs to learn to smile more or he's going to get permanent wrinkles on his face. Perhaps I'll gift him wrinkle cream for his birthday… whenever that is. He was born, right? Frankie was the man made in a lab. Would it be weird to ask for confirmation?

"It's a housewarming gift," I blurt. Out of my periphery, I see Frankie's eyes drift to my discarded pants and narrow, and I quickly work to kick them away.

He didn't see that, did he? Nope. I'm gonna go with a big fat "n" to the "o" to the "p" to the…"p" again?

"You're gifting us our own plant for a housewarming gift? In a house that we technically don't own and have been living in for years?" Vin asks dryly, but Violet perks up.

"How's Mason?" she asks, and I feel myself deflate. Of course she would ask about him. Why wouldn't she? He's her mate and boyfriend. I'm just…the stupid friend.

I shove the self-deprecating thoughts aside and remind myself that I'd rather have Violet in my life as a friend than not at all.

"He's sleeping. Would you like to see him?" I extend a hand toward her, and her eyes glow brightly as she struggles out from between the two men. Vin growls, holding her to him, and murmurs something in her ear too softly for me to make out.

After a moment, she blows out a breath and says, "Give me five minutes. Apparently," she elbows Vin in the stomach, "I need to put clothes on."

"You're naked, for fuck's sake," Vin growls, and Violet releases a derisive snort.

"I'm dressed in air, thank you very much. Now kindly fuck off."

I'd prefer if you didn't wear clothes and continued dressing in air, but that's not something a bestie would say. And I'm the best bestie that ever bestied this world.

Oh god.

I'm so fucked.

∼

Ten minutes later, we're upstairs in Mason's bedroom, Violet perching on the edge of the bed. Her tiny hand rests on Mason's sweaty forehead, feeling his temperature, before she trails it down his cheek to cup his chin.

Mason murmurs something incoherent, his features twisted in sleep, but doesn't wake up. I made sure of that when I put him under hours earlier.

"Is he in any pain?" Violet asks softly, grabbing his hand and holding it tightly between both of hers. A softness invades her expression, a sort of vulnerability I've never seen before. It makes my throat close up and my heart gallop like a runaway stallion.

"No, Cheese Curd," I assure her. "He's having good dreams."

When I left him, he was in a meadow made of candy canes and lollipops while a dream version of Violet strutted around completely naked, grabbing pieces of candy at random and shoving the entire thing into her mouth with exaggerated moans. Mason has a very strange imagination. And apparently…a candy fetish? Who would've thought?

"I didn't know it got this bad," she confesses softly, not peeling her gaze away from the sleeping man. His chest rises and falls steadily, and her eyes focus on that repetitive motion as they glaze over. "I knew about his addiction, of course, but I didn't know…" She swallows. "I didn't see…"

"Don't blame yourself for this," I tell her, wondering if I should place my hand on her shoulder and squeeze reassuringly. I want to—God, do I want to—but something holds me back. Fear, perhaps, that she'll reject me? I no longer have my plant as a barrier between us. It's just me, her, and my dick hole. "You're doing everything you can to help him."

"Am I?" A breath of humorless laughter escapes her. "I wasn't here when he needed me."

"Because you were kidnapped. You shouldn't apologize for that, my sweet cheese curd."

"Cheese curds aren't sweet," she points out absently, and I can feel my heart rate pick up speed as icy dread glides down my spine.

She's on to me!

Say something mean, Barret! Say something mean! Get her off your scent.

"Your face is definitely not sweet," I manage to stutter out. And when she whips around to face me, one of her golden brows quirked, I give myself a mental high five.

Nailed it.

"Thanks for that, Boo Bear," she tells me sincerely, returning her gaze to a sleeping Mason. "I needed to hear that."

She needed me to tell her that her face isn't sweet?

Oh god. I failed again.

Curse my superior wooing capabilities.

"We need to talk about Cal," she continues, her words churning the contents of my stomach—human liver, actually, if you were wondering. She once again twists around to face me, her expression uncharacteristically pensive. "About the man he killed—"

"There's nothing tying him to the murder. No one can prove it was him," I interrupt, my heart thrashing, twisting, burning.

Cal's my best friend, my lover, and the thought of him being punished for avenging me...

Insidious fear wreaks havoc on my insides.

"To be honest, I haven't seen him much since you disappeared. Maybe once or twice, if that," I whisper, lowering my gaze to my bare toes as they wiggle against the carpeting. I don't want to see the accusation in her gaze, the hatred and anger at me for abandoning the man we both care about.

If my theory is correct...

Well, only Violet's presence is capable of calming him.

"Barret," she begins, and I hear her rise to her feet though I don't look away from my piggy toes, "where is he?"

There's a tiny seed inside of me—a little nugget I like to refer to as my happiness. My next words don't just destroy my teeny tiny nugget. They stomp on it, chew it up, and then poop it out.

My happiness is now shit.

A shit-iness.

Since I've been brought to detention, I lived with the motto that "thou boat shall not be rocked." I'll just steadily row, row, row my own boat gently down the stream, disappearing into the mist glissading over the water, never to be seen again.

But now, I'm standing smack dab in the middle of the sinking ship, bouncing from side to side with a dorky ass grin on my face. Water sloshes over the sides as people scream at me to "stop rocking the motherfucking ship or you'll kill us all!" But dammit, it's too much fun to stop.

"I don't know." My left toenail is slightly longer than my right. I'm gonna need to make sure I get that cut as soon as monstrously possible. "I don't know where Cal is."

Or how to stop what he is becoming.

CHAPTER 17

CAL

Everything hurts.

My wings, my face, my very soul.

I wince, twisting to and fro as I attempt to get a good look at my broken wing in the dirty mirror.

I don't even know why I'm here at the moment, if I'm being completely honest. Detention, in the upper levels of the academy. My home for the better part of…one hundred years? Give or take? Maybe I'm being too fucking dramatic.

I suppose you can say the *worst* part of one hundred years, though I don't regret for a second meeting Barret, who has become my best friend and lover.

I can't help but recall the first time I ever met the Boogeyman…

I've gotten used to the upper levels of the school. The graffiti on the walls, the haphazardly placed desks, the cement blocks splashed with white paint, the cracked sinks, the bathrooms in desperate need of a wash.

Home sweet fucking home.

Honestly, I don't even know why I'm here. What I've done surely isn't as bad as some of the other monsters. Helping creatures find their fated mates? That's not a crime, at least in my eyes.

No, the crime is the way the monster council reacted, slaughtering my family without a shred of remorse or guilt.

Anger burns like fire in my gut, rushing up my throat like bitter acid.

But Prodigium Academy has the mentality of guilty until proven innocent. And me? A sex demon with fairy blood? I didn't stand a chance in this bigoted society—a society where victims are blamed and perpetrators are victimized.

I wasn't a monster when I came to Prodigium Academy and was immediately locked in the upper levels. No, I became a monster because of what they did to me. They wanted a monster...and they got one. How could I not become one, after everything I endured? All of the pain and heartache and agony? I became one because—

Oh, I look good.

I survey myself in the bathroom mirror, flexing my brilliant red wings.

"Who's a hotshot?" I ask my reflection with a sultry smirk. "You're a hotshot." I may or may not have finger-gunned myself. Read as—I totally did.

My hair is tousled, disheveled, the thick pink strands longer on the top than the sides. Sprouting from my back, a shade of red darker than my tresses, are a gorgeous set of wings that expand the length of nearly the entire room.

Oh yeah. Even after all this time, Cupid still has it.

"And...I shouldn't talk about myself in third person," I murmur, cupping water in my hands and splashing it on my face. Cupid is the name the other monsters gave me. Don't ask me how or why. Maybe because my first victim—sex victim, not murder victim— didn't understand what I said when I was balls deep inside of her. Either way, I got a reputation.

Why they associate my name with hearts and babies and

diapers, I don't know. I only wore a diaper once, and it was because the woman I was with had a strange kink. I don't just walk around with a bow strapped to my back, shooting arrows of love or whatever at everyone I pass.

The familiar click of a door opening and closing reverberates through the room. My ears perk at the footsteps tentatively traveling down the hall, closing in on where I'm hidden in the bathroom.

It's no secret that the school will send their troublemakers to me. Sometimes, I'll kill them, depending on what they did. Other times, I'll feed on them until they're begging for me. And fewer times than I care to count, I'll let them go.

It's a part of my power. I can sense the intentions of people I meet, sense the light and darkness roaming within them. If my time in detention has taught me one thing, it's that light and dark aren't mutually exclusive. There are facets to every aspect of nature, and human nature is no different. It's my job to see if the dark overpowers the light.

And yes, I admit, it's nice to get my dick wet. Male, female. It doesn't matter. I'm attracted to both.

But that's all it is—attraction. I truly believe I'm incapable of feeling anything else. Besides, who would love a monster such as me? A monster who uses sex to kill? Granted, I don't ever sleep with unwilling victims, but it doesn't change the fact that I do kill.

And I like it.

"Is someone in here?" a low, eerie voice questions. It seems to echo off every wall, every floor, every ceiling tile. I can't tell where it's coming from, and a chill of unease skates down my spine.

Dammit, what is this new guy doing to me?

I'm supposed to be one evoking fear in him, not the other way around.

A slew of angry bees buzzes around in my chest as I push open the bathroom door, poke my head out, and narrow my eyes on the intruder.

At first, all I can see is an odd moving silhouette crawling up the wall. A green light emits from the shadows.

The motherfucking Boogeyman. I would know that magical signature from anywhere. He's almost as infamous as me, stories of his kills whispered in hush murmurs.

A moment later, he steps into view at the end of the hallway, his arms crossed over his chest. In the single hanging light, even I can admit that he's handsome. Not as handsome as me, of course, but a solid seven or eight, depending on how generous I'm feeling. His dark skin blends into the shadows, becoming one with them. I can't discern where he ends and the darkness begins. Green-tipped hair is spiked on the top of his head.

"Boogeyman," I droll lazily, leaning against the door frame.

His eyes take in my glorious appearance.

"Cupid." He nods curtly at me.

Silence descends as I nonchalantly stare down at my nails. Perfectly cut, of course. Even in detention, hidden away from wandering eyes, I need to look amazing. I'm a monster, not a crazy person, thank you very much.

"How did you get here?" I don't bother looking up as I speak. Most people don't deserve my attention.

"I was led up the staircase, through a metal door, and then took a few steps down the hall before you emerged," he answers seriously, and at first I think he's fucking with me. But nope. There's only sincerity in his gaze.

"I meant what did you do," I amend, rolling my eyes.

He frowns. "I told you. I was led up the staircase, through a metal door—"

I cut him off with a wave of my hand. "I meant, what did you do to end up in detention?"

"Oh!" He smiles, as if he suddenly had a grand epiphany. "I killed a man." Shrugging his broad shoulders, he adds, "After he raped and killed a girl."

"Good for you."

Silence.

"How long are you in detention for?" I continue, kicking one leg back and resting it against the wall.

Boogeyman sighs heavily. "Don't know. They didn't tell me when they shoved me in one of the classrooms. You?"

"Eternity. Probably. I don't know anymore."

I'm not gonna lie. The fact that someone else is up here with me makes me giddier than I care to admit. Loneliness has been my only constant companion for years and years and years, sans a few rebellious students. And to have a guy as sexy as Boogeyman...

My eyes travel over him in a new light, and my cock hardens. Yeah, I'm a shameless hussy. Sue me.

"Since we're going to be here together for a while..." I trail off, taking a suggestive step forward and licking my lips. "Want me to pound into your asshole until you're screaming my name and then suck you off?"

As tactful as always.

Boogeyman opens his mouth, closes it, and then opens it again, gaping at me with a slack jaw.

"Uhhh...sure?"

"Perfect." I step closer to him and immediately pull down his sweatpants, revealing a semi-hard dick. Without preamble, I push him against the lockers face first and trail my hand over each of his ass cheeks.

"I'm Cal, by the way," I introduce, pulling my pants down to free my own cock.

He huffs as I tease my head against his puckered hole.

Dammit, where's the lube when you need it? I'm not so much a monster that I'll enter him without proper preparation. I'll just have to change the order around—suck him off first and use his cum as lubrication for his ass.

See? Smart thinking solves all the problems in the world.

"Barret," he says as I drop to my knees and turn him around to face me.

"Well, Barret," I begin, licking his slit. "We're going to have some fun in detention, aren't we?"

The memory carves a smile onto my face, though it immediately fades when I catch a glimpse of myself once more in the dusty, dirt-streaked mirror. My eyes...

My beautiful, perfect eyes...

I hesitantly lift a hand and touch just underneath the right one—currently a splotch of dark ink in my tan face. The rage inside of me, the rage growing and growing with every passing second... It's unlike anything I've ever experienced before.

I've always considered myself a calm man. Cocky, yes. Arrogant, most definitely. But angry? Vengeful? That's not me. I didn't even retaliate when my entire family was murdered after the monster government discovered my unique powers revived dormant mate bonds. Not when I was tossed up here, never to see the light of day until just recently.

I'm the monster the world tries their hardest to forget about, tries to shove underneath the bed to live out the rest of his days in the darkness. Most of those monsters don't choose to be there. They're forced to hide because they're too different, too weird, too strange, even by monster standards.

Violet's one of the only people who hasn't looked at me like a beast.

Violet...

A moan of longing escapes me before I can contain it.

Violet. My best friend. My confidant.

And apparently, my fated mate.

I didn't know it, didn't suspect it, until the night I killed Alex's father. All I remember is being consumed by an almost incandescent rage over Barret's death and this desperate need to protect Violet no matter the cost. I needed to eliminate the threat to her one way or another, and nothing—and no one—could stop me.

I turned dark, cruel, sadistic, my mind contaminated by bloodlust. Only seeing her sweet face pulled me out of the dark abyss I found myself in.

Where is she?

Oh god.

Where's Violet?

My hands grip the countertop as the familiar tendrils of darkness wrap around my brain, squeezing, squeezing, and squeezing until I feel lightheaded from it. My wings flex on my back, wanting desperately to take to the air. Fly away. Fly to her.

I need to go to her.

The last thing I remember is a spurt of uncontrollable rage. And then I ran into Jack and Hux. And then we fought…

Horror engulfs me, drowning me in an explosion of lava.

Fuck. How could I have fought Violet's mates?

I didn't kill them, but I did leave them in just as bad of shape as I am currently.

My eyes drift to one of the many bruises decorating my torso, and I wince. I probably broke a rib or two, though I can't bring myself to care.

Nothing matters.

How could I have abandoned my mate after the second game? How could I have allowed my bloodlust and darkness to consume me? What if something happened to her? What if she didn't make it out of the game—

I dismiss the insidious thought before it can truly form.

I would know innately if anything happened to her. Our souls are connected, twined together in a way that can't be undone. We're inexorably connected, she and I. I can try to ignore it all I want, but a part of me will always crave her, always desire her.

It both terrifies and exhilarates me in equal measure.

Something crunches behind me, and I spin around automatically, my teeth bared as a growl rumbles through my chest. I don't relax my taut posture even as the headmaster steps out from around the corner, his arms raised in the air in a placating manner.

"Easy, boy," he tells me in that cold, impassive voice of his. It blows through my veins like an Arctic wind. I don't bother to chastise him for referring to me as a boy, despite the fact I'm ten times his age. His ice-blue eyes are practically archaic, rife with horrors I can't even begin to describe.

And considering the fact I watched my entire family get slaughtered, that's saying something.

"What do you want?" I barely recognize my voice. It can best be described as a guttural hiss. My wings beat up and down erratically, and all I want is to fly, fly, fly away. Away from him. Away from here.

Away. Away. Away.

"Easy," Headmaster Gray repeats, his eyes calculating as they survey me from head to toe. A tiny flicker of self-consciousness penetrates the red haze that has taken over my mind. I've lived my life being the most beautiful person in the room, so it's a metaphorical kick to the balls to be stared at with such distaste and haughty disapproval. Fuck, I need to shower, pronto. And maybe cut my pink hair. And maybe hit the gym... Am I getting flabby? Fucking hell. I can't be getting flabby.

"I asked you a question, Headmaster." I don't dare take a step closer, not wanting him to see me as a threat. I may be relatively unhinged at the moment, but I'm nothing compared to the professor-slash-headmaster-slash-deadly assassin. I've heard stories of the monsters he killed, and they don't evoke the warm and fuzzies. More like the shit yourself senseless fuzzies.

Though I can't imagine shit being fuzzy...

"I wanted to discuss the final game of the Roaring, Mr. Calcabrina," he says, acknowledging me by the name I was born with, not the one I chose for myself. I fucking hate that name. Calcabrina. It's a name that belongs to a little boy who laughed with his brothers and sisters, told his parents he dreamed of changing the world, and then watched his entire family get cut down by jealous, malicious monsters. The name died with them, buried underneath seven pounds of dirt, never to see the light of day again.

I know I won't be able to get rid of the name fully, but the way Headmaster Gray says it makes me uneasy, as if he knows more than what he's telling me. There's something astute and clinical in his ice-blue gaze, reminiscent of the looks the monster council gave me when they discovered the truth about my abilities.

And then chose to take matters into their own hands.

"What about the Roaring?" I cross my arms over my chest and quirk a brow, one of my wings ruffling in agitation. It bangs against the mirror hard enough to leave behind a crack, but neither of us flinches. His stare remains fixed on me, unblinking.

I wonder how hideous he thinks I am. Like, on a scale of one to ten, do I make him want to vomit, or does he secretly want to bone me? I swear to Zeus, if I'm not at least a six, I'm gonna throw myself out a window and—

"You have one more round to win if you ever want a chance to reclaim your freedom," he continues, and his dispassionate words rush through me like the winds of a hurricane, leaving me colder than I can ever remember being in my life.

Freedom.

Fuck, freedom.

The sun hanging bright in the sky, a glorious yellow fire-ball that burns your retinas...

The smell of freshly cut grass and musty books from the academy's ancient library...

The canvas of blue high up above, speckled with fluffy clouds...

And then Violet, with her curly blonde hair, angelic features, and impish smirk.

I'll willingly spend my days in this hellhole if it means being with her. But I refuse, absolutely refuse, to remain here now that I found her. I don't know what the future holds for us—not with our relationship currently tarnished by the blood staining my hands—but I do know that I'll fight for her with all of the darkness and evil simmering inside of me.

They wanted a monster, and now...

Now they got one.

The smile I give Dimitri can best be described as a baring of teeth. There's not a hint of anything remotely warm about it. "I'm playing, Headmaster Gray." I take a step forward, and Dimitri takes an automatic step backward, though his expression doesn't change in the slightest. Not even a twitch. "And I'll win."

Or die trying.

CHAPTER 18

DIMITRI

I've been told I'm an idiot before.

Granted, those people usually found themselves at the end of a very sharp and pointy sword, their blood pooling around them in a crimson ocean, but I have been insulted once or twice in my life.

I've never believed them until now.

You're a fucking idiot.

I repeat those four words in my head as I stalk through the upper levels of the academy, barely able to focus on my surroundings or my prior conversation with Cal. No, my mind—and attention—is utterly consumed by a five-foot-nothing female with golden tresses I yearn to wrap around my fist and pouty, kissable lips.

The same lips I kissed just a few hours ago as she writhed against me, her gorgeous, naked body a feast for my eyes. The darkness constantly pressing against me, surrounding me from all sides, isn't as difficult to navigate when she's near, a fact I both hate and love in equal measure.

A similar sensation to what I feel in her presence.

Hate and love have always been so close together, after all. Sometimes, it's impossible to decipher between the two of them. My father once described it to me as a pendulum that won't stop swinging. It'll rapidly alternate between the insidious pollution of hate and the heady, all-consuming feeling of love. You won't even know which one you're currently experiencing until it smacks you in the face, demanding your complete attention.

I suppose that's just one of the many things that makes Violet so dangerous. Not the girl herself, necessarily, but my volatile emotions concerning her. I'm a beast on the best of days, a monster on the worst, and she brings out a side of me the likes of which the world has never seen.

I can practically hear my father's chiding voice pulsating through my head.

Weak.

Stupid.

Foolish.

Of course, he'd get distracted shortly after that final word, usually by his own reflection, but his criticism would stick with me.

Loving someone only makes you weak, a fact that has been drilled into my head time and time again. The second you love, you develop a vulnerability, and in our world, a vulnerability has the capacity to completely annihilate you. If my enemies were to get word about Violet...

My internal musings are interrupted by a low cough coming from the room directly to the right of me.

I freeze, my hackles rising, as my hand drifts to the blade I always keep hidden on my body. I pull it free, relishing the cold metal in my hands, and take a stealthy step in the direction of the intruder.

As the headmaster, I know all of the comings and goings

at Prodigium Academy, including the monsters that have been put into detention. Only Cal and Barret have been assigned the upper levels, so unless something happened that I wasn't privy to…

I pull the door open and press the tip of my blade beneath a man's chin, forcing his eyes to me. My hold on the blade momentarily falters as a familiar man turns to stare at me, pain gripping his features.

Hux—or is it Jack?—looks awful. His face is covered with bruises and fresh blood, and his dark hair cascades forward in clumps.

When his cheeks drain of all color, fear manifesting in his eyes, I drop my blade into the scabbard and take a step away.

"Jack," I say, a frown pulling at my lips. "What are you doing up here?"

He swallows heavily, moving to push up his glasses before seeming to remember that he doesn't have them on. With his black hair hanging the way it is, I can't see the long, jagged scar I know to be carved through one of his cheeks.

"I got detention." There's a hitch to his voice I've never heard before, and he shuffles from foot to foot, his eyes continuously flicking toward the blade. I resist the urge to roll my eyes.

If I wanted him dead, he'd be dead already. He should be grateful that I'm in a generous mood.

"And, pray tell me, what did you do to earn detention?" We usually only send the worst of the worst up here, the monsters too sick and sinister to remain on Earth but too powerful to kill.

Like Cal and Barret.

"I didn't do anything," Jack pleads, and the sincerity in his words is strong enough to knit my eyebrows together.

"That doesn't make any sense."

"I was framed," he continues, and I swear he looks

seconds away from crying. "And I know you probably don't believe me—"

"I don't know enough about the situation to draw any sort of conclusion," I tell him, though I can feel my heart stuttering with something akin to…warning? No, that doesn't seem right. Anger, perhaps? I can't quite name the emotion resting on the tip of my tongue.

But if he's here…

What does it mean for Violet?

I'm under no disillusion that this man—or men, as the case may be—isn't one of Violet's fated mates. If she discovers the truth about where he is, it'll destroy her, and consequently, it'll destroy me too.

Which is why I'm really fucking sick of exhibiting these blasphemous things people call emotions.

"I'm heading back to my office now. I'll look into your case file," I tell him, keeping my voice cool and dispassionate. Expressionless. No matter how hard he looks, he won't be able to see beyond my apathetic mask. It's what has kept me alive in this world for so long.

"I don't want to be here," Jack whispers, scratching at his neck absently. "I need to be with…" A blush stains his cheeks as he ducks his head, but I know what he was going to say.

He needs to be with Violet.

His mate.

Because he can offer her everything I cannot and will not.

"Can you send a message to Violet from me?" Jack blurts, and when I don't respond, he hurries on, "Can you tell her that I'm here? That I'm okay? And tell her…tell her I didn't do any of the things they're accusing me of. Tell her it was Balor."

Balor?

Where have I heard that name before?

I take a step away from him, but something has me pausing. My hand grips the door frame tight enough to turn my knuckles white as I debate my next words. After a moment, I grit out, "You are still allowed to compete in the Roaring, despite your detention." Jack's head snaps up, hope filling his eyes. I don't know why his hope causes my own chest to inflate and pound enthusiastically in my chest, but it does. This is unlike me. I don't give monsters *hope*. "And the rules we give to all detention students apply to you as well."

Jack swallows heavily, once again attempting to push up an imaginary pair of glasses. "What rules?"

"More of a reward," I tell him, my lips curling away from my teeth, though I can't quite tell if it's a frown, smile, grimace, or something else entirely. "If you're able to win the Roaring, you're also granted your freedom. We gave the offer to Barret and Cal, and as headmaster, I'm extending it to you as well."

Weak.

Stupid.

Foolish.

What is Violet doing to me?

She's messing with my head, that's for damn sure. I can't differentiate up from down, left from right, top from bottom, good from evil. Everywhere I look, her face pops up, her eyes sparkling with emotions I yearn to articulate. Those lush lips of hers open and demand me to do better, to *be* better.

I fucking hate it.

No, I fucking hate *her*.

"There's a chance we can be free?" Jack breathes, that dangerous hope once more flaring to life in his eyes.

"There's a chance for everyone in this godforsaken world to be free," I reply vaguely, already moving down the hall in the opposite direction. "But that doesn't mean it's going to happen."

Before he can respond, I plug in the familiar code at the

end of the hall and step into the stairwell. The metal door shuts with a bang behind me, but I don't immediately move. My feet are cemented to the ground as fear lacerates my chest.

Violet.

I need to see Violet.

That damn, stupid monster.

SHE SITS BESIDE HER FATHER'S BED IN THE HOSPITAL, THE steady *beep-beep-beep* of Dracula's heart monitor a surprising comfort. An IV full of red blood is connected to his arm as he sleeps. He's a fighter, that's for damn sure. A god-blessed dagger through the heart would've killed any other monster, but not Dracula. He refused to fucking die, holding on to the tendrils of life with both hands and yanking with all his might. The cantankerous shadow I normally see in Vladimir Dracula's expression is absent as he sleeps, giving him an almost serene appearance.

But I'm not a fool.

Even unconscious, the man exudes danger and unpredictability, just like his adopted daughter.

His insufferable, beautiful, annoying, perfect, infuriating daughter.

Violet squeezes her father's hand as she watches him, emotions glistening in her vibrant eyes. She brushes at his cheek, whispering in a voice too low for me to hear, before dropping her forehead to their combined hands.

I watch from the shadows, a silent sentry, and ignore the pounding of my heart, the intensive tug that demands I go to and comfort her. That tug is nothing but a fool, the same as I am. A fool Violet made of me.

No, I refuse to be that weak, stupid, foolish boy my father always accused me of being. Violet is a job, nothing more.

I'll protect her, look after her, ensure her safety…

But I won't let her in.

Because I know that the second I do, she'll own me.

Who the fuck am I kidding?

That girl already owns me, no matter how much I fight it.

No, I'm gonna have to be smart about this.

You want me to fall in love with you, Violet Dracula? You want to make me your monster to wield whenever you snap your dainty fingers?

Fine. Do it.

But just know that if you push me too hard…

I'll snap.

And I don't think either of us will survive that inevitable break.

CHAPTER 19

"**D**o you have to go?" Mason runs his knuckles across my cheek as I nuzzle against him, my naked leg lying over the top of his.

We sit on a blanket in the middle of a bright pink field. The sky up above is colored a vibrant shade of yellow interspersed with streaks of orange and red. A brilliant tree line of purple and blue dot the horizon like a clump of mushrooms.

"I do." I lean forward to press a kiss to his chest, directly above his heart, as he smooths a hand over my bare shoulder. "Fuck, I wish I could stay here forever."

"But you have a life waiting for you." His voice is heady with self-loathing and unbridled bitterness as he reluctantly releases me. "And that life doesn't include a drug-addict boyfriend recovering—"

"Hey!" I interrupt, pushing myself up to glare down at him. In this dream world he constructed, he doesn't need to wear his gray beanie. Instead of snakes, brown hair feathers across his forehead and cheeks, currently wet with sweat from our...um...exercise. Well, to be completely honest, this is probably the only cardio I'm gonna *participate in anytime soon. Running and me? We don't really have a good relationship. Now, donuts and me, on the other hand...*

Our ship name is Vinuts.

"Don't try to sugarcoat things, Pinkie," Mason growls out, and my heart cleaves in two at the reproach I see in his eyes, the heartbreak. "I'm a fuck up."

"You're sick," I interrupt immediately. "And you're trying to get yourself better. Don't ever act like your addiction is an inconvenience."

"I just wish I could be the type of monster who—" I shut up his self-deprecating ramblings with a heated kiss. My tongue plunders his mouth as he groans against my lips, his cock hardening almost instantly.

"You're the type of monster who has always been there for me, even from the very beginning," I tell him sincerely, brushing a hand down his cheek. "You're my best friend, my confidant, my cock buddy—"

He snorts before he can stop himself. "Cock buddy?" His lips push out into a dramatic pout. "Is that all I am to you, Pinkie? A piece of meat? A piece of hard cock?"

"We haven't even had sex yet, technically." I roll my eyes as a flush burns my neck and cheeks.

While we've had fun together in this dream landscape, we both agreed not to do the chitty chitty bang bang, if you know what I mean. I don't think either of us want our first time to be in a world that doesn't truly exist as he struggles with his addiction to Fairy Blossom. That doesn't mean we can't do other R-rated things, though.

The wicked things that man can do with his tongue...

I squeeze my thighs together as prickles of desire run across my skin.

I rather like his tongue. A lot. It's a skilled tongue. A pretty tongue. A thick tongue. A hard tongue. A long tongue. A—

Wait.

Am I talking about his tongue or his cock?

I do like the taste of his cock in my mouth—

Mason begins to plant tender kisses down my throat and to my breasts. He sucks on one of my nipples as his hand lowers between my thighs, stroking me in tandem.

"Maybe you shouldn't have stopped cold turkey," I pant as my fingers grip his brown hair. Don't get me wrong—I like the luscious locks, but I much prefer his beanie and snakes. They're more...him. And I fucking love him. Errr. Like him. Care about him. Have strong feelings for. How am I able to say 'I love you' to Vin and Frankie without any problems, but here, in Mason's arms, I chicken out? Is it because I was sexually sated and my defenses were lowered with the other two? Or is it because I want to confess my feelings, both to him and to myself, outside of this dream realm? "There are treatment centers that—"

He bites down on my nipple hard enough to hurt as he plunges his thick fingers in and out of me. "No, Pinkie," he murmurs against my breast. "I need to do this. You know that. Fuck, it's my own fault for allowing myself to get so bad. How can I ever protect you—"

I grab his cheeks with my hands and force his face back to mine, kissing him with a fierce intensity that leaves us both breathless.

"Don't." I squeeze even harder until he has duck lips, something I'd normally find comical if I wasn't in such a bad mood. "You're fucking perfect, Mase."

"You're perfect," he responds reflexively, and I grin, planting a chaste kiss to the corner of his mouth.

"Are we gonna do a perfect off? Because I'll have you know, I—" Something tugs at my chest, and I hiss out a curse. Mason reluctantly removes his fingers from my wet core, sadness sparking in his eyes.

"You have to leave?" He phrases it as a question, but we both know the answer.

"I'll be back," I promise, knowing he needs the reassurance that I won't abandon him, that I care about him, that nothing has or will change between the two of us.

I also want him to know that my feelings for him have expanded from mere friendship into something more...but the words get caught in my mouth, trapped before it even touches my tongue.

"Goodbye, Mason." I kiss him one final time, hoping to translate everything I'm too frightened to say out loud through that tiny clash of lips.

Since I joined Prodigium Academy, I fought monsters, hate groups, and discovered I'm the daughter of two powerful and terrifying supernatural beings...

Yet, I can't say three teeny tiny little words to one of my boyfriends.

Way to go, Violet.

Way to fucking go.

~

I'M RIPPED OUT OF MASON'S HEAD WITH A GASP, MY HEART beating a mile a minute as I blink rapidly against the blinding artificial lights in Mason's bedroom.

Barret releases my hand as soon as he notices I'm awake, taking a step away from me with an indecipherable expression.

"Thank you," I breathe, capturing his hand and holding it tightly between both of mine. Because of him, I'm able to visit Mason's dreams, if only for a few hours every day. Because of him, Mason doesn't feel as alone anymore. Because of him, my boyfriend can rest with no pain. Because of him...

"Don't mention it," Barret mumbles, not meeting my gaze as he runs a hand through his green-tipped hair.

My eyes narrow.

What's gotten his panties in a twist? Or boxers, as I learned the other night when he attempted to shield himself with a plant.

Is it universal boxer twisting day? Is it some sort of national male holiday that I didn't see on the calendar?

"I need to go eat some cheese," Barret murmurs, already pushing himself out of the room.

"Barret, why the fuck are you acting so weird?" I call to his back, trying to ignore the pang of hurt that accompanies his hasty retreat. "Was I making sex noises again in my sleep? Because I'm sorry about that. Honestly. My brain and vagina don't have filters, apparently. That doesn't mean you need to run like your boxers are on fire!"

Vin, who's entering the room the same time Barret leaves it, freezes, his eyes traveling over my face as his lips curl downward.

"Do you ever think about what you say before you say it? Or do words just leave your mouth without conscious thought?" he asks sincerely, cocking his head to the side. I sort of wanna punch him for his insult, but…

My man doesn't lie.

"I could think about what I'm gonna say before I say it," I confess, my eyes drifting to Mason's sleeping form. His long lashes flutter against his rosy cheeks, but his features are no longer creased with pain—just another thing I have to thank Barret for. If the fucker would *let* me. "But what's the fun in that? Spontaneity allows you to live a longer and happier life."

"I don't think that's true," he points out, stepping farther into the room.

"Um…who said it's not true. Your ex? Shell boobs?" I thrust my hip out to the side, my lips curling down distastefully as it always does when I mention Cheryl fucking Ness.

Ugh. The bane of my existence. Life would've been so much easier if she had just died in the games. But alas, children still cower in terror when she walks down the street and she still makes annual visits to underdeveloped countries to suck the blood out of their goats and cows. Fucking she-devil.

"How is he?" Vin nods in Mason's direction, his features softening as he stares at his best friend.

I run the tips of my fingers down Mason's cheeks before sighing and allowing my arm to fall to my side. "Good. He's not in any pain, thank Zeus."

Well, maybe not Zeus, since he's a little coo-coo in the head.

"He's going to be fine, Violet," Vin reassures me, extending a hand for me to take. I accept it with a tiny smile, allowing him to pull me out of Mason's room and down the staircase. "He's a tough asshole, and we both know he's gonna fight tooth and nail to get back to you."

"I know." I give his hand a squeeze as we stop in the living room and he grabs his leather jacket off the hook. The dark material molds to his sculpted body, and my mouth practically salivates. My time with Mason in the dream world has revved me up, and I have a desperate need only one of my men can fulfill. "I'm just worried…"

"About?" He pauses, turning to face me with a quirked brow.

How have I once feared this man? Hated him? Where I once saw cunningness, I now see vulnerability and fear for his friend. The harshness of his features is juxtaposed by the frown tilting down his plush lips and the warmth emanating from his gaze.

Vin is proof that people can change for the better.

That *monsters* can change.

"I just hope that the Mason who wakes up is the same Mason who went to sleep, you know?" I confess, my heart rate picking up speed at my impulsive confession. It's not something I even admitted to myself, let alone to another person. But it's the truth.

I know about addiction. Yes, the memories implanted in my head are fake, but it doesn't change the fact that I watched my mother die from Fairy Blossom. Even when she tried to get better, she inevitably relapsed, the pull to the drug too great for her to ignore.

What if that happens to Mason? What if I lose him before I even really got him?

"Vi," Vin once again reclaims my hand and gives it a squeeze, "Mason cares about you more than anything in this fucked up world. He'll fight this. I promise you. He'll fight until he's incapable of fighting anymore."

"That's exactly what I'm afraid of," I whisper breathily, and Vin offers me a sad smile, one that doesn't quite reach his eyes.

"Come on. Let's get you some dinner. You're probably starving."

"FOUR SCORE AND SEVEN YEARS AGO…I SHIT MY PANTS IN THIS cafeteria," I muse as we step through the heavy doors. Natural sunlight spills into the room from the floor-to-ceiling windows that look out to the grounds beyond.

It's not overly crowded today, a fact that fills me with immense relief. The last thing I want to do is be around… people. Ugh. The mere thought has me shuddering. Why do most people in this world have to suck so hard? And not the good type of suck either.

"Remind me again why I find you attractive?" Vin murmurs as he keeps a respectable distance between my body and his. The last thing we need is any of the monster hunters seeing the two of us together. Right now, they believe I'm trading blowjobs for protection. If they discover the true nature of our relationship, it won't just be my life on the line…but his as well.

No, we need to maintain our distance from each other while we're in public. No one can know the truth, or our lives will be forfeited. And I rather like my life unforfeited.

As in, alive.

I like being alive.

"I just want some blood," I all but whine, my eyes traveling to the feeding rooms with longing. When the vampire-hating assholes took over campus, they also monopolized the rooms that would allow me to drink in peace outside of the safety of my dorm room. Not only that, but they slaughtered all of the human blood donors—something I find so fucking repulsive, I get sick to my stomach even thinking about it.

"I know, baby. You can feed off of me when we get back to the house. For now, have a tiny bit of bagged blood," Vin murmurs as he steps in front of me, purposely walking two paces ahead of me. I want to pull him back toward me, link my fingers with his, but I curl my hands into fists and ignore the temptation. I can see a few of his relatives sitting around a cafeteria table glaring daggers at me. The last thing we need is for them to see me getting cuddly with their esteemed leader.

As Vin pushes his tray down the cafeteria line, I head to the cooler and grab a bag of stale blood. Just another thing the vampire haters implemented to ruin my life.

And no, I'm not being dramatic.

They say "bitches be crazy," but the real crazies are the ones trying to reform the world to fit their point of view.

Unlike most vampires at the school, I'm lucky to have men I can feed on when I'm thirsty. However, I can't allow the vampire haters to *know* I have veins at my beck and call.

Or neck and call, pun intended. To keep my men safe, I often force myself to drain a bag of blood in the cafeteria every couple days. Ugh. It's like drinking piss.

The things I do for love.

Though I *do* wonder where my need for blood comes from, since I'm not technically a vampire. Maybe it's the demon in me?

"Violet!"

And speaking of the devil…

I use my teeth to rip open the blood bag and slurp obnoxiously as Alex stalks forward. I give him a dismissive once-over, my eyes drifting from his tousled black hair, to his dark tattoos, before resting on his lip piercing. If he wasn't such a raging douche, I would say he was attractive.

But calling him attractive makes me want to vomit, and I rather like my bagged, tepid blood *inside* of me.

His eyes—chips of russet mixed with obsidian and a startling contrast to his pale face—lock on mine as he glowers. He crosses his huge arms over his chest, and my eyes instinctively dip to the tattoos rippling and flexing on his sinewy forearm. I can't quite tell what they are, the colors blending into one another seamlessly, but if I had to take a guess, I would say it's a cock. Or a decapitated head. Or a bloody tampon. Or a—

"Where the fuck were you?" Alex hisses, lowering his head so he can get in my face.

Excuse me?

Ex-fucking-cuse me?

"Get the fuck away from her!" Vin bellows, discarding his tray and lunging forward. I place a hand on his chest before he's able to attack Alex. We're already garnering an audience, and the last thing we need is him getting into a fistfight over my honor.

"You just fucking disappeared!" Alex rages, and his

muscles tense beneath the fabric of his dark shirt. "And now you reappear acting like—"

"I don't owe you any explanation." I keep my voice soft and low as I take a step closer. My hand clenches around the blood bag. "I could've been off fucking the entire monster council and it wouldn't have concerned you."

His eyes and nostrils flare simultaneously as something dark crosses his handsome face.

"You're a bully," I continue. "An asshole. And quite frankly...an idiot." Without preamble, I lift my hand and squeeze out all of the blood onto his head. "And you can go fuck yourself, Alex."

Without giving him a chance to retaliate, I spin on my heel, grab a second blood bag, and move toward an empty table. There's gonna be hell to pay for my petty retaliation, but I don't care. Alex, and the rest of this goddamn school, need to realize that there will be consequences for the way they treat me.

Who does Alex think he is confronting me like that?

With my back toward him and the cafeteria line, I half expect him to attack me. I know it's what I would do if the situation was reversed. I brace myself, my muscles bunching together...

But instead, I see him out of my periphery walk out of the cafeteria, his face carefully blank as he wipes at the blood on his cheeks with his sleeve.

He doesn't look back.

"Yeah, you walk away, goth asshole. Don't let my foot hit you in the ass on your way out," I mumble under my breath, not at all cackling like an evil movie villain.

I totally cackle.

Vin moves to sit with his family, though he makes sure to keep me in his direct line of sight. Because I have problems, I make hideous faces at him while he shakes his head in exasperation, attempting to focus on whatever his sister, Vanessa, is saying. I subtly look in both directions, ensuring no one is paying me any mind, and pull down my shirt and bra, freeing one of my tits.

The expression on Vin's face? Fucking priceless. He looks halfway between aroused and annoyed, his eyes shifting from side to side as if he's gonna kill anyone he catches staring at me. I pinch my nipple as he practically begins to salivate, his hand clenching around his fork until his veins pop. Arousal darkens his eyes.

I have half a mind to spread my legs under the table and begin fingering myself like a shameless hussy with a libido that rivals even Cal's when my eyes lock on a pair of ice-blue ones entering the cafeteria.

Dimitri's steps falter as embarrassment and desire run amok inside of me. His eyes are like shards of glass, sharp enough to do irreparable damage, but underneath his cold countenance is barely veiled lust and warmth.

Awkwardly, I shove my misbehaving tit back into my bra and fold my hands on top of the table, attempting to act nonchalant as if I hadn't just been pinching my nipple in a crowded cafeteria.

Dodododododo. Nothing to see here, folks. Oh! Look! An airplane! Shinyyyyyy. Focus on the shiny airplane and not on the tit. Not. On. The. Tit.

Dimitri's throat bobs, but he resumes his confident gait as he walks to the front of the cafeteria. He pauses and then clears his throat.

"Attention!" His booming voice has everyone in the cafeteria freezing, all eyes turning in his direction. Dimitri Gray is a fucking magnet that attracts people to him, and nothing can convince me otherwise. His white-blond hair gives him an aloof, dangerous vibe that is only exacerbated by the unforgiving glint in his eyes.

It's sexy as hell, if I'm being completely honest. If you have a thing for psychopathic murderers...

Not that I do. Nope. Not me. Nada.

I mean, it's not as if I have a search history on my computer for "therapists who specialize in helping girls get over murderous assholes and fictional characters you wish would choke you."

Dimitri waits until the usual whispers and fidgets have been snuffed out before continuing. "It has been brought to my attention that cheating has played a huge part in the second round of the Roaring."

A few gasps ripple through the crowd, but Dimitri doesn't react. And all I can think is...

What the fuck are you up to, you sexy, evil warlord?

I meet Vin's eyes and his brows scrunch together, but he simply shakes his head, letting me know he has no idea what's happening either.

I don't like this.

Not one bit.

"Because of that," Dimitri continues in a booming, regal voice, "we have a new contestant who will participate in round three." His eyes ensnare my own, and I feel my heart play a dangerous game of hangman in my throat. As in, it hangs there awkwardly as I struggle to breathe. "Violet Dracula..."

Murmurings erupt throughout the crowd, but I don't break eye contact with Dimitri. His words tumble through my head like loose change as my body turns cold.

"...congrats on making it to the final round of the Roaring."

Oh...

Fuck me.

CHAPTER 20

VIOLET

The combined heat of all of their glares burns my skin, licking at my arms and shoulders like blistering flames.

I awkwardly clear my throat, shuffle from one ass cheek to the next, before standing.

Dimitri gives me a look as if to say, "What the fuck are you doing?" while Vin pinches the bridge of his nose. Vanessa flashes me a sheepish smile but quickly turns away when her cousin whispers something in her ear. Probably something about me.

"Hi," I begin, waving my hand back and forth in the air. When everyone continues to glare at me, I drop it back to my side. *Talk about a tough crowd.* "I'm Violet Dracula. I'm a Libra. Umm…I like long walks on the beach, a little bit of anal play, and sucking on—"

"Sit the fuck down, whore!" someone hollers, but I'm not able to see who it is. To be completely honest, it could be any of the monsters glaring up at me with acrid-like stares. Vin's eyes turn as black as pitch, while Dimitri's right hand clenches into a fist.

Fuck, I desperately wish one of them was standing beside me right about now. Or if not them, then Mason, Hux, Jack, or Frankie. I need Mason's playfulness and his ability to look at life with unbridled joy and excitement. I need Hux's protective intensity and the way he can make a grown man cower with just a single, eloquent look. I need Jack's calm, compassionate disposition and Frankie's logical one.

I need all of my men with me.

Clearing my throat, I try again, "I would just like to say—"

"Shut the fuck up," a feminine voice screams, and I wince.

I try for humor, because, really, what else can I do? I'm a damn good comedian. "I like *opening* the fuck up."

Vin facepalms himself, and Dimitri's left eye begins to twitch. Even Vanessa, who's supposed to be my bestie, winces.

My words slam into me like a wrecking ball, along with the implications of them.

Oh…

Didn't think that one through, Violet.

"I meant—"

"You!" The belligerent voice has me tensing, ice coursing through my veins. I recognize that voice…

A second later, Mr. Van Helsing—aka, Douche Extraordinaire and Vin's dad—comes barreling through the cafeteria doors, his head lowered like a charging bull. And in this scenario, I'm the billowy red flag.

"Oh…oh fuck," I exclaim when I realize that he's charging at *me*.

"What's the meaning of this, Stefan?" Dimitri demands, stalking forward with a lethal grace and intensity that I don't find sexy in any way, shape, or form. Not at all. Definitely not sexy.

Stefan's vitriol-filled eyes shift to my face and harden almost immediately. A monster-sized cock gets lodged in my throat—a metaphorical cock, you perverts—and swallowing becomes virtually impossible.

"I know it was you," Stefan hisses, leaning down so his rancid breath washes across my face. I hate how much he looks like his son. I fucking despise it.

However, when I stare up into his arresting face shrouded with anger, I have no doubt that this is what Vin's going to look like in a few years, when gray hairs begin to form on his head and lines ravage his smooth skin.

I just pray Vin never stares at me with as much hatred as Stefan currently does.

"Father?" Vin moves to stand behind his father, and despite his attempt at nonchalance, I can see the violence teetering just beneath the surface. He's seconds from completely decking his father...and consequently revealing the truth about our relationship in the process.

Monsters begin to scurry out of the cafeteria in all directions like ants being stepped on at a motherfucking picnic. Every single one of them can sense how close we all are to exploding...and no one wants to be around to deal with the aftermath.

"I know you did it," Stefan hisses, baring his teeth at me.

I swallow. "I don't know what you mean."

"You killed Christopher!" His upper lip peels backward into a sneer. "I know it was you, bitch!"

"Allegations without proof get you nowhere, Mr. Van Helsing," Dimitri states drolly, his own lips thinning into a straight line.

"I don't even know who this Christopher is," I protest. There's something about the deadened look in Stefan's eyes that has my heart pounding erratically. A flickering red warning sign bursts to life inside my head, sparking at intermittent intervals with every second he stares at me. This man… He doesn't just want to hurt me. He wants to fucking destroy me. Kill me with his own two hands if he has to.

Family Halloweens are gonna be so fucking awkward if I ever become his daughter-in-law.

Not that I want to get married to Vin or anything…

Or do I?

Nope, I definitely don't.

Or do I?

I really—

"You killed Christopher!" Stefan thrusts a photograph in front of my face, so close that I'm forced to cross my eyes in order to stare at it. When I see what he's presenting to me, all of the blood drains from my face.

That man…

I know him.

But I didn't kill him.

Cal did.

Alex's dad—Christopher, apparently—stares back at me with lifeless eyes, blood coating his skin and hair.

Fuck. Fuck. Fuck.

"I know it was you," Stefan continues, his voice a low hiss. He takes a threatening step closer, and both Vin and Dimitri move in tandem, their muscles bunching. "And I'll prove it."

"I don't know what you mean," I hiss, lying through my fucking teeth. "I didn't kill him."

"We found his body in a club's backroom earlier this morning," Stefan continues, his dark eyes flicking first to Dimitri and then to his son. Something indecipherable distorts his features—grief, perhaps?—before he conceals it. "And lo and behold, our cameras saw little Miss Perky Tits heading in the same direction around the time he died."

First…

He called my tits perky. Does that mean he's starting to like me?

And second...

If he saw me, then that means he saw Barret as well... though for some reason, he's determined to place all of the guilt and blame on me. That's okay, though, because I don't want to drag Barret or Cal into this mess.

To be completely honest, I don't want to drag myself into this mess either, but beggars can't be choosers.

"Until you can find sufficient proof—" Dimitri begins, but he cuts off abruptly when Stefan places a hand on my shoulder. Before I can even blink, the monster hunter is shoved across the room and both Vin and Dimitri move to stand protectively in front of me, the latter wielding a long blade that he points at Stefan's chin. "I ask that you don't place your hands on my students, Mr. Van Helsing, or we're going to have a problem." His voice is cold and dispassionate, but I can see the rage hovering just beneath the surface, sparking through his veins like electrical wires.

Stefan turns hate-filled eyes onto me, his lips twisting into a sneer. "I'll find my proof, bitch, and when I do, I'm gonna look forward to ending your miserable existence."

"Good luck with that, asshole." A bark of bitter laughter escapes me. "You won't find any proof because I didn't kill him."

Stefan growls, muttering something under his breath too low for me to hear, before jumping to his feet and brushing a hand down his suit coat. I imagine it's hard to remain dignified and aloof when your ass was just handed to you by a school's headmaster.

"This isn't over," Stefan warns, a promise and a threat in his voice.

"Yes, it is," Dimitri says coldly.

Stefan levels one final glare in my direction before

storming out of the cafeteria. The doors slam shut ominously behind him, leaving me alone with Vin and Dimitri.

Both men immediately turn to stare at me.

Say something intelligent, Violet. Say. Something. Intelligent.

"So…that was fun," I babble. "First, I discovered I'm allowed to compete in the Roaring once more—thank you for that, by the way." I turn toward Dimitri, though I still want to punch his nuts for the way he treated me the other day. "I know you lied to help me…though I don't really know *why* you want to help me. Or why you want me to compete when you were so adamant that I shouldn't in the first place." I shake my head before focusing on Vin. "And thank you for sorta sticking up to your father for me. I didn't kill the asshole Christopher."

Dimitri's lips purse as he crosses his arms over his chest. "I still don't want you to compete in the Roaring," he confesses, his tone carefully indifferent. "But unfortunately, some of the gamemasters were aware that your escape room was not the one they set up for you. I couldn't very well confess the truth, so I allowed them to believe your game had been tampered with. And as for Christopher…" He takes a step closer, and I swear he's somehow able to steal all of my body heat. Vin's eyes shift between the two of us, his brows dipping, but he doesn't comment. "I don't believe you killed him."

"Thank you. I didn't kill—"

"But I *do* believe you know who killed him and are covering for him," Dimitri finishes, and it feels like the Abominable Snowman himself has stepped into the cafeteria and lowered the temperature by one hundred degrees. Goosebumps pebble on my arms as I struggle to keep my expression placid.

"I don't know what you're talking about," I manage to say after a moment of silence.

Dimitri's white brows quirk upward. "I would think very, very hard about who you're protecting, Ms. Dracula." He begins to move toward the door Stefan exited through before stopping and turning toward me. "And if that person would cover for you, just as you're doing for him."

"Again, I don't know what you're talking about." Irritation rumbles through my chest at what he's implying. I know Cal, and more than that, I trust him. I know without a shred of doubt that he would do the same for me in a heartbeat.

Which is why he can never know that Stefan is looking into Christopher's death. He'll turn himself in without an ounce of hesitation in order to spare Barret and me.

"I have a message for you," Dimitri interrupts my internal musings, his voice almost dismissive.

"What's the message?" I ask, exchanging a wary glance with Vin. I don't like this abrupt change in topic.

Messages and I don't really go well together. Usually, these messages are along the lines of, "You're gonna die painfully." Or, "I'm gonna kill you."

Why can't I ever get messages that say, "You're super sexy and pretty and have a good booty?"

"Jack and Hux are in detention," Dimitri tells me.

And everything inside of me…stops. I swear for a brief second, my heart stops pumping blood, my lungs stop taking in air, and my brain stops functioning. Dark specks claim my vision, and only Vin's hand around my elbow keeps me upright.

No.

No.

I refuse to believe that.

"Detention?" I gasp out, horror squeezing my ribs hard enough for them to snap in half. "How is that possible?"

Dimitri's face is grave, cut from ice, as he responds. "I

looked into their case file, and apparently, they're wanted for over ten counts of murder, if not more."

"Murder?" I exclaim, my voice high-pitched and alarmingly squeaky.

I'm not oblivious to the beasts that hide inside of my friends' bodies, the beasts that hunger for blood and death, but I know that Hux or Jack aren't stupid enough to kill someone and get caught. They're especially not stupid enough to kill more than ten fucking people during the Roaring, where every move you make is analyzed and dissected.

"I'm still looking into the details," Dimitri tells me, once again adopting that cool, impassive tone that makes me want to punch him.

"It must be the..." Vin glances at me out of the corner of his eye, his jaw clenching.

It must be the mysterious third entity sharing their head space.

"Balor, you mean?" Dimitri queries, surprising me. I had no idea he knew about that. About *him*.

Did Jack and Hux tell him?

Is he involved somehow?

Vin's frown deepens, distrust flaring to life in his gaze. "How do you know that name?" he demands, his tone scathing.

"Because they told me," Dimitri answers. His ice-blue eyes shift to me. "They also told me to tell you that they're safe... and that they'll come back to you."

Tears begin to well in my eyes, but sheer determination and stubbornness keep them at bay. But fuck! Detention? For murder? They'll be up there for hundreds and hundreds of years, if not more. I was lucky I only got half a day, when the usual sentence is one hundred years or longer.

Vomit coats my tongue.

"You know they didn't kill anyone." My voice wobbles, and I mentally chastise myself for that sliver of weakness. "Dimitri, please," I plead.

But if I expected him to care—to actually give a damn about me or anyone else, for that matter—I was sorely mistaken. If anything, his eyes seem to harden further, reflecting like shards of ice in the bright fluorescent lighting.

He really doesn't care about me or my men.

He truly is as cold as he wants the world to believe he is.

"Goodbye, Violet," he tells me, already turning to exit the room.

"Dimitri, you can fix this!" I call to his retreating back. I try to stumble forward, try to charge after him, but Vin tightens his grip around my elbow, holding me steady. Still, I can't help but scream after him, "You're a selfish prick, Dimitri Gray, you know that? Fuck you!"

He pauses, the muscles in his back rippling as if he's holding himself at bay, before taking an audible breath and pushing open the door.

And my heart…

It shatters.

CHAPTER 21

VIOLET

Stupid Dimitri with his sultry stare and those intense, unwavering blue eyes and his cleft chin and his—

Stupid Dimitri.

Stupid. Stupid. Stupid.

With a growl, I slam my bedroom door shut and all but throw myself onto the bed. All I want to do is sleep for a billion and a half years and then wake up when all of this shit is over.

My birth parents.

Balor.

Christopher's death.

It's all too much for me to deal with.

And now, my sweet Jack and Hux are forced to stay in the upper levels of the academy, alone and probably worried sick. I debate the merits of sneaking up there and visiting them—as I did with Cal and Barret—but worry about what will happen if I get discovered overrides my rebellious spirit. With the Roaring in full swing, monsters are everywhere. I literally can't step outside my dorm without running into at least twenty of them.

But that doesn't mean I won't try. I just need to be safe and smart about it all.

What if the man I meet on the upper levels isn't Jack or Hux? What if it's...Balor? His name settles in my stomach like an immovable boulder as bile coats my tongue. A part of me feels intense indignation and anger that someone would dare try to impersonate one of my men, but that tiny sliver is overshadowed by fear—because I have no idea how permanent this change will be and how strong Balor truly is.

Balor.

Where have I heard that name before?

It rests on the tip of my tongue, and I just know that if anyone in this godforsaken world would know it, it would be Dracula, who's currently unconscious in one of the monster hospitals.

I wonder if the library would have any information on the sadistic asshole. Maybe I could check out a book and—

A knock sounds on the door, pulling me out of my thoughts. I tense instinctively, because that knock could belong to an entire flurry of enemies. Let's be honest, I have a shit ton of them. Cheryl fucking Ness. Alex. Stefan. That's just a tiny list of many who want to see my head on a silver platter.

"Vi?" Vanessa's soft voice filters through the wood. "Are you in there?"

Slamming my feet on the ground, I hurry forward, pulling the door open to see Vanessa and Cynthia standing on the other side of the threshold.

Vanessa, as always, looks fierce and unapproachable, her dark brown hair brushed into a tight french braid that emphasizes her modelesque cheekbones. Her bronze skin, a similar shade to Vin's, glints with a slight layer of sweat, as if she just came from a particularly intense training session. Twin swords crisscross on her back.

Beside her, Cynthia stands with her arms crossed over her chest. Her long, stringy black hair cascades around her face in dirty clumps in desperate need of a wash. Her white, billowy dress hangs off her slender figure, revealing jaundice yellow skin interspersed with streaks of gray. I notice that her right eye is slightly lower on her face than her left one, as if she struggled to make them even when she stuck them in her head this morning.

That's right. Cynthia has an entire collection of body parts she takes on and off every morning and night. Imagine a Mr. Potato Head…or a Mrs. Potato Head, as the case may be. Now, imagine that the potato is actually very slender and a color that fluctuates between yellow and gray. And of course that the potato is human-sized.

That's Cynthia for you.

Right now, she currently has her DD breasts on. Have you ever seen a pair of DD breasts? Well, let me tell you…they just kinda sit there like two bean bags. Her white dress does very little to conceal those monstrous things. When she bends forward slightly, one of her ginormous tits pokes free. It's gray. With a yellow nipple. And pus.

"It's rude to stare at someone's boob, Violet." Cynthia's voice is laced with amusement as she attempts to wrangle that blasted thing back into her dress. In the process, her hand slips free and falls into her cleavage. Literally.

She doesn't bother to retrieve it as she once again folds her arms over her chest, one of them sans hand.

"You got a new pair," I point out like a true friend.

Ladies, the key to any lasting friendship is to comment on her boobs, especially if they're new. A simple, "Hey, you have large knockers" can go a long way toward developing a lasting and healthy relationship.

"Let us in." Vanessa, my designated best friend because I licked her and she's mine, shoulders past me and steps into my room.

The dorm room used to belong to both Cynthia and me, but after the two of us got into a fight, she moved out. The last I spoke to her, she confessed that she's living with her fated mate, Pete the Pumpkin.

And I'm still living…alone. Here.

It's not as if I don't have options—Mason casually brought up moving in with him and the others on more than one occasion—but there's a sort of finality about living together that has my heart thumping and palms sweating. And not the sexy type of thumping and sweating, either.

The guys and I… We haven't really talked about what this all means. Frankie confessed weeks ago that he was my fated mate, but the others haven't really been as open. I know the truth and they know the truth, but we haven't had the hard conversation that defines what we mean to each other. I don't even know if I can technically call them my boyfriends, though the thought of them with any other girl besides me makes me extremely stabby.

Which is ridiculous, considering I have feelings for all of them.

Not that you care about being hypocritical, Violet.

Clearing my throat, I focus my attention on Cynthia and Vanessa. "What are you guys doing here?"

"We haven't really talked in a while," Cynthia answers, taking a single step into the room and shutting the door behind her. She leans against it with her arms still crossed, her wayward hand still awkwardly sticking out of her boob cage.

"I wanted to talk to you about what happened in the cafeteria today." Vanessa winces, shame filling her face, but I wave away whatever apology she wants to say.

"It's not your fault that your dad is a raging dick," I say, and then freeze. "Shit. Sorry. I didn't mean to call your dad—"

"He *is* a raging dick." Vanessa rolls her eyes as she sifts through the books sitting on my nightstand. She grabs a copy of *How to Dismember a Human Body* and begins flipping through the pages. "I didn't know you were in this class," she says, in regards to the book.

"Next semester." I perch on the bed beside her, swatting at her legs to give me more room. "And your dad…is he going to cause problems?"

One of Vanessa's manicured brows cocks upward. "What do you mean?"

"I mean, he's accusing me of murder, Vanessa." I volley my gaze to include Cynthia as well, who's currently turning her mouth upside down to resemble a frown. "And they're not just going to put me in detention like they do with the other monsters. Because of who I am, because of who my father is, they're going to kill me."

And I can't even begin to imagine what will happen when they discover the truth about Lucifer and Hera. And I'm saying when, not if, because in today's monstrous world, secrets can never remain buried for long. They always find a way to make themselves known, clawing to the surface like zombies.

"I won't let that happen," Vanessa tells me resolutely, raising her chin into the air.

"What can you do to stop it?" I gently place my hand on top of hers to take the sting out of my words. "I don't mean that in a negative way, my beautiful, perfect designated best friend. I just meant…your father is dangerous. I don't want to see you or Vin hurt."

"We can handle ourselves." Vanessa returns my squeeze before flicking her gaze toward Cynthia. "But enough about my douche of a dad. Cynthia, is it true you found your mate?"

Cynthia's face practically lights up at Vanessa's inquiry, and I half wonder if the Woman in White placed candles inside of her skull. It wouldn't be the first time she had done that—a total fire hazard, but what do I know?

I'm so happy Cynthia was able to find her fated mate. Our friendship broke for a lot of reasons—one of which included me accusing her of being a murderer and her retaliating by buying my sex doll and using it as target practice with a baseball bat—but the biggest discourse between the two of us were her unresolved feelings for Mason. She was in love with him, desperately so, but he didn't even know her name. When the two of us became friends, she got insanely jealous.

But that's not the only reason I'm happy Cynthia found her mate. Yes, I'm grateful that we've steadily been rekindling our friendship, but more than that, I want her to be happy. She deserves it.

"Pete's amazing," Cynthia gushes, finally taking the last few steps into the room to sit on the bed beside us. This occasion feels monumental, as if she wasn't just stepping into a room but choosing to walk back into my life as well. A wide smile unfurls on my lips at seeing her so animated.

She looks fucking radiant.

"Have you been sucking on his pumpkin stick?" Vanessa teases, and Cynthia throws her head back in laughter.

"Oh my god!" She covers her face with her hands—well, her hand. Her right wrist just kinda awkwardly thumps her chin. When she lowers her arms, her eyes sparkle mischievously. "But yes. Yes, I have."

"How about you, V?" I ask, hitting her shoulder with my own. "Any guys capture your attention?"

"Any girls," she corrects, a delicate blush staining her cheeks. "And maybe one…"

Before I can demand she tell me more—I'm a greedy little ho when it comes to gossip—another knock sounds on my dorm room door.

"Are we expecting anyone else?" I ask, my brows raised.

"No." Vanessa's lips purse as she stealthily gets to her feet, unsheathing her blades from their twin scabbards as she moves. In less than a second, she has the door open and the tip of her blade underneath a familiar man's chin.

Frankie doesn't even blink as his eyes drift from Vanessa, to Cynthia, and then to me.

"Good grief, Frankie!" I exclaim, jumping to my feet as Vanessa reluctantly puts her blades away. She gives Frankie a narrowed-eyed stare before reclaiming her seat on my bed. "Vanessa could've shish kebabed you."

"Give me some credit." Frankie runs a hand through a wayward brown curl that tumbles in front of his face. "I'm harder to kill than you think."

"I know how hard you are to kill," I grumble, scowling. Even after all this time, I still have nightmares of Frankie getting stabbed in the heart by our ex-headmaster.

"What are you doing here, Flubbernugget?" Vanessa asks lazily, and when I give her a glare at the insult, she simply shrugs, completely unrepentant. She's known the guys for years and considers them friends, if not second brothers, so I can't blame her too much for her teasing.

"I wanted to take Violet out." Warmth invades Frankie's eyes, defrosting some of the ice that has been prevalent there for far too long. Every day, a little more of that frost melts, revealing the vulnerable man underneath it all.

"Like on a date?" Cynthia perks up instantly.

Frankie bites down on his pillowy lower lip. "I know it's not ideal timing, considering the final round of the Roaring is tomorrow, but..." He shrugs helplessly as something radioactive and explosive erupts in my stomach.

"I would love to go on another date with you, Frankie," I whisper, biting down on the girly squeal that wants to escape. I can at least pretend to be dignified, for fuck's sake. I'm so fucking dignified, the Queen of England wants to invite me over for tea and cookies.

Cynthia and Vanessa don't have the same chill as me.

Both screech like banshees—pun intended—as they grin wickedly at me.

"I'll do your makeup!" Vanessa coos, already flying off the bed and toward my bathroom.

"And I'll do your hair and pick your outfit," Cynthia adds. Her eyes narrow as they travel over me before she nods once. "I'm thinking white and billowy. What do you think?"

<h1 style="text-align:center">CHAPTER 22</h1>

The last time I went mini-golfing, it was when my dad was going through a phase. An 'I like using and recycling bones after I kill the person' type of phase. He would use the femur as a golf club and a portion of the pelvis as a ball. His version of the sport became so popular that another monster bought the rights to it, decided to use an actual eyeball instead of a pelvis as the ball, and thus...bone golf was born. Or bone ball, as the kids like to say.

Me. I'm the kid.

The bone golfing course Frankie brings me to is cute in its simplicity, with low hanging rafters twined with sparkly fairy lights and walls depicting some of the world's most famous monsters. I catch a glimpse of an oil painting of Dracula—wearing nothing but a speedo as he winks at the artist. A pang of sadness hits me as I stare at my dad's smiling face...before that sadness distorts into disgust, because ew. I've seen more of my dad in that one painting than I ever wanted to in my life. Gag. I'll need bleach to scrub my eyes after that. What monster wants to see her dad in a speedo? Especially when said dad is still fighting for his life...

Don't think about that right now, Violet.

The course itself is located inside a corrugated iron warehouse that most humans believe to be abandoned. With good reason, because if one of them were to accidentally set foot into here, they would lose their shit. Humans tend to be frightened of things they don't understand, and us monsters? We're the definition of that.

A castle made entirely of bones and held together by intestines rests in the center of the room, a tunnel going directly through the middle. Each hole features a similarly macabre object—a werewolf's head in mid-shift, his eyes gouged out and his mouth opened in a silent scream to reveal a hole. A mermaid gutted down the middle, so the player is forced to hit the eyeball through her cut-up tail and into her mouth. A vampire devoid of any fangs.

Bone ball. And all of this is thanks to my dad.

Frankie accepts a golf club and eyeball from the bored-looking monster manning the front desk. When I attempt to grab my own, she glares at me, her lips pulling away from her teeth to reveal sharp canines. Her lack of body hair proves that she's not a werewolf, but I can't figure out what supernatural creature she is. Perhaps a fairy? A siren?

"We don't allow your kind here," she hisses, and I realize that she must be a gorgon with diluted blood. No snakes for hair but all the venom and bite.

"I'll have you know"—I glance down at her name tag, my nose wrinkling— "LeeAnn, that my daddy invented this sport."

A single black brow raises, revealing a sliver of pale green scales I hadn't noticed earlier. She must be a siren then. "You call your father daddy?" Judgment and derision drip from her tone, accompanied by a haughty twist to her lips.

"I call everyone daddy," I respond, deadpan. "Just last night, I called Frankie daddy in the bedroom. Isn't that right, Frankie?" I turn toward him with a quirked brow, and he simply blinks at me, unsure of what to do next.

"I called her mommy too," he says in a completely expressionless tone. When LeAnn looks away in disgust, he winks at me conspiratorially. Not the direction I wanted him to take that, but A-plus for effort.

"Just take the damn things," LeeAnn snaps, shoving a club made of bones into my right hand and the hard eyeball into my left. I have no idea what they've done to the eyeballs to make them so hard. Maybe it's a special liquid that Merlin or even Frankenstein created and—

Frankie gently grabs my elbow and drags me toward the first hole. This one has dark-red carpeting with a simple skull we need to maneuver the ball through before it can enter the hole on the other side.

I very much like things entering holes, especially things that have to do with balls. Balls, holes, and me? We're besties. We go way back.

"I haven't played this in… God, it's been forever," I confess as Frankie places his eyeball on the ground and attempts to line the golf club up with it. "And by the looks of it…you've never played this game before." A tiny laugh escapes me when Frankie ducks his head in embarrassment. He doesn't blush—a product, I'm sure, of his lack of organs—but he does appear rather sheepish.

Why do I find a flustered Frankie so damn adorable? I sorta want to have his babies right about now, in a non-creepy way, of course.

"I looked up the best date ideas online and stumbled across this one," he confesses, releasing the club to run a hand through his shaggy brown hair. "I didn't even realize your dad invented the sport until you told me. Well, told the worker." He flashes me a sheepish smile. "I take it you're an expert?"

"There's no reason to be embarrassed, Frankie." I move up behind him and trail my fingers down his arm. His eyes fixate on where I touch him as goosebumps pebble on his skin. He may be an experiment, a creature made in a lab, but he's more real and vibrant than most people I know. I can practically feel the heat emanating from his body, warming me from the outside in. "You saw me naked," I continue, point-blank. "At this point, neither of us should ever be embarrassed around each other."

His eyes turn hot, burning with liquid heat at my words. A delicate blush rises to my own face when I think about what we got up to the other day with Vin. The way Frankie's cock vibrated inside of me...

Yup. Not going down that hole—pun intended—right now. I can think about sexy times with Frankie later, when we're not in public and my dad's grinning face isn't staring down at me from the wall.

Frankie's eyes burn with banked fire as his gaze makes a slow, leisurely pathway from my feet to my head, stopping only at my chest before meeting my eyes.

"I never felt this way about anyone before," he whispers, and I feel myself drowning in his gaze, drowning in *him*. His unique, spicy aroma bombards me, and I close my eyes and breathe it in deep. "I thought I was incapable of feeling love for another person. *Lust* for another person. And then you..." He trails off, shaking his head as if he still can't believe it, as if a part of him is maybe still denying our connection. "The day you stepped onto campus was the best day of my entire life," he confesses.

My heart flutters, and I feel lighter than ever before, as if there are thousands of tiny bubbles buoying me up. I'm flying, disembodied and hundreds of feet above the ground, and only Frankie's penetrating stare is keeping me tethered to the world.

"Oh, Frankie…"

"And I don't know what's going to happen next," he continues, ensnaring my gaze. Even if I wanted to, I don't think I could look away. Beneath his brooding, cold countenance is so much warmth, so much yearning for a love he didn't think was possible. "I don't know what's going to happen with the games, with Jack and Hux, with Cal and Barret…but I do know I'm going to be with you the entire time."

Love and lust run amok inside my chest, and I desperately want to breach the distance between us, take him in my arms, and show him once again how much he means to me. I want him to fuck me against the castle made of bones as the red artificial lighting spotlights our coupling. I want to claw at his skin, tear at his neck with my teeth, wrap my lips around his hard cock…

Frankie turns away and focuses on the hole once more, almost as if his heartfelt confession embarrassed him. He's usually so aloof, so cold, that I imagine it *did* frighten him, in a way. He probably doesn't know what to think anymore.

Instead of forcing him to talk, I step up behind him and wrap my arms around his stomach, resting my chin on his back, since I'm not tall enough to reach his shoulder. My hands cover his on top of the golf club as he goes still beneath my body.

"Violet…" he breathes, a hint of reproach in his voice, as if he doesn't know quite what to say to me.

"You're holding the club all wrong," I breathe as I move his hands down the golf club, heat migrating wherever we touch. "This way will allow you to have more control over the ball." My crotch presses against him as I reposition both of our hands on the golf club. When I step up onto my tiptoes, I'm able to brush my core against his ass. I pause, something occurring to me, before blurting out, "Have you ever been pegged before?"

Real smooth, Violet. Real smooth.

Frankie, who'd been in the midst of trying to hit the eyeball, loosens his grip on the club and tosses it across the room in the middle of his swing.

I do what I always do when I find myself in these awkward situations.

I backtrack like hell and attempt to justify my weirdness.

"Being pressed against you like this, I realized you have a really great ass," I rush to say, moving my hands from his stomach to his ass and giving each cheek a squeeze like they're clown noses or some shit. When he tenses, I press my forehead against his back in a handless attempt at a facepalm. "I just meant I want to put a dildo inside your asshole. Or a finger. I put a finger inside of Vin's asshole before, and he seemed to like it. I mean—"

Frankie spins around, biting down on his lip to contain his smile. "Violet?"

"Yes?"

"You're cute when you ramble about pegging." He grips my chin and plants a tender kiss to my lips before releasing me. His breath feathers against my skin as he whispers, "And no, I haven't ever been pegged before. But I'm down for anything as long as you're the one doing it."

Heat rushes to my core, drenching my panties, and I'm sure my eyes are dilated with desire. My breath escapes my parted lips in embarrassingly loud gasps.

"I just have fantasies of pegging a fucker until he screams. If you're down for anything, I have some daydreams that involve space cowboys, anal beads, and a skirt that—"

"Can you guys hurry along? Some of us want to fucking play," an angry voice demands from behind me, and I turn to see none other than Cheryl fucking Ness and Alex the Asshole standing behind us, waiting for their turn. Cheryl was the one who'd spoken, her eyes now narrowed as she crosses her arms over her chest.

And Alex...

Absolute hatred distorts his features as he glares at first me and then at Frankie. His lips pull away from his teeth as he bares them at us.

"Of course the whore would be talking about pegging," he snaps, directing his vitriol-filled gaze onto me.

Frankie takes an automatic step in his direction, his muscles tensing and his eyes flashing with the promise of violence. "You watch your mouth—"

"Hey," I grab at Frankie's arm to restrain him, "he's not worth it."

Alex glares at me. "I think I just vomited a little in my mouth. What asshole would be desperate enough to fuck a bitch like you?" His gaze dips down my body, his scowl deepening at whatever he sees. Or whatever he *doesn't* see.

I simply roll my eyes, refusing to rise to his bait. He's not worth my time. Or my attention. He's just a pathetic man who needs to tear everyone else down in order to make himself feel better. If anything, I feel sorry for him. I imagine he just learned about his dad's death and is blaming me for it, just like everyone else is.

"Come on, Frankie," I tell my boyfriend. Because that's totally what he is. I'm refusing to allow him to say anything differently. "We'll finish our game of golf and then I'll let you fuck me senseless in the bathroom."

Alex snarls in rage, his hands clenching into fists, but I simply grin and wink at him before pulling Frankie with me toward the second hole.

This battle of wills continues for all eighteen holes—Alex and Cheryl remain a single step behind us the entire time, the former's eyes hurling daggers into my back with his dark, obsidian stare tinged with red.

It's only when Frankie's returning our supplies to the store clerk does Cheryl step up to me, tapping me on the shoulder. I turn toward her, my lips already twisting into a scowl, but surprisingly, her face is devoid of confrontation. If anything, she just appears…tired.

"Shouldn't you be with your boyfriend?" I ask, already preparing myself for her verbal assault.

Gah. I still can't believe both Vin and Mason slept with her. Actually…I don't want to think about that. At all. I don't want to think about my men with any girls, especially girls as gorgeous—and as wicked—as Cheryl fucking Ness. I'll just scrub that thought from my mind, thank you very much, and pretend that Vin and Mason are both virgins.

"Alex isn't my boyfriend, and he doesn't want to be," Cheryl responds with an eye roll. Her lips compress into a grim line.

"You guys were looking awfully boyfriend and girlfriend-ly a few minutes ago," I point out, remembering when Alex pressed Cheryl against the wall directly in front of my dad's crotch—ew—and began to kiss her senseless. When I turned to face them, wondering who was dying painfully because they were both making horrible gasping sounds, I saw Alex's eyes fixed firmly on me as he pulled down her shirt, allowing one of her blue tits to spring free. Her seashell tit. No joke. I simply rolled my eyes, grabbed Frankie, and kissed him until I completely forgot about Cheryl and Alex's disgusting display.

Alex didn't kiss Cheryl again the rest of the night, almost as if he didn't want to be repulsed by the sight of me kissing Frankie in retaliation.

"Isn't it funny?" Cheryl asks, cocking her head to the side. I don't know where Alex went, but I'm assuming he's doing the same as Frankie—returning the supplies that we used to the front desk.

"What's funny? Your face?" I retort like a true badass. My insults are next level, I swear.

Cheryl's eyes turn slitted. "No. Not my *face*." She sneers. "Honestly, I don't know what all of these men see in you."

"A charming personality and big tits," I respond without pause, and I swear Cheryl's lips twitch upward in the beginnings of a smile for a millimeter of a second. Just as quickly, she smooths her expression over and glares at me.

"Vin left me because he fell in love with you. Same with Mason."

"Vin left you because you cheated on him with Mason," I point out, grimacing.

"And you cheated on both of them with each other," Cheryl retorts with an indignant huff.

Anger flares inside of me, white-hot and blistering in its intensity. "First, I didn't cheat on anyone. They knew about each other and supported it," I snap before I can stop myself. The last thing I want is to accidentally reveal the truth about our mating bond, but fuck this shit. And fuck her. I won't have her insulting me and my relationships like that.

"Look," she rolls her eyes, "I'm not trying to be a bitch—"

"You're always a bitch," I point out.

Another one of those tentative smiles graces her face. "True." She sighs suddenly, her shoulders drooping. "Look, what I mean to say is…I'm always second best to you. First, Vin, because he fell in love with you. Then, Mason. And now, even Alex is consumed by his hatred for you that he can't focus on anything or anyone else."

"Alex?" A bark of sharp laughter escapes me.

"I'm not saying he's in love with you or anything," Cheryl

huffs. "The exact opposite, actually. He hates you so damn much that he's incapable of loving another person. He even chose to bring us here tonight on a 'date' because he heard you were going to be here with Frankie." She pauses, pulling at a strand of her orange-red hair and twisting it around a light blue finger. "Look, what I'm saying is everyone has a strong reaction where you're concerned. Either that's love," her lips curl, "or hatred." She squares her shoulders and meets my gaze head-on. "I just want you to stay away from me, okay? Because the second I get to know a man, you steal their attention away from me. Just leave me the hell alone and maybe…maybe we won't have to be enemies."

CHAPTER 23

I wrap my arms tighter around Violet's waist as I stare up at the cotton candy pink sky. My dream world is lighthearted and whimsical…just like I am. Everything is colored in pastel shades, with a sky and ground that change colors constantly, depending on my mood. Currently, the grass is a shade of dark purple, the color almost replicating the slash of lipstick on Violet's pouty, kissable, blowjobable lips, and the trees in the distance are orange.

"I don't want you to remember me like this," I whisper, tightening my arms around her almost imperceptibly. She stiffens in my arms, twisting up onto her elbows to peer down at me. One of her golden brows rises.

"Happy? Content?" she queries, something dark and dangerous lurking in her tone, as if she's just daring me to argue with her.

I sigh heavily. "Weak. Trembling. In bed. Sweaty." Disgust fills me at what she must be thinking. In here, in this dream world, we can pretend that the rest of the world doesn't exist, that I'm not a major fuck up struggling to overcome his addiction. But there's going to be a time soon where we'll both have to face reality.

And my reality?

I'm a major screwup with a list of problems a mile long.

"Mason…" Violet's voice holds a hint of warning and reproach as her gorgeous eyes narrow. "Don't talk about yourself that way."

"Do you want to know why I started taking Fairy Blossom, Pinkie?" I don't wait for her to respond, continuing on as my muscles lock together tight. I can't quite speak coherently around the sudden lump that manifests in my throat. "Because I knew I was unlovable. Because taking drugs was the only thing I had control over. Because I wanted to escape the voices in my head constantly reminding me that I'll never be good enough, that I'll never live up to my mother's expectations. I can't even take you on a date, Vi. Not like Frankie can." I can't quite hide the note of self-loathing that seeps into my voice unbidden.

Anger floods my system, dark and caustic, before I can adequately contain it. But fuck, I should be with Violet right now, dammit. I should be taking her boning and to fancy restaurants and—

Her lips press against mine, a soft and soothing presence, and I automatically open my mouth to allow her tongue entrance, determined to deepen the kiss. Her hands roam across my broad shoulders as she pushes me back onto the blanket, positioning her lithe body so she now straddles me. Her eyes hold my own as she presses her palms into the center of my chest, holding me down. Not that I want to go anywhere…

"I don't ever want to hear you talk shit about yourself again, do you hear me? You, Mason, are one of the best people I know. You were my friend when I first arrived at

Prodigium Academy, and you remained my friend long after, regardless of what life threw at us. And I mean literally threw at us. Remember when you jumped in front of a smelly fish to save me? You're the most lovable, perfect, sexiest monster I know."

My lips tug up in a cocky smirk before I can stop it, even as my heart thunders at her heartfelt, sincere words. "To be quite honest, Pinkie, I had alternative reasons for being your friend." My hand snakes out to flick at the button on her jeans. "I wanted to get into your pants."

A bark of shocked laughter escapes her as she grins at me. That smile is so beautiful, so fucking perfect, that I'm momentarily at a loss for words. The damn girl struck me speechless with just a simple smile. I'm so, so whipped where she's concerned. She has my penis wrapped around her pinkie, and I fucking love it. My balls? Yeah, she's just casually carrying them in her purse as souvenirs. They're sure as fuck not attached to me anymore.

She leans down to kiss me a second time, her crotch pressing enticingly against my rapidly hardening cock, but I push at her shoulders before she can take it a step further. "I'm not having sex with you in a fake world," I huff, though my body screams at me. I want nothing more than to sheathe myself inside her tight pussy—the pussy I dream about way too often than should be normal.

She smirks, running a hand through my shaggy brown hair I wished onto myself when I first arrived here. It's just another thing I always wanted to change about myself. What sane person would choose to have venomous, evil snakes for hair? There's a reason I always keep a beanie on my head, and it isn't because I think they're stylish. I know Violet claims to love my snakes, but I can't help but wonder if she's lying to make me feel better.

What girl wants to fear being turned to stone in the middle of an orgasm because my beanie becomes askew?

"Who said anything about sex?" she asks with a quirked brow, amusement dancing in her vibrant eyes. "What do you think of me, Masey? That I'll take advantage of a sick and vulnerable man?" She places a hand to her chest in mock offense as a pout pushes out her plush lips.

I give her a cocksure grin, my hands moving up her body to cup her ass through the fabric of her jeans. I love it when she wears those cute, frilly, pink skirts, but damn. There's something about Violet Dracula in skin-tight jeans that drives me fucking insane. I've always been an ass man, and Violet's ass? It's phenomenal. Probably the best ass I've ever seen, and I'm not just saying that because I'm desperately in love with her. If she were to do a booty off, she would win in a landslide. Though…

The thought of any man who isn't one of her boyfriends seeing her ass makes me a little murdery. Just another thing the two of us have in common—we both like to kill people who…for lack of a better word…infringe on our territory. We're both possessive as fuck.

"Just because we can't have sex, doesn't mean we can't play," Violet purrs as she presses a tender kiss to the corner of my lips. Her grin is decidedly impish as she stares down at me, and I push myself onto my elbows, my eyes devouring her from head to toe.

"What are you thinking, Pinkie?"

She moves away from me and to her feet, and a whine escapes my lips before I can contain it. But dammit, I like the way her body feels pressed against mine, her soft curves molding to my hard ones. She simply grins, winking flirtatiously, as music begins to reverberate from the trees. I don't recognize the song right away, my attention utterly captivated by this stunning creature before me. But it's a sultry, sexy beat that has my hips jerking before I know it like a goddamn stripper.

Violet begins to sway her hips as her hands travel down her body, stopping only to cup her breasts through the fabric of her shirt.

"I like where this is going…" I groan, placing my hand into the waistband of my own jeans to cup my junk. It's so fucking hard right now, I could probably pound a hole into her if I wanted to. Picture a jackhammer breaking through concrete—that's Mr. Mason right now.

And yes, that's one of the many nicknames for my cock. The others include Torpedo, Goliath, Pussy Destroyer, Jingle Balls, and Pussy and the Cockroach. There are probably more, but my brain seems to be jammed, repeating only a few words over and over again. Violet. Boobies. Pussies. And booties.

Violet's hands travel to the hem of her shirt as she slowly drags it over her head, revealing a toned stomach and the swell of her breasts barely contained by her black bra.

Amusement burns inside of me. "Are those bats on your bra, Pinkie?"

Because of course, Violet would have bat bras. Of course.

"Why?" She cocks her head to the side with a mischievous smile. "Do you want to have a closer look?"

Do I want to…? Do bears shit in the woods? Is the sky currently pink and the grass purple? Does my cock have the capacity to break a girl's pussy in two? What type of asinine question is that?

She unhooks her bra and tosses it at my face before I can even respond to her question. I swat at the fabric before glancing down at it, confirming that, yes, there are pink bats scattered throughout the fabric.

I place the bra down beside me and bite down on my lip as my gaze roams back toward Violet. Fuck, her tits are incredible. Each one is easily a handful or two, the pink nipples hard enough to cut glass. She smirks at me, reaching up to tweak both nipples while maintaining eye contact.

I can barely focus on her through the baking, pervasive heat running rampant through my body at her little show.

"Come here, Pinkie," I say, giving her the come-hither gesture. "Let me taste you."

"Which part of me do you want to taste?" she teases, dropping her hands to the clasp of her jeans and slowly pushing them down her toned legs. She turns at the last second, giving me an unrestricted view of her ass, as she bends down, her breasts dangling enticingly. She's only wearing a pair of pink panties—the source of her nickname —that leave very little to the imagination.

"You're killing me here, Vi," I moan as I lift my ass to shrug my jeans farther down my legs. My cock springs free, the tip already dripping with precum, and I use it as lubrication to stroke myself. "I want to pound into your sweet pussy so bad." I gesture her toward me once more. "Get your ass over here before I spank it red."

"Kinky," she teases as she skips toward me, and I don't know where I want to look—her pussy, her pink panties already wet with her arousal, or her bouncing breasts. When she gets onto her knees, I don't hesitate to wrap an arm around her back and guide her tit into my eagerly awaiting mouth. She gasps in shock and pleasure as my tongue swirls around her beaded nub before I suck it completely into my mouth.

"Mason…" she moans, my name a prayer on her lips. And I'm not gonna lie—a surge of smug male satisfaction cascades through me at the reverent way she says it. Like, *yeah. That's me, fuckers. Having her moan my name in less than two seconds of tit play. Care to beat my record?*

"I want you to sit on my face," I tell her, pulling away to meet her bright gaze.

She doesn't need to be told twice.

In the next second, her panties are discarded beside her bra and her pussy is hovering directly above my lips. I wrap my hands around her thighs and pull her down completely, wanting to lose myself in her sweet, addictive scent. Everything about Violet is addictive. I need her more than I need air to breathe, more than I need my next hit of Fairy Blossom or my mother's approval.

Violet is…everything.

I push my tongue inside her slick folds and begin to lick her enthusiastically. She turns almost frantic as she moans my name, bucking her hips, and I push her thighs farther apart to drink from her. My tongue laves the entire length of her, from her clit to her anus and then back again, repeating this rotation until she's mindless with pleasure. I latch on to Violet's clit and graze it between my teeth.

Violet chants my name as she rides my rather skilled tongue, if I do say so myself. Her muscles tense, then a scream erupts from her lips.

Her juices run down my chin as I attempt to swallow everything I can, loving her tangy, sweet scent. Just like Violet—sweet and sour in equal measure. Kind and fierce.

"Fucking hell," Violet moans as she collapses on her back beside me, her eyes fluttering shut in sated content before reopening once more just as abruptly. Her smile turns wicked as she glances at me out of the corner of her eye. "Shall I return the favor, little Masey?" She crawls toward me.

"Little Masey?" I ask in mock outrage. "I'll have you know that—oh my fuck!"

Her sweet lips wrap around my cock as her tongue swirls around the tip.

"Hmmm. Mason de la cream," she purrs, pulling away from me to flash me a wink. "My favorite dessert."

"You cheeky minxy." I swat at one of her ass cheeks, hard enough to leave behind a red handprint. "Just suck me already, dammit, before I combust."

Her nipples graze the top of my thighs, and I reach between our bodies to roll the right one between my fingers. I desperately want to kiss her, to have our tongues dance together in a passionate tango.

Claim her.

Make her mine.

The need grows inside of me until I fear I might burst.

I've never felt this way about another living soul before, but I can't deny that my body burns for Violet in a way that it hasn't for anyone else. I already know I'm in love with her, and that she's my fated mate, but this…this feeling…it extends beyond even that. I'll follow her to the afterlife if need be, and if there's a life after that, I'll follow her there too. My love for her is a twisted kind of obsession that goes beyond logical and rational reasoning. I'm pretty sure I'm incapable of coherent thought where Violet Dracula is concerned.

And as she takes me in her mouth, her hands cupping my balls, I know I'm a fucking goner. Maybe I've always been. Fuck if I know.

I'll do whatever she asks of me, whenever she asks it. If she wants my hand, I'll cut it off with a happy smile.

Desperate for something to do, for a way to have her experience just as much pleasure as she's giving me, I grab at her ass and pry her cheeks apart. I lift my head up to prod at her anus with my tongue, and she gasps, releasing my cock with an audible pop.

"Mason!" she gasps, surprise coloring that one word.

"Shush," I say from where my mouth still connects to her

skin. I swat at her ass cheek with one hand while still holding her apart with the other. "We're in a dream world. We can do whatever the fuck we want. *I* can do whatever the fuck I want. And if that includes tongue fucking the love of my life's asshole, then so be it."

Eloquent, I am not.

"Love of your…?" She freezes, and when she speaks next, there's a note of awe in her voice. "Mason, do you love me?"

I begin to kiss her ass cheek as my fingers travel to her core, already wet and ready for me despite her previous orgasm. "I thought that would've been obvious, Pinkie. Anyone with eyes could tell I'm utterly obsessed with you."

My words seem to break something inside of her, her breaths escaping her lips in shallow bursts. "I want to feel your cock inside of me," she moans, releasing my cock from her lips a second time and standing. She spins around, her feet still on either side of my hips, and slowly lowers herself down.

"Pinkie…" My hands reach for her hips as my eyes flutter shut, ecstasy already coursing through my veins despite the fact I haven't entered her yet…

But just before my hands can come into contact with her smooth, unblemished skin, someone begins to cough dramatically, the noise coming from directly behind me. I cant my head to the side, my eyes narrowing, to find Barret staring at us with stark disbelief…and hunger.

He shields his expression before Violet can see.

"Shit. Sorry to interrupt," he murmurs, red entering his dark cheeks.

Violet stands abruptly, and Barret's eyes dip to her swaying breasts before lowering to her exposed pussy lips. I wait for the jealousy I know I should feel, the rage at having another man stare at my girl, but it never comes, a fact that confuses the ever-loving shit out of me. Maybe it's because I know that he's cool?

That he's not an asshole? That he's Violet's friend? I want to say it's because I know he doesn't think about her that way, but if the banked fire in his eyes is any indication, he definitely does.

"What is it, Barret?" Violet asks softly, her brows dipping low with concern.

"Mason's waking up," Barret answers. He can't seem to decide where to look. His gaze volleys from Violet's naked form, then to mine, and then back to hers before he finally lowers it to his feet. "I'm going to pull you both out of the dream world right now."

"Wait...am I better?" I ask, sitting upright. I severely doubt it. When unconsciousness claimed me days ago, I was a shell of a man, a shell of myself. I find it hard to believe that a few days of detoxing changed that.

Will my body still be ravished by shakes? Will sweat still coat my skin as I force myself to go about my day, forcing a smile I don't truly feel? Will Violet still look at me with pity in her gaze, pity she tries to hide? I know she claims that she doesn't see me as less of a man because of my addiction, but how could she not? I'm a fuck up, an addict, a piece of shit who can't take care of himself let alone a mate.

She knows it, I know it, and the world knows it.

I don't think I'll ever be good enough for her.

"It's hard to say," Barret confesses, scrubbing a hand through his green-tipped hair. "But your body is rebelling against my dream hypnosis, so I think it's time that we woke you up and go from there."

Violet's eyes gleam as she pulls me to my feet and clasps my hands in both of hers. She doesn't seem to care that my cock is pushing against her stomach and that she's still completely naked. "Mason, this is good news," she chirps excitedly, and my frown deepens.

"Violet..."

"You're going to be okay," she tells me, giving my hands a squeeze. "I promise."

"And if I'm not?" I can barely voice the question running amok inside of my head as fear and hope battle for dominance.

What if I'm still a shell of myself?

What if I give in to my addiction again?

What if I'm not strong enough to fight?

At my tentative question, her smile turns softer, radiating from her eyes in palpable, genuine waves. It's impossible to doubt the sincerity of her next words when she speaks. "If you're not, then I'll still be with you every step of the way. You can't get rid of me that easily, Mason. I'm just excited to see you in the land of the living once again."

"Huh?" Barret pipes up, his tone rife with confusion. "Mason isn't dead, Cheese Curd. He's just sleeping. I don't know why you think that he is, but I can assure you—"

"Boo Bear," Violet flashes him an adoring smile, one that has him ducking his head with another blush, "I was just using a figure of speech." Turning back to me, she presses up on her tiptoes to peck me on the cheek. Her soft breath flutters across my skin, and I can't help but think that this is what I'm fighting for. For her. For our future. For our happily ever after. "I love you too," she whispers softly.

My heart flutters wildly at her confession, and I desperately want to slide my cock inside of her and finish what we started before Barret interrupted. I want to tell her how much better my life has become since she stumbled into it, how much she means to me, how my heart races for only her, but before any one of those cheesy as fuck statements can leave my lips, the world around me vanishes and darkness descends.

I blink my eyes rapidly, noticing first the hanging bulb of

my bedroom directly above me and then the two faces peering down at me with concern.

A fine layer of sweat coats Barret's skin as he releases my hand and then Violet's, but I'm already turning away to focus on the love of my life.

Her eyes swarm with unshed tears as she throws herself into my arms.

"Oh, Mason!" she sobs, kissing me senseless. I wrap my arms around her waist—hating the fact that in the real world, she still wears clothes—before glancing at Barret over her shoulder. He stares at her with such intense yearning and love that a twinge of sadness runs through me.

Dude, I feel ya. I felt the same way once upon a time—loving a girl I believed would never love me back. Now look at me.

Kissing the girl I once thought would never care about me the way I do her.

Barret swallows convulsively, looking away before Violet can catch him staring. His eyes meet mine, and I give him a nod of acknowledgment, choosing not to mention the adoring look on his face a few seconds earlier.

"Thank you," I whisper, knowing what he did for me. Putting me in the dream world, for one, but also using his gifts to allow Violet to visit me from time to time. I know that he would've needed to touch both of us and put a shit ton of his power into the connection, and I also know he wouldn't have done that for just anyone.

The Boogeyman has fallen in love with Violet Dracula.

And unfortunately, she doesn't know.

I can't say anything to her either—it's not my secret to tell —but if the despondent look flashing in Barret's green eyes is any indication, he's going to remain silent for as long as he can.

"How are you feeling?" Violet asks, pulling away to survey my body.

The shakes have stopped, and I'm no longer covered in sweat, so I take that as a win.

"I think…I think I'm okay," I whisper, stunned. I can't remember the last time I was 'okay.' Maybe when I was a boy? Before I discovered the allure of Fairy Blossom? Fuck if I know. Offering her a teasing smile, I drop my gaze down to my hard cock. "You want to know what's not okay?"

"What?" Her eyes widen with alarm.

"Big Mason. He needs some loving." I pout dramatically as she throws her head back in laughter.

"Little Mason is so damn needy," she jests with an eye roll.

"Only for you," I say, grinning up at her.

And for the first time in forever, I feel…hope.

Maybe our story *will* end in a happily ever after.

Or maybe…

Or maybe we're doomed before we've truly begun. After all, monster books aren't romances—they're horror novels.

VIOLET

"It's Violet, bitch," I murmur to myself as I stand on the edge of the grassy field. Behind me, and in front of the main academic building, are row after row of bleachers, all of them filled to the brim with monsters eagerly awaiting the third and final game.

The game that will determine who is truly the winner of the Roaring.

"Oops I did it again," I continue to mutter, doing squats. Frankie stands on one side of me while Mason takes the other, both of them looking delectable in their academy-issued T-shirts and gray shorts. I'm grateful to see that Mason is looking ten times better, color actually returning to his pasty cheeks and his eyes glimmering with mirth. "Hit me baby one more time."

Vin leans forward so he can see me around Mason's strong, muscular body. "Violet, what the fuck are you doing?"

"Exercising," I pant, before dropping down. "Burpee time!" I fall completely on the ground, prepared to do a push-up and then jump back to my feet, before deciding…I like the ground. The grass is soft on my cheek.

I continue to move my hands up and down, to give the guys the impression that I'm super athletic and into fitness.

"Do you see them?" I ask breathlessly, because let's be honest…all of this working out is taking a lot of me. I'm gonna need a donut and chocolate bar, stat, or else risk going into a coma.

"What 'them' are we referring to?" Vin surveys the crowd with cold eyes, his gaze snagging on his parents for a long moment before moving to his sister. Vanessa dropped out of the third round of the Roaring at Vin's urging, so now we don't have to worry about her getting hurt or injured if she loses—which she would've needed to, if she chose to stay. She knows how important it is for Cal, Barret, Jack, and Hux to win the game.

None of the Van Helsings are paying us any attention, thank God—I'm definitely not in the mood to be glared at by my family-in-law.

"Jack, Hux, Cal, or Barret," I hiss, stretching my arms above my head…before immediately dropping them back to my lap after my muscles begin to sting.

I haven't seen Jack or Hux since before the second trial, before fucking Balor entered their head and caused them to murder innocent people. Before they were shoved into the upper levels of the academy, where I'm unable to get to them. Trust me. I tried. Dimitri—the fucking prick—must've known I would've gone after them, because he changed all of the locks and codes that once allowed me access to detention.

He can take his snowy-blond hair, his glacial blue eyes, his sexy as fuck face…

Where am I going with this?

Oh yeah. He can take all of that and shove it up his butt.

I'm sure it'll be right at home with the stick already present there. I'm surprised it doesn't poke out his eye with how high up there it is. Maybe that's why he's such an asshole—it ran through his brain. Does Dimitri Gray have a brain injury from the stick up his ass?

I haven't seen Cal in a while either, though I know he's around. Watching. Stalking. Waiting. A part of me wants to warn him to remain far, far away, because the last thing we need is Vin's dad sniffing around us. Around *him*. But... I miss him. I miss my best friend.

I miss Barret, too, which is completely ridiculous because he's still around. He's just not...present. It's almost as if his mind is a million miles away—more so than usual—despite his body being in the same room as us. He hasn't even called me cheese curd in...God, how long has it been? Too damn long.

He better not be calling any other girl cheese curd, or I swear to Zeus I'll zap his ass to kingdom come with...

A taser?

What do people zap asses with?

Note to future Violet—go to Target and ask the nice store clerk which toy I can use to zap a man's ass with.

There are a *bunch* of asses I want to zap. Dimitri's, for one, because he's a dick and I can. Barret, for ignoring me. Cal, for ignoring me. Jack and Hux, for ignoring me...though I can't really blame them for that one. The fault lies solely in Balor.

Fucking asslicking Balor.

I search the crowd of monsters waiting to compete in the final game but can't see any of them. Are they purposely avoiding me? Did something happen?

My eyes accidentally collide with Alex's, which narrow into thin slits. I glare back at him but stop when I start growing cross-eyed. Instead, I stick out my tongue like a mature monster and focus back on the makeshift stage erected in the center of the field.

Dimitri, as always, adopts a haughty expression as he surveys the crowd. I try to meet his gaze, but it brushes over me as if I'm nothing but an insignificant bug to him. I try not to let it bother me, try not to allow it to flay me open, but hurt sneaks its way inside of me before I can stop it.

As always, when Dimitri speaks, the crowd goes silent. Even Cynthia's mother—one of the most powerful banshees in the world—stops screaming her head off to listen.

"Good evening, ladies and gentlemen, and welcome to the final round of the Roaring." He doesn't shout, but then again, he doesn't need to. The audience hangs off his every word as if he's Zeus or some shit. He's not, by the way.

Zeus has a way bigger cock.

Not that I think about his monster dick often. I don't want to see my sort of stepdad's ding-a-ling, thank you very much. It can remain in his pants or in my mom's—

Do not finish that thought, Violet Dracula. Do not finish that thought.

Thoughts of my birth mom make my mind travel back to the last time I saw my dad. In the hospital bed. Unconscious. His face gray as he battled against death.

My throat tightens as emotions permeate my system.

I can't lose Dracula. I can't. He's an asshole, but he's *my* asshole. Yes, he kept secrets from me, but I truly believe he did what he did because he loves me. The world can't know the truth about my birth heritage.

A flash of red captures my attention, pulling my thoughts away from Dracula and my birth givers, and I turn eagerly to see bright, shimmery wings surrounding pale pink hair. I jump to my feet in excitement.

Cal.

My heart lurches, thundering in my chest, but I can't talk

to him with Dimitri droning on at the front of the crowd. I can't do anything, really, except stare in his direction wistfully.

Why is he ignoring me?

Is it because he killed the man he thought killed Barret?

Honestly, I don't even blame him. I would've done the exact same thing if I were in his shoes. Only it would've been a little bloodier.

I am a vampire, after all, and that's our specialty.

I search the crowd surrounding Cal to see if Barret's with him, but come up empty. My brows draw together in alarm.

The two of them are best friends, lovers even, and they've always been thick as thieves. What the heck is going on? Why aren't they together?

"For the final game, you will be split into teams of two," Dimitri continues, and this time, his eyes land on me. Something indecipherable flickers to life in his ice-blue gaze before he forces himself to turn away. It happens too quickly for me to get a read on, but I can say with certainty that it's *not* constipation in his gaze. Or only a little constipation. Maybe gas. "You and your partner must complete the task *together* in order to win." He emphasizes the last word with a wry grin tugging up his luscious pink lips. Lips that have sucked on my clit only a few days earlier—not that I'm going to think about that. My head is a Dimitri-free zone. No siree. I will *not* think about Dimitri tongue fucking me on his kitchen bar. "I have chosen the partners personally."

Ahhh. So that explains the smirk. Dimitri cheated the system.

Well played, Headmaster Gray. Well played.

"Whoever's with Violet needs to stay on guard at all times," Vin murmurs out of the corner of his mouth. He's not even staring at Dimitri. Instead, his gaze is fixed solely on Stefan Van Helsing, the smug little prick.

"He's not even competing," Frankie points out, pushing his glasses back into place up his nose. "Do you really think he'll pose a threat?"

"I know my father," Vin growls out, his hands clenching into tight fists. "If he can't do something himself, he'll just hire someone else to do his dirty work for him."

"And there's not a shortage of monsters that won't want a taste of Dracula's daughter's blood," Mason adds grimly.

A burst of laughter bubbles out of me before I can contain it. When the three of them stare at me like I'm insane, I begin to laugh even harder, bringing my hand up to cover my mouth in order to stifle the sound. Feeling the need to elaborate, because they're seriously killing the mood, I say, "It's funny. A taste of my blood. Get it? Because I'm a vampire? And they hate vampires? Irony at its finest."

Vin shakes his head from side to side, his hand creeping up to pinch the bridge of his nose. He gives me a look that clearly reads, 'What the fuck am I supposed to do with you?'

Honestly? I don't have an answer to that. He chose me, so he's kinda stuck with me now. He has no one to blame but himself.

Dimitri, still standing on the raised podium, begins the tedious task of reading off the pairings for the final game of the Roaring.

I burn with restless energy and anticipation, jogging in place, as Mason glances at me out of the corner of his eyes.

"Pinkie?" He cocks an eyebrow.

"Yes?"

"You're not moving, sweetheart. You're simply lifting your hands up and down like you're running." His lips twitch in amusement as I stare down at my body.

"I'm jogging in place," I protest instinctively.

"Your feet aren't moving."

"I'm stationary jogging. My arms are getting quite the

workout…Dear Lord, I'm tired. Is it dinner time yet?" I dramatically begin to fan myself as my eyes dip to the vein in his neck. If I salaciously lick my lips like a girl in a porno, will he let me ride his—I mean, suck his cock—I mean, suck his blood?

Damn hormones. Giving me visions of sugar tits and ball-sacks dancing through my head.

"How are you so goddamn tiny?" Vin shakes his head as if he still can't believe it, and I can't help but puff out my chest indignantly.

"I'll have you know, asshole, that I had a salad last week."

Frankie's nose wrinkles. "You had a green-colored peppermint chocolate."

"And the whole time, you kept screaming, 'Get that unholy vegetable away from me! Be gone, Devil! Be gone!'" Mason adds, amusement lacing his voice.

I huff and cross my arms over my chest, pouting. "It was traumatizing. I thought I accidentally ate a piece of lettuce."

"…Vin Van Helsing and Mason Gorgo," Dimitri reads, and Vin and Mason exchange nods of camaraderie before turning toward me as one.

"We're going to do everything we can to help you in whatever game we're in," Vin tells me seriously, seemingly forgetting about our previous conversation where he implied that I should be fat. But I'll remember.

I'll *always* remember. We're gonna be in rocking chairs, and I'll randomly point out this exact moment to win an argument. I just need to shove it in my brain for safekeeping.

Mason nods his assent, pulling my wayward attention back to the conversation at hand. "So make sure you keep an eye out for us."

"I can take care of myself, guys," I protest with an eye roll. But inside, I'm giddy. Something about their protectiveness makes me hot down under.

"Just because you can, doesn't mean we'll let you," Frankie tells me, placing a hand on my shoulder and giving it a squeeze. When he pulls away, I feel something on the fabric of my shirt that hadn't been there prior.

Keeping my voice low, as to not be overheard by the others, I ask, "What is this?"

"A tracker. One that will go unnoticed by the scanners," Frankie confesses unrepentantly. Most guys would be embarrassed or sheepish to be caught putting trackers on their girlfriends, but not my Frankie. He simply holds my stare and blinks. "We won't go through losing you again."

"Good call, man," Vin tells him.

"Smart," Mason agrees.

"You're all idiots." I roll my eyes, but my attention is already diverted by Dimitri as he calls off more names.

To my great amusement, Cheryl is paired up with the Bog Monster. I don't know if Dimitri did that to get back in my good graces or what, but I'm glad.

Hux and Jack—or Balor, that slimy asshole—is paired up with Barret. Cal is with Frankie.

Only one name hasn't been called.

Dimitri's white brows dip with confusion as he glances from side to side, his eyes landing on two of the game masters. Their white hair makes me believe that they're brothers, perhaps descendants of a snow creature, though one is tall while the other is short and stubby.

"There must be some mistake," Dimitri says coldly, not caring that murmurings had erupted through the crowd.

"No mistake," the man on the right says with a shake of his head. "Read the final pairing, Headmaster Gray, so we can get on with the game."

"We made some minor changes," the other says with a rictus grin.

Dimitri's lips compress in a thin line as his hand clenches

around the paper, crinkling it. For a moment, he doesn't speak, but when he finally does, I feel as if the breath has been siphoned from my body.

"Alex Mortem." Dimitri turns toward the striking man with obsidian eyes and hair and matching tattoos. "You'll be paired with Violet Dracula." He swallows convulsively as I feel everything within me grow ice-cold. No. This can't be happening. Not *him*. "Let the final round of the Roaring begin."

CHAPTER 25

VIOLET

Well, fuck me with a duck and call that duck Donald, because this is *not* what I expected to happen.

I would've happily been paired up with the slimy Bog Monster over Alex. Hell, even Cheryl fucking Ness would've been a better partner in crime than the stony, murderous necromancer.

Alex's eyes turn into slits as he spews vitriol my way, his hands clenching into fists by his sides. Unsure of what to do, I wave awkwardly and then give him the sexiest set of finger guns known to mankind.

His brows furrow, pulling low over glowering eyes, but I continue to shoot him with my fingers for the hell of it, imagining the entire time that my hands are full of *real* bullets.

Vin's hand on my shoulder reclaims my attention.

My guys have pulled me into a tight huddle, concern decorating their handsome faces. Frankie's hand begins to tap against his side in agitation as his shrewd gaze roams over the crowd, calculating all of the monsters present. They pause on Stefan for a moment longer than necessary before flicking to Dimitri still standing on the raised podium.

Dimitri, for his part, looks fucking pissed. At least, I'm assuming he's pissed. It's always hard to tell with the stoic headmaster. Sometimes, I think he's pissed, and he's actually super horny—case in point, his apartment the other day. Other times, I think he's horny, and he actually wants to snap my neck.

Why do men have to be so complicated?

"I don't like this," Vin growls out, his arm muscles rippling as he crosses them over his chest. I really, really shouldn't pay attention to the tribal tattoos on his forearms that dilate when he flexes. I really, really shouldn't imagine leaning forward to lick them, tasting his salty, bronze skin. I wonder if his skin would taste the same way his cock did. Hmmm. An experiment for another day.

Frankie would be so proud of me. I'm becoming a scientist, just like him. My question—what does Vin's arm muscles taste like, and not in a cannibal way? My hypothesis—like his cock, but only a little sweeter. My conclusion…

I lean forward before I can stop myself, my tongue darting out like a poisonous frog, but Mason catches the back of my head, his hand tangling in my blonde curls, before I can lick my prey.

"What the fuck are you doing, Pinkie?" Amusement, confusion, and concern distort his handsome face, but he still manages to flash me a tiny smile.

Oh…

Oh shit.

My thirsty ass was about to go all lollipop on Vin.

Save it for the bedroom, Vi. Save it for the bedroom.

"Nothing." I blink innocently as I flash them all a wide

smile. A smile that hopefully says, 'I wasn't envisioning licking you like an ice cream cone.' Not that I think they would mind…

Vin's frown deepens, but he doesn't comment. Instead, he turns toward Frankie with a dark brow raised. "How does the tracking device work, exactly? I'm assuming we're not going to be allowed cellphones and tablets wherever we're traveling."

Frankie pushes up his glasses with the pad of his middle finger and clears his throat. He glances surreptitiously in both directions before holding out his right arm, palm up. Without preamble, he pulls back a sliver of skin just above his wrist, revealing blinking lights and metal machinery.

I gasp before I can stop myself, and Frankie turns toward me, his eyes completely impassive. Not hard, necessarily, but guarded, as if he's afraid my opinion of him will change because I finally get to see what he keeps underneath his smooth, unblemished skin.

Without acknowledging any of us, he presses a button near the bottom of his palm, and the screen nestled inside his wrist lights up. Two dots materialize on the screen—one blue and one pink.

"I take it I'm the pink dot," I murmur in amazement, desperately wanting to take a step closer and run my fingers over the strange piece of machinery inside of him. I stop myself though, knowing that he won't appreciate my comfort right now. He'll probably mistake it as pity, which it's most definitely not.

I love all my men the way they are. Frankie's mechanical parts. Vin's domineering personality. Mason's snakes. Hux and Jack's shared body. I wouldn't change one thing about any of them.

"And I'm blue," Frankie confirms with a curt nod. He

glances toward Vin and Mason. "I didn't have enough time to make trackers for you guys as well."

"That's okay," Mason tells him, scratching absently at his cheek. It's something he's been doing often, though I don't dare call him out on it—twitching. I wonder if he's trying to stop himself from reaching for a joint. My heart lurches with fear that he'll relapse before I shove it away, reminding myself that Mason is one of the strongest men I know.

"You and Cal just need to find Violet as soon as you can," Vin agrees, his eyes fierce. "And Mason and I will do everything in our power to catch up with you guys as well."

"Do we even know what the last game is?" I interject, fear causing my stomach to twist and tighten. Last year, the monsters played a fucked up game of Chutes and Ladders, where every wrong move they made led to their death. Usually the painful kind. The year before that, it was an epic fight to the death with squirt guns. And before *that*, the organizers recreated a macabre version of Candy Land. You did *not* want to visit the grandma.

Suffice to say, I don't have a lot of confidence that this next game will be easy.

What if I get kidnapped again?

As always, my mind travels back to the second game, where Dracula and Dimitri sat me down and told me about my birth parents. And then Medusa crashed the party and threw even more information at me about prophecies and what not. She claimed an oracle told her about all of this, but who is this mysterious oracle? And why are they talking about little ole me?

God, it feels like that happened years ago, not days. I still can't wrap my head around it all.

All I know for certain is that it's going to come back to bite me in the ass.

Shit like this always does in the monster community.

"Violet." Vin's fierce eyes meet my own as he holds my stare. He lifts his hands as if to place them on my shoulders before remembering himself and fisting them by his sides. I resist the urge to roll my eyes.

"You can touch me, you know," I tell him. "I would be shocked if Stefan and the other monster hunters aren't aware of your feelings for me by now. You aren't exactly subtle."

He growls. "They can't know how I feel about you."

"Then you need to stop being so damn obvious," I tell him with an exasperated huff. Does he think his parents are stupid? I mean, they're probably a teeny tiny suspicious that their son—the world's fiercest monster hunter—spends all of his time with Dracula's daughter and protects her from her enemies. Unless they think he's just using me for my delectable body. I do have a good one. My boobs? Top-notch. My ass? Bottom-notch.

"We need to go." The familiar, growly voice comes from directly behind me, and all three of my men stiffen and growl as Alex shoulders his way through the crowd. His multiple piercings glint in the waning sunlight as he scowls at me, absently brushing at a strand of pitch-black hair.

Alex takes the whole 'goth and mysterious' thing to a whole other level. Well, maybe not mysterious. It's not a mystery that he wants to see my head on a spike and bathe in my blood.

Side note—I've bathed in blood before. Surprisingly, it does wonders for your complexion.

"Let's get this over with," I grumble, but before I can take a single step in the asshole's direction, Mason grabs at my hand and spins me around to face him.

He devours my mouth, his hands roaming over my body and cupping my ass. He gives it a tight squeeze before reluctantly releasing me and turning me toward Frankie. Frankie doesn't hesitate to resume where Mason left off, only he doesn't grab at my ass but instead massages my tits. When he finally releases me, I turn toward Vin expectantly…only to remember that he has to pretend to despise me. At least, kinda despise me.

His eyes smolder with banked heat, and before I can take a step away, he curls an arm around my waist and pulls my body flush against his.

In a voice loud enough for his eavesdropping family to hear, he snaps, "When you get back, I'm tying your sorry ass to my bed and putting my cock so far down your throat that you choke on it. Do you understand?"

Under my breath, I whisper, "As if I'll ever let you dom me, baby." His eyes flare with heat as I continue on with a sultry, secretive smile. "When we get back, I'm tying you to the bed and riding your cock until you're begging for more." I stealthily reach around his body and cup his hard ass. Just as quickly, I release him.

"Violet…" he rumbles, but I can't quite tell if my name is a warning to behave or if he's begging me to keep going.

Flicking my gaze toward the hunters, knowing I have to play the part of a submissive female, I say in a louder voice, "Oh, you great, merciful master. Let me suck your juicy cock until my…um…stomach gets bloated with your creaminess."

Nailed it.

Mason facepalms himself, Frankie frowns, and Vin once again pinches the bridge of his nose.

"For Zeus's sake, Violet…"

"Do you want me to keep up the dirty talk?" I whisper, once again glancing toward Vin's family. Stefan looks disgusted, his face taking on an unnatural green tint, and even Vanessa seems a little queasy.

"No," Vin adamantly protests.

"I don't know how I'm going to survive without your hot dog to keep me nourished!" I say in a loud voice, winking at

Vin when he glares at me. I'm totally killing this sub-game. "Oh, your salty, musky hotdog. How do I survive without the dog in my bun?"

"We need to go, dammit," Alex growls from behind me, and I turn toward him in feigned innocence. His right eyebrow is twitching, that damn piercing reflecting the sunlight back at me, and murder shines in his obsidian gaze.

Does someone not like it when I talk dirty to Vin?

Hmmm.

I must be so repulsive to Alex that he hates even thinking of me having sexual relations with other guys. Asshole.

"I was just talking about being dominated by Vin," I say, blinking innocently. I'm so damn innocent, you can just put me in a nun's outfit and ship me off to a convent. "He likes deep-throating me. Wait…I like deep-throating him. Is there a difference on who deep-throats whom?" I tap my chin contemplatively. "Obviously, it's his cock being shoved down my throat—and I mean wayyyy down. I half expect myself to get pregnant because it touches my uterus—"

"Oh my god," Vin murmurs, his voice nasally from how hard he's pinching his nose.

Alex's gaze, if possible, turns even darker, the black eating the crimson. "Shut the fuck up."

"With a cock in my mouth?" I respond with a bright smile.

And for a second, for a brief, brief second, stark lust shines in his eyes before he masks it.

What the fuck?

What. The. Fuck?

Is he one of those perverts that gets turned on by the thought of any girl sucking a cock? Does he like the idea of sucking a cock himself? Is it the thought of *me* sucking a cock that turns him on?

I dismiss that last thought immediately. I would rather

stab myself than ever put my mouth anywhere near his diseased, filthy cock. That thing has probably been inside Cheryl, and ew. Well, I guess it's not ew, because Vin and Mason also put their cocks inside Cheryl and I rather like their cocks. But it's ew that they put their cocks inside her in the first place.

Ugh. Now I want to kill the bitch.

"We need to line up," Alex insists, reaching for my arm. I step backward at the last second so his fingers graze my skin instead of grabbing hold.

"I can walk without you manhandling me, asshole," I huff, tossing a blonde curl over my shoulder. "I don't like people leaving marks on my skin outside of the bedroom."

I begin to move toward the line of paired-up monsters, all of whom appear to be stepping through a portal manned by Dimitri. His blue gaze, however, isn't fixed on the monsters in line.

It's directed at me.

I give him a mock salute and move to join the line, Mason and Vin stepping directly behind me. Frankie leaves to go find Cal—who's still avoiding me, that asshole—and Barret is...

Well, I don't see him, Jack, or Hux anywhere.

Worry for Barret briefly erodes the annoyance I feel toward Alex and this situation, but I tell myself that Dimitri paired them up because Barret is the kindest monster of them all. And also the deadliest. I have no doubt he can hold his own without harming Hux or Jack if Balor makes an appearance.

Fucking Balor.

"Be careful, Pinkie," Mason whispers from behind me, just as Alex and I step forward in line. Somehow, we've made it to the front and now stand before a glittery silver portal leading God only knows where.

Dimitri's glacial eyes travel over the two of us, his lips thinning.

"Is it our turn to step through, old man?" I ask him, and Alex begins to choke on the other side of me at the rude way I addressed the headmaster. But Dimitri deserves all that and then some for the way he treated me.

Dimitri's brow creases with annoyance. "Yes," he tells me curtly, already turning his attention elsewhere. Apparently, I'm not worth even a second of his precious time.

Once again, I tell myself that this shouldn't hurt me, that I don't even like the asshole, but pain unfurls inside of me regardless.

Alex glances at me out of the corner of his eye and then steps through the portal. I make a move to follow him when Dimitri clasps my wrist and pulls me to a stop.

He doesn't move his gaze in my direction, but I know his complete and undivided attention is on me. Goosebumps pebble on my arms as he slowly releases me before anyone can see.

I pause, waiting.

"Be careful, Violet," he murmurs, his low voice barely audible over the thumping of my heart. "Just remember that two wrongs don't make a right."

"Um…okay?" What does he expect me to say to that? I'm not in the mood for fortune cookie bullshit.

"Just remember, Violet," Dimitri tells me softly. And then, without preamble, he pushes me through the portal.

The fall only lasts a few seconds, but the same sickly sensation from before twists my stomach into dozens of tiny pretzels. I land on my knees roughly, pain shooting through my bloodstream, before slowly rising to my feet.

Fortunately, my brain isn't mush this time around, but it still takes me a few seconds to adjust. And when I do, my eyes widen in alarm.

We appear to be standing in a...tunnel? Cave? Maze? Hell if I know.

Walls crafted entirely out of brittle bones surround us. The ground, in contrast, is nothing but compacted dirt.

I spot femurs and skulls and ribs...all packed together to create walls that I doubt we'll be able to break through. If I had to hazard a guess, I would say that it's enchanted with magic to keep it durable against almost any monster attack.

Gray sky shines above us, the sun steadily sinking beneath the bone prison. I have no doubt that it'll turn dark as pitch in the next hour or so. Something glimmers just at the top of the bone walls, sparkling at intermittent intervals.

A forcefield, to keep winged monsters from flying out.

"We're in a maze," Alex breathes from behind me, and I spin in alarm, having forgotten he was there.

"I once went to a cornfield maze with my father," I babble, taking a step away from the striking, terrifying man. "It was during Halloween, and Dear Old Dad wanted to perform an experiment and see how many 'boos' it took for grown men to pee their pants. It took two, by the way. But that could've been because I was holding a chainsaw." I continue to step away until I find myself at a fork in the maze. "Now if you don't mind..." I turn away, prepared to go in the opposite direction of him, but before I can take more than a step, he has me pushed against the bone wall. His hand tightens around my throat as he bares his teeth at me.

"Choke me harder, daddy," I say breathlessly, flashing him a smile to show that he doesn't scare me.

Even though he does. He truly does.

His grip isn't tight enough to hurt, but it has enough pressure to remind me that I'm not in control, that he can snap my neck at any possible second. Sure, I could fight him back with my vampire strength and speed, but will I beat him? He has anger and rage on his side. I just have…a snarky personality. And boobs. I do have boobs.

"You heard Headmaster Gray," he hisses, his breath fanning across my face. I expect it to smell bad, like dead skunks or farts or shits or something, but instead, I get a waft of minty freshness. Does the asshole just keep breath mints in his back pocket or something? And am I allowed to have one? "We need to complete the game together in order to win. That means both of us have to make it to the exit."

"Orrr…" I give an exaggerated gasp as his hand tightens around my throat, his hard body pressing against my own. I swear I feel his cock brush against my hip, but that could be a weapon he snuck through the portal. "Or we could separate and hope for the best. Yeah? I vote that one."

His eyes flicker briefly to my lips before meeting my gaze with a piercing glare. He releases my throat as if I disgust him, as if I'm the one who smells like dead skunks and shit and farts.

"Either we live together or die together from now on, Violet Dracula," he snaps, already heading down the direction I had chosen for myself. He doesn't wait for me to follow, but I know that I don't have a choice in the matter. If I want to get out of this maze alive, I need to do it with Alex. Fuck my life. "Come on."

CHAPTER 26

HUX

"**W**here's my precious treasure?"

It's almost an obsession inside of me, this need to see her and ensure that she's okay with my own two eyes. It's been way too fucking long since I held my beloved in my arms.

Correction—it's more than an obsession. I might literally go insane if I don't get to her.

You're already insane, Jack deadpans in my head, but he doesn't protest as I storm through the maze of body parts. We appear to be in a section made entirely out of hearts—each one thumping rhythmically in tandem to the pounding of my footsteps against the dirt.

"We'll find her," Barret says from behind me, hurrying to keep pace with me. For such a large, terrifying man, he's surprisingly slow.

"If I don't find her soon, I'll tear the nearest person apart limb from limb with my bare hands," I growl out.

Barret's eyebrows dip. "But I'm the closest person

around," he points out, sounding confused. "Does that mean you'll rip me limb from limb?"

"I'll rip everyone limb from limb," I assure him with a growl. I just need to find my precious treasure. The world will stop spinning as soon as she's in my arms.

"You can't rip everyone limb from limb," Barret protests as he finally catches up to me. His green hair sways in agitation on his head. "The world has, like, over a thousand people in it, I'm pretty sure. It'll take you a long time to go door to door and tear all of their limbs off."

"Are you questioning my ability to massacre everyone on this Earth?" I ask, puffing out my chest as anger coils through my stomach, dark and mordant.

"I'm just saying…it seems highly improbable that you will be able to kill everyone before someone takes you down," Barret says reasonably. That makes me even angrier, and I struggle to hold on to my tenuous rage. We don't yet know how—or if—Balor will come back, so for now, we need to keep control of our emotions.

Even if all I want to do is murder this Boogeyman with my bare hands, rip his head clear off his shoulders, and—

Behave, Jack chastises. *He's Violet's close friend.*

We already had to deal with her other close friend attacking us! I roar, remembering the fight with Cal. Both of us escaped with our lives, but not without a multitude of bruises and lacerations.

Cal wasn't himself, Jack states simply. *Just be relieved that we're out of detention and have a chance to gain our freedom.*

Anger floods my system, washing away my good mood from earlier—I always get in a good mood when I think about killing people. To Jack, I ask, *Is it wise to have our freedom?*

For the first time in my life, I'm the voice of reason.

Usually, that weight rests solely on Jack's shoulders, but the question slips out, unbidden.

Jack's mental voice is hesitant, tentative even, when he asks, *What do you mean?*

With Balor still inside of us, I say, my frown deepening. *I mean, is it safe to be around my precious treasure with him still sharing our body?*

I was thinking about that, Jack admits, and I imagine that if he were the one in control of our body, he would've shrugged meekly. *I remember something Frankie said about being able to separate our souls from this body...* He trails off, but instantly, my curiosity is piqued.

"So you're saying I could be with my precious treasure without Balor getting in the way?" I ask out loud, and Barret turns toward me in confusion. I point to my head, indicating that I'm speaking to my brother, and he nods once in understanding.

Yes, I believe so, he tells me. *But we'll have to talk to Frankie.*

"I've always wondered what it would be like to motorboat my precious treasure's bosom," I tell Jack sincerely as wonderment cascades through me.

Barret stumbles over his own two feet, turning in my direction with wide eyes. When did he get so damn clumsy?

How do you know what motorboating means? Jack asks in alarm.

I was introduced to something called a pornographic by Mason, I respond, recalling images of the magazine Mason supplied to me. It's fascinating how far behind I am on all things sexuality. If I want to woo my beloved, I need to study rigorously.

Umm...Hux? Jack's mental voice is laced with amusement and something akin to exasperation. *What you're envisioning is not a porno.*

What the bloody hell is it then? I demand, grunting.

Do you know what a porno even is? Jack asks instead, ignoring my question.

My brows furrow in annoyance as we turn right at a fork in the maze. From here, the beating hearts transform into piles and piles of bone, a bright red liquid seeping from an unknown source near the top of the wall. Blood, by the looks of it.

Of course I do. I'm not an imbecile.

Then what is it?

Is this a trick question? What exactly is Jack playing at?

A porno describes ways to decorate a house to fit your beloved's deepest desires, I respond. Turning toward Barret, I ask, "Have you ever thought of motorboating Violet's bosom? Mason says females quite enjoy it."

Hux! Jack admonishes, almost as if he can't decide if he wants to be angry, annoyed, or amused.

What is his issue with me?

Barret's eyes widen imperceptibly as a flush stains his dark cheeks. His hair begins to sway even more, almost as if his entire body is made up of electricity.

"Wh-why do you want to know?" he stutters out.

Hux, what do you think motorboating bosoms means? Jack demands.

Obviously motorboating is the thing you do with the sucker.

The sucker?!?

Yes. I nod my head once. *The thing you use to clean the carpeting.*

What the heck are you going on about? Jack demands. I send him a mental image of the object in question, and shock reverberates down the bond we share. *You mean...you mean a vacuum?*

Is that what it's called? Mason must've been confused when he explained it to me. But I suppose you could say I want to vacuum my precious treasure's bosom.

A deep sigh echoes through my head before Jack questions, *And what do you think bosom means, Hux?*

Obviously a bosom is... I struggle to articulate what I mean and instead send Jack an image of Violet's dorm room.

And Mason taught you this?

Why does Jack sound so amused? He's usually the kind one, but he's not acting so nice now.

Yes.

Was it before or after he gave you a home design magazine and told you it was a porno to pleasure a lady?

A home design magazine? Surely not. Mason's my friend. He wouldn't—

He did, Brother. Jack chuckles good-naturedly.

Blinding rage breathes down my neck, colder than winter in Antarctica. I hate when people make a fool out of me. Fool me once, shame on me. Fool me twice...you die.

I growl sharply, my hands digging into my thighs, as I envision punching Mason's smug, grinning face in. I might show mercy—because he was ill for a while, according to my sources, and he is Violet's mate—but he'll still pay in blood for messing with me.

"We're at a dead-end," Barret tells me, pulling me out of my murderous thoughts. I turn toward him in surprise, only to see that he's right. The way in front of us is nothing but sickly yellow bones dripping with red blood.

"We need to retrace our steps. I'm sure we'll be able to sense our precious treasure when we get close to her," I tell him, spinning on my heel to face the opposite direction. It didn't even occur to me until now that I used 'our' instead of 'my.' But Violet is *my* precious treasure, not Barret's. Besides, he doesn't even like her like that.

I wouldn't be too sure... Jack murmurs in my head. But his ominous words flee from my thoughts when I see that the entrance to this particular tunnel has also been closed off.

We're trapped.

"What the bloody hell?" I murmur in alarm, baring my teeth as if I'm capable of biting through the blood-soaked bones. I glance above me, toward the shimmering forcefield, before twisting in a slow circle. In every direction, I see nothing but bones and blood. No exit. No escape.

"What do we do?" Barret asks nervously, his green hair twitching as he scrubs his hands down his side.

"We can't go over," I growl out. "Maybe we can go through?"

Doubt it, Jack answers. *The bones are probably reinforced with dangerous magic.*

Before I can formulate a response, a high-pitched scream echoes from the other side of the bone prison.

A *familiar* high-pitched scream.

Violet.

"Precious Treasure!" I roar, something dark and insidious crawling up my throat like a beetle. No. This can't be happening. No!

I throw myself at the nearest wall, ramming my fists against it with all my might. Guttural screams leave my parted lips as I do everything within my power to get to her, to find her.

"Help me!" Violet screams in absolute terror. My precious treasure should never feel terror, not when I'm alive to save her. If something happens to her, I'll keep my promise to Barret. I'll kill everyone in this godforsaken world.

"Precious Treasure!" I begin to claw at the bones, desperate to escape, to go to her. One of my fingernails gets caught in the bone, breaking free with a sickening snap, but I barely notice the pain. Jack's panic merges with my own, exacerbating my own rage and fear, but I don't stop. I can't stop.

A loud roar echoes from beside me, and I barely have the

chance to move out of the way before Barret barrels forward, his head bent like a charging bull. He's nearly three times the size of his human form, so tall that he has to bend at the back in order to not hit his head on the forcefield above. Even still, a strand of wispy green hair touches the magic above and disintegrates instantly.

Not that he notices.

His dark skin shines with a green sheen as his huge hands grab at the bones creating the maze. Power emanates from him in palpable waves, so thick and intense that I feel something catch in my throat.

With a roar, he pulls at the bones until they curve inward, unveiling a passageway.

I don't hesitate to race through the entrance he created, running in the direction of Violet's shrill, terrified screams.

"I'm coming, my precious treasure!" I bellow, jumping over a fallen skull.

And then I see her, and everything inside of me turns ice-cold.

Her head is bent to the side, her glassy eyes staring up at me with unshed tears. Blood runs in rivulets down her cheeks from a wound on her head.

And her body…

I've never seen so much blood on one human body before.

"No! Violet!" I roar, dropping to my knees beside her. I want to touch her, but I'm terrified that I'll hurt her even more. She appears so fragile, so weak, her eyes rife with pain and fear. Terror poisons my blood, and I just know that if I lose her, there'll be no stopping me, no reigning me in. I'll kill every single person in this maze in order to avenge her, friends be damned. "Violet!"

Slowly, her lips part as if she wants to say something.

Blood cascades down her chin as she opens and closes her mouth.

Behind me, I hear Barret's roar of rage and his huge footsteps thundering toward us. But I can't focus on him. I can't focus on anything but the love of my life dying before my very eyes.

"No!" I don't know who I'm screaming to, or who will even listen, but the noise scratches at my throat like sandpaper as tears stream down my cheeks. I'll willingly give up my heart if that's what it takes to keep Violet Dracula alive.

And then...

She smiles, a sardonic twist of her lips, and vanishes before my very eyes.

"What...?" I gasp in alarm, staring at where she once was. "How is this...?"

An illusion! Jack exclaims, and even his mental voice is nothing but a rasp of pain. *This is good, Hux. It was a trick of the maze. Violet's not dead! She must be—*

Brothers, thank you for inviting me to the party. The accented voice cuts Jack off in mid-sentence. My muscles lock up tight as I sense the intruder probing at the edges of my mind, demanding release.

Balor.

No! I roar, fighting with all my might. I can't sense Jack any more, and that terrifies me more than anything else. Well, almost anything else. I still can't quite shake the pain of losing Violet.

It's that pain he latches on to, that moment of vulnerability and weakness where I dropped all of my defenses and lost myself to my grief.

Before I can scream, can shout, can warn Barret, Balor grasps on to my essence and tugs with all his might.

I'll take it from here, Brother, he tells me.

And then I lose myself to the familiar darkness.

CHAPTER 27

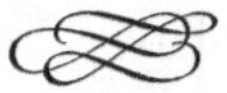

VIOLET

"You know," I begin conversationally as I veer right down a tunnel of skulls, "most people are crabby because they have tiny dicks. Do you have a tiny dick, Alex? Is that why you're so cranky all the damn time?"

He growls sharply under his breath, though his eyes don't flit in my direction. Instead, he remains alert, his posture tense and ready for anything.

"Why?" he mocks me with a wry tilt of his lips. "Do you want to look?"

"Sorry," I say lazily as I move onto a ledge made of tibia bones. I hold my arms out on either side of myself for balance and begin to venture forward at an annoyingly slow pace. Well, annoying for Alex, who can't help but glare at me. "I actually have bad eyesight. I'm not sure I'll be able to see it."

"Do you ever shut the hell up?" he snarls. Apparently, I found his breaking point—talking about his tiny dick.

I pretend to consider his question carefully. "Yes, actually." When he turns toward me in surprise, I elaborate with a cheeky smile and wink. "When my mouth is full of cock."

He throws his hands up into the air in exasperation.

"You're the most infuriating woman I ever met," he growls out, quickening his pace so he's a few steps in front of me. My eyes land on his broad back and the tattoos visible just above the collar. I half wonder what all of his tattoos mean—assuming they have meanings, of course—but I'd rather stab myself with a god-blessed dagger than ask him.

"Does it disgust you to know that there are some men who actually like me? Want me?" I ask lightly, jumping off my makeshift balance beam and running to catch up with him. He's trembling so badly, I want to tease him about having a seizure. Ohhh. Maybe he's constipated and trying to take a mean shit. You know, the type of shit where you're rocking back and forth on the toilet seat and grunting like crazy.

"I just don't understand why men would put their cocks in filthy whores like you," he bites out, his tone scathing.

Instead of upsetting me, as he probably intended, his crude words make me laugh. Like, I actually throw back my head and guffaw like a maniac. He turns to stare at me as if I lost my mind, his feet stilling. I stop walking as well, though laughter still bubbles out of me.

"I'm sorry…it's just rich hearing that come from you."

"Me?" He seems genuinely affronted and confused, his brows puckering together.

"I'm sleeping with men who actually care about me," I snap out, and he winces imperceptibly, something I would almost describe as pain flickering across his face. He smooths his expression out into cold indifference as I continue on bitterly. "You sleep with someone that you apparently can't stand."

"I'm not sleeping with Cheryl," he bites out, his upper lip pulling away from his teeth.

I laugh again, the noise humorless. "Do you expect me to believe that?"

"I don't expect you to believe shit." He turns away from me with a growl and continues stomping down the path. He's a freaking baby having a temper tantrum. All he needs is an adult-sized diaper and pacifier to complete the look. "Are you coming, or are you just going to stand there looking stupid?"

"You know what?" I once again hurry to keep up with him. Curse his long, muscular legs and my short, stubby ones. "Fuck you!"

"Are you offering, baby?" He winks at me, but there's no mirth in his eyes.

"I wouldn't fuck you even if I were all out of fucks—which I am—and you were the last fuck left to give," I snap, hurling blades with my eyes at his profile.

"Right back at you, baby."

"Don't call me baby," I huff out, annoyance infiltrating my system all over again.

"Why?" He cocks his head to the side in mock curiosity. "Is that one of your boyfriends' little pet names for you?"

"We have a lot of pet names for each other," I retort, speaking out of my ass. "Sugar tits. Plumberry. Sir Cocks-a-lot. Bacon butts—"

"Why the fuck are you calling each other bacon butts?" he interrupts in alarm, once again halting. I almost tumble headfirst into his back before I stop myself.

"You wouldn't understand. You're just not advanced enough." I shake my head sadly. "You'll never get on my level of awesomeness, Ass-ex."

"Ass-ex? Really? Real fucking mature." He rolls his dark gaze. "And why would I want to get on your level? You do realize eighty percent of the monster population wants to see you dead, right?"

The next words tumble out of me before I can think better of them—a brief show of vulnerability and weakness that I despise. "And does that eighty percent include you, Alex?" I hold his dark stare, refusing to blink, to break the fragile connection. "Do you still want to see me dead?"

He doesn't say yes right away, but he also doesn't deny it. He simply holds my stare, and I half wonder if I'm falling through a black hole. That's what his eyes remind me of—an endless black hole, a vortex, that you can become lost in. I imagine they're just as cold and unforgiving as a black hole would be.

"What do you want me to say, Violet?" he whispers, and for some reason, his voice sounds pained. "You killed my dad—"

"I didn't kill him," I interject, for once being completely honest.

His eyes search mine—gauging the sincerity in them, perhaps?—but he doesn't immediately answer. His tongue snakes out to fiddle with his lip ring as a myriad of emotions flash in his dark gaze. Sadness. Anger. Vengeance. Hurt. And then…fatigue. His shoulders slump forward as if he's unable to keep them up underneath the weight of the world, the weight of the expectations placed on him.

I remember meeting his mother, Helena, and her despondent, desperate gaze. I had no doubt that she was getting abused by her piece of shit husband.

Was Alex also being abused?

Does he even mourn his father?

Or does he just think he should?

As quickly as all of those emotions flash across his face, he shuts them down, adopting a look of icy indifference once more.

"If you didn't kill him, then I know one of your little boyfriends did," he says at last, scowling. For some reason, that scowl doesn't meet his eyes. They don't seem angry or vengeful. They just appear…resigned. As if he's accepted the hand in life he's been dealt.

"You don't know anything about us," I say, keeping my voice just as soft as his had been. I don't dare speak above a breathy whisper, as if the walls themselves have ears. Who the fuck is he to think that he's allowed to stare down at me as if I were a giant turd who gained arms and legs and developed a sentient mind? "So don't pretend you understand for a second what we did and didn't do. You don't know what it's like to be hated and hunted. To have complete strangers staring at you with disgust. To watch your dad wither away in a hospital bed because of cruel people. To be scared for your own life every time you venture outside on your own. To have words carved into your arm because you're different."

A single tear cascades down my cheek, but that's the only one I'll let fall. The only fucking one. Pain grips my heart and shreds it with razor-sharp claws.

Alex's face drains of all color, and his throat bobs as he swallows. He seems to be at a loss for words, his eyes like shards of glass.

"You don't know anything about me either," he responds curtly, but I can tell that's not what he wants to say.

I blow out a breath and turn away from him, continuing down the dark path. The sky above is turning a metallic gray, streaks of silvery-white interwoven throughout from the rising moon. I'll give it only a half-hour or so before night completely falls and darkness descends. Hopefully, we'll be able to escape this maze before then. The last thing I want to do is traipse through body parts with Alex at night.

My leg catches on a loose bone, and I stumble forward,

holding my hands out to catch myself and break my fall. Just before my nose can touch the ground, Alex grabs at the back of my shirt and pulls me upright.

"Can you at least be careful?" he snaps, and his sharp tone immediately incites a sarcastic retort from me.

"Can you at least shower? You smell like you spent the day rolling around in shit."

That's not true. At all. He actually smells like pine and mint.

Not that I'll tell him I like his smell.

He glares at me. "Excuse me for saving your miserable life."

"I'm sure I would've been fine," I snap back. "A little fall won't kill me."

"In that case…" He releases my shirt, and the momentum has me falling forward, my nose hitting the putrid-smelling bone on the ground.

"Ow! You fucking asshole!" I holler, grimacing as I glare at him over my shoulder.

Only to find his eyes locked on my ass.

"Seriously?" I snap, pushing to my feet. I hold my bloody nose with one hand as I use my free one to jab at his stomach. "Why do you have to be such a—"

Something growls in the distance, the noise causing every hair on my body to stand at attention. Alex freezes as well, his eyes volleying from side to side as his face drains of all color.

"Violet?"

"Yes?" My voice is nothing but a breath of air. I don't dare move, don't dare speak. Hell, I don't even dare to fucking breathe.

"Turn around. Slowly." My heart hammers in my chest, doing nothing to drown out the blood sluicing between my ears, as I move to do what Alex instructed. My breath leaves me in a loud exhale as I see what has captured his attention.

Monsters.

Dozens of them.

Surrounding us.

Oh…fuck.

CHAPTER 28

VIOLET

Have you ever seen honest-to-God monsters before? And I'm not talking about monsters like Alex and me. No, I'm talking about ferocious, dangerous beasts with canines and claws and torn ears. The type of beasts that inflate your heart with blinding terror and steal the breath from your lungs.

I count at least fifteen of them, if not more, lurking behind the walls of the maze. They each are a different type of beast, but they all have one thing in common—the desperate and irresistible need to eat me like a goddamn hamburger.

Some of them resemble dogs, but they're not as cute as Biscuit—the monstrous pup Frankie semi-adopted that now lives in his house outside of campus. No, these creatures are disgusting and putrid-smelling, their bodies almost leathery in appearance and paper-thin. I can see their vibrant red veins pulsating with every step they take beneath their pitch-black skin. Their ears resemble that of Siberian Huskies, curled triangles, but the very top is chewed away. Instead of a normal tail, long, spindly coils of chain cascade behind them, digging into the dirt.

The other monsters are just as hideous. One has a face that consists of nothing but serrated, yellowing teeth and blood-red eyes. No nose. No ears. No hair. Its lanky body crawls forward on his hands and knees, his butt in the air. And I'm saying it's a he, because I can clearly see a red rocket beginning to form as saliva drips from his sharp teeth. Apparently, the thought of eating us makes him horny.

Gag.

"Frankenstein's experiments," I breathe in horror as I spin in a slow circle. More beasts crawl up behind me—one appearing to be made up entirely of skinned arms and legs, the muscles bright red and pink. Another has razor-blades stuck to her face, giving her a distinct robotic look. Another resembles a huge spider with claws sprouting from its hairy body. More and more continue to surround us, each more awful than the last.

And there's no Frankie here to reel them in, to convince these hideous creatures not to kill us.

"How good are you at fighting?" Alex growls, already lowering his head as he prepares himself. I don't know what he expects to fight these monsters with, considering the fact that he wasn't allowed to bring any weapons into the maze with him, but I don't dare ask. Mindful ignorance and all that bliss.

"Um…" I rack my brain desperately and finally blurt out, "I once punched myself in the face. Does that count?"

Alex mumbles something under his breath that might've been, "We're so fucked," but I could've misheard him amidst the growling and roars of hungry, ravenous monsters.

"We can fight them off," I insist with a confidence I don't truly feel. Mentally, I'm reaffirming his initial assessment of being "so fucked." But I'm going to add to that and say we're gonna be fucked sideways, backward, over a barrel, under a table, inside a bathroom stall, and then on the grassy fields of the White House itself.

We're so, *so* fucked.

"I have an idea," Alex says, already reaching for a bone that protrudes out of the wall of the maze.

"You gonna bone them to death?" I ask, incredulous, and he gives me a droll look at my phrasing.

"This section of the maze doesn't seem to be reinforced with magic," Alex explains, pulling more bones away from the maze wall and tossing one to me. "This was probably the gamemaster's design."

"So what's the plan?" I question softly as one of the hounds takes a step closer, his teeth bared and a growl rumbling from its chest. I bare my teeth right back at it, because I'm petty and vindictive like that.

"Come here." Alex gestures for me to take a step even closer to him, and I spin so we're back to back.

"We fight?" I don't dare speak above a whisper as another one of those evil fuckers ventures toward us.

Before Alex can answer, the monster with a face made of teeth lunges forward.

I stab at it instinctively with my makeshift weapon, hitting its stomach and eliciting a gasp of annoyance and rage from the beast. Oh hell. Apparently, all I served to do was piss it off even more.

"Hi, nice, pretty monster," I coo. "Please don't kill me."

"Are you really trying to have a conversation with that thing right now?" Alex asks as he stealthily dodges the attack of one of the canines. He spins, kicking out, and his foot lands squarely in the monster's stomach. Before another one can charge at him, he turns back to the maze wall and begins to rip apart more pieces of bone.

"What are you doing?" I bellow as sharp teeth dig into my ankle. I cry out in pain, glancing down to see the razer-blade chick eating at my skin like a goddamn psychopath. I can be pretty damn kinky when the mood calls for it, but ankle biting? I put my foot down on that one.

I stab at her head with my bone, listening to the satisfying crunch of something in her skull breaking. Hopefully her brain, but I wouldn't be too confident, considering she's still moving and growling and glaring.

And Alex...

He's a lethal weapon. A machine. A dancer.

He flies through the enemies' ranks with a cold-hearted focus and a lethal intensity I can't help but admire. He slashes and ducks and jabs, his features aloof and cold.

"Violet, come here," he instructs as he jerks away before a beast can put its teeth into him. I do as he instructs, praying that he won't decide to sacrifice me to the monsters. I'm not really sacrificial material. I'm definitely not a simpering virgin. Unless they want to sacrifice an annoying smart-ass with a mouth full of acid, they got the wrong gal.

"What's the plan—Alex!" A strangled scream gets caught in my throat as Alex shoves me with all his might. At first, I think I'm falling right into the eager teeth of the predators surrounding us. Terror flays me open, momentarily blinding me, as an icy chill caresses my skin.

Instead, I find myself flying backward through the air, through the opening in the maze wall Alex created when he ripped apart the bones.

I have only a second to see his face on the other side of the wall, terror splayed across his features, before the maze closes before my very eyes, the bone pieces reconnecting as if by magic.

"Alex!" I scream in alarm, but it has turned deathly silent. I can't hear him, the monsters, or...anyone. Anything. The silence surrounds me like a sickly tar, pervading my system, and I feel a cold sweat break out on my skin. My heart beats unevenly as terror floods my system.

I can't pull my gaze away from the now-closed maze wall. Alex…

He sacrificed himself for me. Sure, he didn't know the maze tunnel would reform as soon as I was through, but he still got me out first. I don't know how I feel about that. One part of me still wants to assume the worst of him—that he planned to abandon me, that he wanted me to die by myself, that this is all a part of some evil scheme, but a tiny piece of me knows that's not the case.

Alex truly chose to save me before himself, and now he's facing an army of beasts. Alone.

An emotion I can't quite identify clamps down on my heart, squeezing the organ until it's weeping blood. Guilt, perhaps? Fear for him? I don't know what it is, but it clogs my airways, embedding itself deep in my heart like a sliver of wood.

Okay, what do you do now, Violet? I whisper to myself, stumbling to my feet. All I can see in every direction are walls of bones and skulls. The steady drip, drip, drip of blood echoes around me.

"You got this, Vi," I tell myself out loud, giving myself a literal pat on the back. I can be my own cheerleader, dammit, and I sure as fuck don't need someone to come and save me. I'll save my men this time, or my name isn't Violet mother-fucking Dracula.

And maybe…

Maybe I'll save Alex as well.

My heart flutters in my chest when I think about his sacrifice, the repetitive *thump-thump-thump* turning uneven as fear and alarm mingle together in a toxic cocktail of emotion. I don't know if I'll be able to forgive myself if he dies because of me. I hate him, yes, and I doubt that will ever change, but I don't think he needs to *die*. He saved Barret, for fuck's sake, and now, he saved me. That's the type of heroism I don't think I can ever repay.

As usual when faced with stressful situations, I begin to sing softly under my breath. "I'm a badass bitch, going to be rich. Momma don't live in a ditch. Because she's...a switch." I nod my head seriously, already planning my mixtape for these killer lyrics, and choose a pathway at random to travel down.

For some reason, Dimitri's words from just before I entered the portal echo in my head.

"Two wrongs don't make a right."

At the time, I thought he was talking about Alex and our rivalry. I thought he was telling me not to retaliate against the evil necromancer. But maybe...maybe he was giving me a clue. A hint. A way to escape this fucked up maze.

But what exactly does he mean by that?

Two wrongs don't make a right...

So is he telling me to go right? To *not* go right? To go in the wrong direction and then go right? What even is the right direction?

Ugh. Why does he always have to speak in code and riddles? Why can't he ever look me in the face and go, "Hey, Violet. You know what you need to do? You need to suck my cock, for one, because I'm horny as fuck for your sweet booty. And also...you need to make three right turns, two left ones, and then go straight for five minutes to get out of the maze. Now get to cock sucking, you beautiful, perfect woman."

A girl can wish.

Something moves in my periphery, the barest flash of shadow, and I turn in alarm. My heart thunders in my chest, racing up my throat, but...

There's nothing there. Only darkness—cloying, tangible darkness. Night has fallen, and only the silver beam of the moon and collection of stars up above provides lighting. Menial lighting, but light all the same.

Why couldn't Dimitri have snuck me a flashlight or something?

Something cracks, snaps, breaks, and my pulse skitters.

"Who's there?" I demand instinctively, proving that I'm as dumb as everyone claims I am.

What stupid girl says "Who's there?" and doesn't die right away? Haven't you ever seen a horror movie? The dumb blonde who shakily yells, "Who's there?" is always the first one to get stabbed by the serial killer.

Welp. You might as well own it, Violet, because you dug your own grave already.

Infusing my voice with false bravado, I add, "I have a weapon, and I'm not afraid to use it."

That's totally a lie. I dropped my bone when Alex ninja kicked me into the hole, and I'm scared out of my mind. But make it till you break it and all that. Or is it fake it till you break it? Make it till you break it?

Note number two for future self—look up the correct saying.

"There's a lot of money for your death, little Dracula," a low voice purrs a second before the figure makes himself known.

A gasp gets lodged in my throat, joining the furball already present there, and terror keeps me immobile.

"You're...You're the Pumpkin Man."

His jack-o-lantern face breaks into an eerie grin, one revealing the candle lit inside.

"That's right. You heard of me, I presume?"

Yes. Your son is mated with my roommate, I think but don't say as I take the man in.

He's tall, nearly a full foot taller than me, and has a body made up entirely of muscle. He reminds me of one of those gym rats who spends every day and night working out and lifting weights. His pumpkin head is the size of two soccer balls morphed together, his triangle eyes rimmed with yellow. A brown stem protrudes from the top of his head, a single leaf connected to the wood.

"You look good enough to eat." His macabre grin broadens, and then a large, slimy tongue shoots out of his mouth like a frog.

I don't even have time to scream before his tongue wraps around my throat and he drags me toward him.

<h1 style="text-align:center">CHAPTER 29</h1>

CAL

I see only red, only blood.

It distorts my vision, consumes my every thought, and evokes the type of stone-cold lethality inside of me that terrifies most people.

My mate…

My Violet…

She's gone.

My wings flap against my back, demanding that I take to the air, but the damn forcefield prohibits me from doing so. Instead, I'm forced to wander aimlessly through the maze, my mind consumed with thoughts of Violet as a black fog descends across my mind like wispy smoke, eclipsing all rational thought.

I left Frankie in my dust, though I didn't hurt him. I hadn't felt the need…something we both should be grateful for.

Violet.

I need to find Violet.

I'll be the first to admit that I've been avoiding her, terrified of how she'll react to the unexpected revelation that she's my mate. The incubus part of me desires her lust and love, but the dark fairy inside of me? He wants her compliance. Her blood. Her body. Her soul. Her...everything. He demands that she fall on her knees for him and bow her head submissively.

The thought terrifies, ratcheting my heart rate up a dozen notches. The last thing I want to do is scare Violet away. She knows about the two sides of me, but she doesn't truly understand the plurality of my nature. The fairy blood inside of me is mercurial, hot one moment and stone-cold the next. It feasts on blood, sin, and violence, the same way my incubus devours lust and sex. The resulting combination is immensely toxic and downright terrifying.

So I kept my distance.

And I watched.

I watched as she worried over me, her teeth nibbling her plush lower lip. I watched as she tried to reach Jack and Hux...the same men I attacked only a few days earlier. I watched as she researched everything she could about the prophecy—a prophecy she doesn't know I'm aware of.

When I first heard the ominous words, I was confused. Was she going to take over the empire Dracula built? Become the queen of vampires?

But the more I watched, the more I learned, and the more I began to understand that not everything was as it seemed. For starters, Dracula isn't her real father. No, that position is reserved for the monster who lives beneath the ground, who revels in sin and darkness much like myself.

Lucifer Morningstar.

And her mother?

This took me a little bit longer to configure, shoving pieces together and praying something would stick. I did some research, unbeknownst to Violet, and the only woman Lucifer had ever been intimate with nine months before Violet's birthday was Hera, the queen of the Gods.

So what does all of this mean for her? For us?

The thought of anyone taking Violet from me has rage spiking my bloodstream, cascading through me in a wave of liquid heat. I bare my teeth, growling low in my throat, and envision snapping the neck of anyone and everyone who tries to harm her.

You can imagine the outcome when I stumble across the Pumpkin Man towering above Violet, his orange face twisted into a rictus grin.

I don't even think. One second, I'm standing at a fork in the maze, my wings batting in tandem to my rapidly racing heart and a cold rage dousing my skin, dampening the flames that have ignited. And the next…

The next I'm stalking forward, vengeance and death at the forefront of my mind. I don't hesitate to wrap my hands around the monster's neck and twist with all my might. Violet gasps in surprise, but the sound barely penetrates the mindless rage consuming me.

As the Pumpkin Man falls to the ground, his triangular eyes somehow even wider in his orange head, I lose my fucking mind.

With ruthless abandon, I stomp on his head, laughing maniacally as pumpkin guts spew in every direction. They douse me, the bone walls, and Violet, but I don't stop. I can't stop. Black and red color my vision, an enticing combination of violence and rage I can't escape from.

"Cal…"

He needs to pay.

He needs to suffer.

He needs to—

"Cal!" Violet places a hand on my arm, and I turn toward her with a growl, my elongated teeth bared in warning. She doesn't flinch, doesn't turn away, as she holds my stare with a defiant one of her own. Her chin twitches upward almost imperceptibly as my eyes roam over her body, cataloging it for injuries. Relief fills me, momentarily dampening even the blinding terror and anger, when I don't see a single scratch on her perfect skin.

"Mate," I growl out, completely forgetting about the Pumpkin Man and stalking toward my new prey.

"Mate?" Her voice hitches in surprise, the cocksure grin from mere seconds ago fading.

I place my hands on either side of her head, caging her against the wall of the maze. Her pupils dilate, her breathing growing uneven.

"Mate," I repeat, my voice guttural, nearly unrecognizable.

"Cal, I haven't seen you in days." Her voice is heady with distress and pain, and a strange noise emits from my throat before I can stop it—a whine and a growl combined. Her distress mirrors my own, and I hate myself for putting her through that, for making her suffer when all I ever wanted to do was protect her. "Where have you been?"

I want to answer her, want to explain everything, but I can't focus over the incessant pulling and tugging in the center of my chest. The pulling that demands I go to her, be with her, love her.

"Mate," I repeat. It seems to be the only word I can say. My brain is quite literally fried, nothing but a steaming wreckage of smoke and charred bodies.

"Cal, I don't know what you mean," she says softly, though she sounds hesitant. Unsure. "I don't think I'm your mate."

I take a deep, shuddering breath, attempting to get the words out through a throat that feels suddenly too tight. "Tell me you don't feel this connection between us. Tell me…and I'll go away."

Everything inside of me roars in protest at my offer, but I know I'll do it. For her, I'll do just about anything.

I don't know for sure how I feel about Violet Dracula—if it's love or merely lust, friendship or something else entirely —but I know I need her like a human needs oxygen and a banshee needs liver. I need her sass, her sultry grin, her babbling nonsense.

I need *her*.

Her eyes dip to my lips for a fraction of a second before lifting to meet my gaze. Lust momentarily darkens her features, accompanied by a healthy dose of surprise, as if she didn't expect to feel that emotion toward me.

I don't know what happens next—if I lean in or she does —but suddenly, my arms are around her waist as her lips devour mine. Or my lips devour hers. I can't tell for certain.

I continue pressing her back until she's flush against the maze wall, my hands roaming desperately over her perfect body. She gasps, the noise traveling straight to my cock, and begins to climb me like a tree.

Mate.

Mine.

Those two words play on repeat in my head as I cup her ass, allowing her to wrap her toned legs around my waist. I grind shamelessly against her, my cock pressed against her core, as she grapples with my shirt, pulling it over my head. It gets stuck on my wings, but that doesn't seem to deter her as she tugs at it desperately.

"Cal…" she murmurs, seemingly in a daze as her hands hesitantly hover over my body. I know I'm handsome—I mean, have you seen me?—but to have her stare at me with

such reverence actually humbles me, something I didn't
think was possible. I like the way she looks at me with half-
mast eyes, as if I'm the only man she sees, the only one she
adores.

"Touch me," I growl out, gyrating my hips against her
again.

"Cal…"

"Touch me."

She doesn't need to be told twice.

With a feverish intensity, she begins to kiss me once
more, her hands caressing my broad shoulders before
dipping down to my prominent V. The best damn V in the
entire world. She moans against my lips, mindless with
desire, as I break free of her kiss to pull her hideous red top
over her head. Her sports bra comes off next, and I duck my
head to take one of her hard nipples into my mouth.

"Fucking hell!" she curses, digging her fingers into my
pink hair as I pull at the sensitive bud, allowing it to slide
through my teeth. I lift my head to meet her stare, and that
same confusion from before splays itself across her beautiful
face now.

"Do you want me to stop?" I grunt out, my voice more
animal than human. More monster than man.

She seems to hesitate, spinning my sincere words over
and over again in her head, before she reaches between our
bodies and pulls my cock free of my shorts. She gives it a
single tug before releasing me.

"No," she breathes out, her lips parted ever so slightly
with desire. "Don't stop."

A sound that is most definitely not human leaves my lips
as I resume sucking on her perfect breast, using the hand not
keeping her up to cup her other breast. She moans, writhing
against the bone wall, as my hand travels down her stomach.

I don't hesitate to shove it inside her shorts and panties, spearing her on my finger.

She gasps, her legs clenching around me, as I begin to fuck her with my finger.

"Mate," I grit out, the word barely coherent. It's a mesh of syllables and air, a growl of a noise.

"Yes, Cal. Yes."

"Tell me what you want," I demand fiercely, holding her bright stare as I rub at her clit.

"I want your cock inside of me," she begs, her words a choked cry.

As if I could deny her anything, let alone something like that.

I drop her legs from around my waist and twist her, so she's forced to put her hands on the bone wall to keep her balance. I tug at her shorts and panties, dropping them around her ankles, and fall to my knees. I kick off my shorts and boxers as well and stroke my dick, taking in her utter perfection.

"Cal, please," she whines, begging. She begins to knead at her tender breasts as my hot breath fans against her perfect, pink pussy.

"My mate should never beg," I rumble out as I shove my tongue inside of her, lapping up her juices. I resume thrusting my fingers in and out of her as my tongue circles her nub, eliciting cry after cry from her sweet lips.

She tastes like ambrosia, the nectar of the gods, and I half wish I could bottle up her flavor. Fuck. She's exquisite. Positively exquisite.

"You taste so fucking good," I growl against her clit as her thighs begin to shake.

"Cal…" she whines.

Without preamble, I jump to my feet and grab the head of

my cock, giving it a few short strokes. Not that I need to. I'm hard as hell for her, just as I always am when she's around.

"I'm gonna go nice and slow, baby, okay?" I tell her, pushing the head of my cock against her tight hole and slowly inching myself in.

She gasps, her body trembling as she struggles to adjust to my girth and length, before she begs, "Move, Cal. You need to fucking move."

I grip her hips, my eyes locking on her bouncing ass, as I begin to thrust in and out of her tight channel. Words of praise leave her lips as I fuck her. Hard, fast, and with all the pent-up aggression and yearning that have been bottled inside of me for too damn long.

I grab a fistful of her gorgeous blonde hair, wrapping it around my hand, and pull her head up so her body is flush against mine. Sweat coats her skin despite the chill, and I reach between us to cup her heavy breasts, twisting her right nipple between my fingers. She mewls, pawing at my arm, and I rest my lips against her ear.

"Do you like that, baby? Do you like my big cock inside of you?" I have the biggest cock of probably any of her mates, and I'm not afraid to admit it. "You're so fucking gorgeous. Do you know that? I like gorgeous things, baby, and you're the most beautiful one of them all."

I release her breast and bring my hand down to her clit, thrumming it in tandem to each thrust of my hips.

"Cal," she whimpers, placing her head on my shoulder and tilting it upward to meet my hooded gaze. Stark desire and lust reflect back at me, and it's that look on her face that sends me over the edge.

My balls tighten, my cock jerking inside of her tight pussy, as a guttural roar escapes me. My orgasm seems to set off Violet's, who screams my name as her fingernails dig into my arm hard enough to hurt. Blood spills, but it only ampli-fies my arousal.

"Mate," I whisper reverently against her ear as her breathing turns uneven.

I know I'm not her only—I'll never be her only—but for just a brief second...

I'm someone.

And that's more than I could ever ask for.

CHAPTER 30

What. The. Fuck?

Seriously, what the ever-loving fuck?!?

My body collapses forward, utterly sated and exhausted from my rendezvous with Cal. He continues to pepper kisses across the back of my neck, his fingers lazily tweaking my nipples.

What. The. Fuck?

Cal.

My best friend.

My…lover?

I care about Cal more than I want to admit, but I never considered him *that* way. At least, I don't think I did. We've always been friends, nothing more, but now, everything has changed.

Mate.

That one word tumbles around in my head as I work to regulate my breathing.

Does Cal think…that I'm his mate?

Am I his mate?

Confusion wars with the lust still running rampant through my system as Cal slowly wraps his arms around me, bringing my body flush against his sweat-soaked chest. I can't say I mind being in his arms, but this entire thing is so goddamn confusing, I'm afraid my head is going to fall off.

When I first saw him advancing toward Mr. Pumpkin Face—or whatever the fuck his name is—I thought he was an avenging angel who had come to drag me straight down to Hell. There was something terrifying in his deadened expression, something I couldn't put into words. His eyes were a shade of red I've only seen once before—when he was killing Alex's father in the club—and black lines were interspersed amidst the red on his wings. I realized that his fairy blood was coming out to play, overshadowing the playfulness of the incubus inside of him.

And then he shoved me against the maze wall, exhibiting a possessiveness and dominance I wasn't used to seeing from him, and…

Well, you know what happened next.

My body flushes deliciously, a deep ache manifesting between my thighs. His cock is no longer inside of me, but I desperately want it to be.

What does this mean? For us? For me and the other guys? I know in my soul that what we did isn't cheating or anything of the sort. How could it be, when it felt so right? So right…yet so confusing. My body and brain can't quite get on the same page, but I *do* know that I want a repeat performance. Or multiple repeat performances.

Fuck.

It once again begs the question—what the fuckity fuck does this all mean?

"You're upset," Cal says abruptly, spinning me around in his arms so that he's able to stare down at me. He's so much taller than me, so much larger, that I want to feel over-whelmed by his presence. However, there's such tender anxiousness in his eyes, such warmth emanating from his pores, that I can't help but wilt into him like a sunflower searching for the sun.

"Not upset," I protest immediately, as my eyes travel over the muscular planes of his golden chest. He really is a gorgeous man, probably the most beautiful one I ever set eyes upon. I want to say that has to do with his incubus allure, but I know that's not the case. It's his soul, his *heart*, that calls to me.

He's incredibly smart and talented, even though he is admittedly conceited. He graduated from Yale with a degree in Molecular Biology. He's funny, witty, and compassionate, even with his fairy and incubus blood. The only crime he even committed—besides the occasional murder that we all do—was help supernaturals find their fated mates.

I still don't understand why the monster council arrested him for that, though I can't help but feel as if everything is connected, as if this is one big conspiracy that I need to unknot.

The prophecy concerning me, and then the other one about Dracula's daughter killing Mason.

My birth parents.

The emptiness of Mount Olympus.

The monster council throwing Cal into detention to keep him from helping monsters find their fated mates.

The fact that I have multiple mates in the first place.

Balor.

The vampire hatred and bigotry.

All of it.

Somehow, all of these things are connected, stuck in a web and just waiting for a spider to devour them whole. But what does it mean? Why does it feel as if I have the pieces of a puzzle but no clear image of what it'll look like when I connect them?

"Violet…" Cal's voice pitches lower, pain darkening his features at whatever he sees on my face. "Do you regret what happened?"

"No!" I rush to reassure him, placing my hands on his shoulders. "Not at all. This is all just…overwhelming."

"Overwhelming," he parrots, his brows dipping low.

"That's not what I meant." I release his shoulder with one hand to scrub it down my face absently. "I just meant…I didn't even know you liked me that way." There. That's the simplest way to describe the turbulent emotions crashing and thundering in my head. I don't regret for a second what we did, but I can't help but feel…bombarded. By him. By my feelings for him. By his feelings for me. By all of it, really.

Cal considers my words thoughtfully, one of his fingers pressing against my pillowy bottom lip. "I didn't," he confesses after a moment. "At least, I'm not sure if I did. You were just my friend at first, and though I could admit you were gorgeous, I didn't dare even think of you this way." He gestures between our naked bodies to clarify what he means by 'this.'

"Why didn't you dare to even think of me this way?" I ask, confused.

He barks out a dry, humorless laugh. "Look at you Violet—you're real, vibrant, fucking hilarious. Basically, you're perfect…and I'm…I like to say that I'm perfect too, but the truth is, I'm not. And I'll never be." His huge wings ruffle, and I can't resist reaching out to touch one of them. I wanted desperately to play with them during sex, but I hadn't dared, not wanting him to stop our desperate lovemaking session. But now…

He freezes, his eyes glazing over in a heady combination of pleasure and pain, as I trace the feathers decorating his gorgeous wings, marveling at the black interspersed with the red. "That's very sensitive," he manages to gasp out.

I grin wickedly. "More sensitive than your cock?" I tease, using my free hand to stroke said cock once. I marvel at the velvety softness over hard steel.

He hisses out a breath through his teeth as I release both his wing and cock. A shudder works its way through his muscular body as his eyes turn half-mast.

"Why do you have to torture me like this, baby?" he croons, crowding against me. The pet name has me biting my lip and clenching my thighs together to keep from jumping him. Again.

But alas, I have to be a responsible adult and discuss our impending relationship…if we're to have one.

"Now, let's get back on topic, please. I want to know everything—when you started feeling this way about me, why you were avoiding me, what this means for us, what this means for you and Barret…" I trail off, giving him a pointed stare that has him blushing. "Because I swear to God, if you made me the other woman and cheated on Barret, I'll never talk to you again."

At least that's one constant in my life. Barret. My sweet, innocent Barret. I don't ever have to worry about him jumping my bones, because he doesn't even think about me like that. And I don't think about *him* like that. At least, I don't think I do…

"I'm not cheating on Barret," Cal declares vehemently. "We have an open relationship, and he knows about my feelings for you. He already said it was okay."

"I don't want you guys to break up because of me—"

"It's complicated right now," he interjects with a shaky exhale, running a hand through his pink hair. "I know that, he knows that, and you know that. But that's not what I want to talk to you about at the moment, after my cock was just inside of you."

Thanks for the reminder. Now my lady boner is back and ready for more. Ugh. I'm gonna have such blue ovaries trying to be an adult.

"You're right. That can wait. Now, tell me everything," I insist.

Another breath leaves him. Another sharp intake and exhale of air. Another weary sigh that has his bare shoulders slumping forward. "I don't know for certain when I started having feelings for you. It might've been one of the times you came to visit me in detention. Or maybe during the Halloween party when we danced together. Or maybe after that when we competed in the first trial of the Roaring. All I know is I started looking at you the way…the way you look at all of the other guys." Self-loathing and a hint of jealousy drip into his tone, but he continues on before I can comment. "I didn't want to say anything and risk ruining our friendship, but when Alex's dad tried to kill you…" A shudder ripples through his body as if he's reliving that moment. "It broke something inside of me. I realized then that you were my fated mate. It's why I went dark."

"Why didn't you tell me?" I hate the fact that my voice wobbles, that I'm unable to conceal the sudden, bitter pain that burns me. "Why didn't you confide in me? Explain yourself? I could've helped you."

"Helped me?" He laughs again, the noise stabbing at my skin like a thousand toothpicks. "Violet, you *just* admitted that you don't know how you feel about the mind-blowing sex we just had. I feel like I took advantage of you—"

"No." I shake my head venomously, stepping forward to grab him once more. "No, don't you dare think that. What we shared was beautiful and amazing. My clit thanks you very much for it, as does my heart, as cliché as that sounds.

You're right, though. It was confusing and unexpected, at least for me, but that's only because I didn't know you felt that way about me. At all."

Something soft manifests in his eyes as he brushes at a strand of my golden hair, pushing it behind my ear. "How could I not? You're the best thing that has ever happened to me, Violet Dracula, and I'd be a fool not to claim you as my own."

"There's a lot I need to tell you—" I begin, but he interrupts me with a sheepish smile.

"I know about the prophecy and Medusa and Zeus and your mates and your birth parents…" He trails off at my flabbergasted expression.

"How in the bloody anus hole did you discover…?"

"I'm a really good stalker," he responds, not a hint of remorse in his tone despite his soft smile. That smile slips from his face, though, with his next words. "There's something really weird going on that goes beyond you."

"I know," I say, rubbing at my arms to fend off the sudden chill. "At least, I suspect there is. Everything seems to be… connected, and I don't know how or why. When I was led through Mount Olympus, it was empty, almost as if all of the gods and goddesses had left and only Medusa, Zeus, Hera, and their guards remained."

"That doesn't make any sense." Cal's brows furrow. "I went to Mount Olympus a few Halloweens ago to bang—" He cuts himself off abruptly, coughing into the crook of his elbow. "To talk to some of the goddesses there," he corrects. "It was rowdy. A nonstop party."

"So what does all of this have to do with me, the prophecy, the mating bonds, and daddy dearest?" I query.

"And Balor," Cal points out. When I glance at him, he offers me another tiny smile. "I may have had a run-in with Jack and Hux up in detention."

"You were able to get in detention?" I bellow, suddenly furious. Dimitri changed the combinations and locks to the upper level of the academy so I wouldn't be able to visit them. That cum stain.

"The magic of detention recognizes me, recognizes my monster," Cal explains. "It welcomed me with open arms."

I grumble, still a little salty that Cal was allowed up there and I wasn't, before focusing on the matter at hand.

"Okay, so you think Balor has something to do with all of this?"

"I can't think of another reason for why he would make his presence known. Why now? Why after all these years?" Cal insists.

"Because he's a bored asshole." I shrug my shoulders. "Why do bored assholes do anything?"

"Power, money, or revenge." Cal ticks each item off on his fingers. "So which one do you think applies to Balor?"

Before I can respond, someone screams my name, garnering my attention.

Cal immediately crouches in front of me, his teeth bared and his body bent forward in preparation to pounce, but relaxes when he sees Frankie, Mason, and Vin heading toward us.

Frankie, seemingly unperturbed by our naked bodies, narrows his eyes at Cal and pushes his glasses up with the pad of his finger. "Hey, asshole. Thanks for ditching me."

Cal huffs, straightening. "It's not my fault my legs are more muscular and can help me run faster," he snaps, pushing out his chest. Even after his sweet, romantic confession, he has to go and prance about like a bird showing off.

Vin glances between the two of us, his dark brows lowering, and at first, I think he's pissed. Guilt rushes up my throat, choking me, and I take a tentative step forward.

But then he begins to laugh, scratching absently at his neck. "Fuck, Vi. Another one?"

"Our girl is gonna have an entire football team of monsters as soon as this shit is done," Mason says with a jovial grin. "Isn't that right, Pinkie?"

"You're not mad?" I don't know why I ask the question—maybe because I'm an idiot and a sucker for punishment, or maybe because I'm desperate to know if I ruined everything we've gradually built.

"Mad?" Vin frowns. "Why the fuck would we be mad? We can sense the mating bond between the two of you."

This time, my brows are the ones that lower in confusion. "You can?"

What is with all of these posturing males sensing mating bonds that I can't?

Mason flashes me another smile. "Yeah, Pinkie. I think it's our own mating bonds with you that help us sense the ones with each other as well. When you and Cal did…" He crudely uses his right hand to make a circle and then stabs his left pointer finger through it.

"Had sex. Yes, I know how it works," I quip with an eye roll. "Unless *you're* in need of a sexual education course…"

"Just checking." He chuckles once before continuing. "Anyway, when you guys solidified the bond, we were able to sense it." He shrugs again.

"That's…alarming and a little sexy, I'm not gonna lie. I kinda want to jump on one of your dicks and pretend it's a pony and I'm a cowgirl," I deadpan.

They blink at me.

"Or…we can continue on through the maze," I concede with a sigh. Curse my responsibility skills. Curse them to the deepest pit of Hell.

"I like option one better," Mason tells me, lifting his hand in the air and waving it around.

"Me too," Frankie deadpans.

"We need to get out of here," Vin tells us all, though he sounds pained. It must suck to always have to be the voice of reason when everyone around you wants to bang. He slides his gaze toward a still naked Cal, his massive cock standing at attention. "Especially if Cal wants to win the Roaring and get his freedom."

The reminder is like a bucket of ice water being dumped over all of our heads. It's easy to forget that at the end of the day, Cal is still a prisoner of the system. If he doesn't win the Roaring, he'll be forced back into the upper levels of the academy for who knows how long.

And I might never be able to see him again.

"We need to go get Alex," I tell them, and when four pairs of eyes turn to stare at me dubiously, I hurry on, "I can't leave unless he's with me. You know the rules of the Roaring." I point in the direction I left the asshole necromancer, praying that I won't find a corpse. I tell myself I only want him alive because I need him with me to win, but the truth is...he saved my life. And now, I'm gonna save his. "Can't you guys trust me?"

"We do trust you, Pinkie," Mason tells me.

"It's him we don't trust," Vin mutters darkly.

"How will we even find him?" Frankie adds, canting his head to the side.

"I know the general location he should be in," I tell them. "If we walk around, we should be able to find him."

I hope.

The guys hesitate, obviously not liking this option, before they nod in unison.

"Come on! Let's go on an adventure!" I tell them fiercely, already stalking down the pathway I came from when the Pumpkin Man found me. I'm honestly surprised none of the guys mentioned the body only a few feet away from us, but then again, they're probably so used to corpses that his doesn't even faze them.

Vin clears his throat, halting me in mid-step.

"Violet?" he asks, cocking an eyebrow.

"Yes?"

"Maybe you should put back on your clothes…"

It takes an hour we don't have to find Alex, but when we do find him…

My heart stutters to an abrupt halt as I stare at his mutilated body on the ground, his chest torn open in more places than I care to count and his face a myriad of bruises and bloody gashes.

"Alex…" I say weakly as Frankie hurries toward him and kneels. He places his fingers against the necromancer's pulse.

"He's alive," he says at last, and relief cascades through my body in a sizzling stream. "But barely."

"We need to bring him with us," I insist, and when all four of them stare at me again, I add, "Remember…I can't leave without him."

But that's not the full truth, and they all know it.

Still, no one presses me for answers when Vin hoists Alex over his shoulders and nods for us to continue walking.

I should want Alex to die for everything he did to me, everything he did to all the vampires in the world, but for some inexplicable reason, I don't. Maybe I'm a bleeding heart after all.

Or maybe…

Maybe I think Alex is one. And if he is, there's hope for him after all.

CHAPTER 31

BALOR

The Boogeyman is going to die.

Sure, he's a strong fighter, a fierce warrior, a passionate advocate for those he loves...but there's no way he can fend off an army of goblins.

A smile curves up my lips when I think about how I left him.

"Hux! Help me!" he bellows, his voice guttural around his massive, hand-sized teeth. He bends at the back, so his head doesn't reach the forcefield above him, and bats at a tiny goblin that runs at him.

Goblins are disgusting creatures, even by monster standards. They have no loyalty to anyone except the Goblin King—a puppet owned by the monster council. As such, goblins are the perfect weapon to use in the maze against unaware monsters. They're only about two feet in height and have sickly green skin covered in warts and pores. Their beady black eyes have no lashes, no irises, just an endless abyss of pupils. Tiny strands of pitch-black hair sprout from the tops of their heads like lava erupting from a volcano. But don't let their sizes fool you—they're fierce little fuckers with razor-sharp teeth and a steely determination to maim and kill.

I grin at Barret, tipping my imaginary top hat in his direction. "No can do, Boogeyman."

His eyes flash in my direction at my accented voice.

"Hux? When did you get an Irish accent?" he demands as he rips off the head of one of the goblins racing at him. More jump on his back, pawing at his skin and sinking their teeth into his neck.

Not a very bright one, that Boogeyman.

So... I leave him. With over a dozen goblins clinging to his body and a bellow of pain and rage slipping free of his bloody lips.

I leave him, and I don't look back.

I smile darkly at the memory, practically skipping for joy.

You'll pay for this, Hux seethes in my head, his wrath intermingling with my own delight and creating a toxic cocktail of emotions.

I decided to be gracious and allow Hux and Jack a front-row seat to what I have planned next. I'm not a complete asshole, after all.

They should be allowed to watch me kill everyone they love.

Don't do this, Jack begs, a tremble in his tinny, metallic voice as he pleads. *Please.*

Begging will get you nowhere, Jack, I tell him with a hum, peering around the corner of the maze at my target.

Violet Dracula and her merry band of misfits.

Currently, the bitch herself is leading the group, singing softly under her breath. Cupid and Medusa's son are on either side of her, while the Van Helsing fucker stands at her back, carrying an unfamiliar male over his shoulders. Frankenstein's experiment eyes the maze with sharp, critical eyes, that analytical brain of his spinning rapidly.

But as always, my eyes are drawn back to Violet, watching her breasts bounce through the fabric of her shirt as she walks. I can't help but imagine pounding into that sweet pussy as my hands tighten around her throat, choking her until her skin turns blue and her eyes bug out of her head. And then, once the life fades from her eyes, I'll continue to fuck her until her body is nothing but a puppet for my pleasure. My own sex doll.

I used the sex doll resembling her more times than I care to admit, kneading those perky tits and rutting into her with wild abandon, but I have a feeling the real thing will be better than anything else in this world.

I'll kill you, Hux rages, pounding against the prison of our shared mind. *I'll destroy you!*

Now, now, Brother, that's not very nice, I tsk, feigning sadness. *Can't we all just get along?*

I'll rip your dick off and—

We share the same dick, I point out smugly. *And I'm going to be putting it inside Violet Dracula as soon as I'm able to.*

Fuck you!

Jack and Hux begin to pound against our head in tandem, and with a sigh of irritation, I dismiss them, pushing them farther into the darkness of our shared consciousness. Stupid, idiotic boys. They should know by now that I have centuries and centuries of experience. While they lived their lives, I learned everything I could about our condition.

More than that, I spent our shared eternity building an empire.

The Formorians.

My people.

My heart and soul.

Currently trapped by Lucifer himself in hell.

But I made a promise when my people were first

kidnapped and locked away hundreds of years ago—I would free them no matter what the cost was.

I smile darkly as my eyes travel over Violet's lithe form.

And that cost?

Violet Dracula.

CHAPTER 32

VIOLET

"We need to find a way out of here," Frankie says after an hour of aimlessly wandering.

Mason, who has taken over carrying Alex for the time being, grunts and lowers himself onto his knees to relieve the pressure on his back and shoulders.

"Dimitri talked to you just before you entered the portal, didn't he?" he questions me. Sweat soaks his skin, dripping down the column of his neck, as a healthy flush unfurls in his cheeks. I have a moment of fear and panic that he's too sick to continue on, too weak, but he stands with another grunt of exertion and grits his teeth through the pain. "What did he say?"

"I thought it was a hint to get out of the maze at first, but now I'm not so sure." I shrug my shoulders but decide there's nothing wrong with confessing the truth to them. "Two wrongs don't make a right."

"Two wrongs don't make a right..." Vin repeats,

scratching at the stubble that lines his jawline. He usually keeps it smooth-shaven, but over the past few days, he's forgotten to shave, hence the dark shadow. I can say with absolute confidence that I love it on him.

"I thought maybe he was just talking about my feud with Alex." I jerk my chin toward the necromancer, who's still unconscious. If we don't get him out of this maze soon and to a healer, he won't survive. Frankie did what he could with the limited supplies we found in the maze, but it won't be enough to save his life.

For some reason, my heart twists into a dozen tight knots at the prospect of his death.

Why does he have to save my life and then get critically injured? Ugh. What a dick.

"Maybe," Mason agrees, returning my attention to the conversation at hand. He grunts, shifting Alex on his shoulders, and Vin walks forward to grab the necromancer from him and carry him once more. "But maybe it's a hint."

"But what does it even mean?" I groan.

"Maybe two left turns and one right turn," Cal suggests, flexing his wings.

"But when would she need to take the two left turns and one right turn? When she first entered the maze? Because if that's the case, there's no way we'll be able to find it back," Vin muses, frustration darkening his features.

"Obviously Dimitri knew that I would never leave you guys," I point out. "So maybe it has something to do with all of us being together?"

"That doesn't make any sense, Pinkie," Mason tells me, leaning forward to boop my nose. I swat at his hand with a growl.

"Don't boop me."

"I'll boop you if I want to boop you." For emphasis, he leans forward to boop me a second time.

"Asshole." I grab at his hand and bite down on his finger when he attempts to boop me again. He hollers out in pain, though that mischievous grin doesn't leave his face.

Cal snaps his fingers in the air as if he has come up with a grand epiphany. "What if the riddle means we can't take any right turns? What if the way out of this maze is only left turns?"

"I don't know, man," Mason says, sounding hesitant, his good mood from earlier evaporating in the face of all that's at stake. "If we're wrong, you're the one who will—"

"I know the risks," he interrupts briskly. "But this makes sense."

"Cal's right," I interject before an argument can brew. "It does make sense."

"Of course I'm right," Cal huffs, straightening out a wrinkle in his bright red shirt. "I have superior intelligence compared to all of you lowly peasants."

"Cal, sweetie?" I blink at him with an innocent smile.

"Yeah, baby?"

"Tone it down a notch."

A sinful grin unfolds on his lips. "You didn't want me to turn it down a notch when I was balls deep inside of—"

"LA LA LA LA!" I sing, putting my hands over my ears and sticking out my tongue. "I don't want to hear about your sexual escapades."

"The sexual escapade was with you," Cal points out, amusement lacing his voice.

"Still gross." I wrinkle my nose. "No one wants to hear about sex. Sex is icky."

"You definitely weren't saying that when I—"

I interrupt Cal again. "Let's get a move on, people. We're burning daylight!"

"It's night already, Pinkie," Mason points out, skipping up beside me now that he no longer carries Alex and linking his arm with mine. As always, I can't stop myself from surveying him from head to toe, gauging his physical and mental state.

"You guys never let me have any fun." I push my lips out into a pout, and Mason uses the opportunity to boop my nose. "I swear to Zeus, Mason, that I'm gonna—"

A loud roar echoes from farther down in the maze. All of us go completely still. Terror thrums through my veins like a live wire zapping haphazardly in all directions as I tighten my grip around Mason's arm. Mind-numbing fear pours acid into my stomach, burning me from the inside out.

All I can picture is a beast with leathery skin hung loose over an emaciated body. Needled teeth. Large, glowing red eyes—

Barret breaks through the wall of the maze like the motherfucking Kool-Aid man, his green hair wildly disheveled and his body twice, no, three *times* the size of his normal one.

My fear and alarm turn into relief…and then that relief turns into trepidation.

"Barret?" I ask tentatively as he locks his eyes on me, power seeming to crackle off his body in palpable waves. As I watch, he shrinks down in size, the bitter countenance from before dropping away to reveal my sweet Boo Bear.

"Violet, be careful," Vin warns, but I ignore him, rushing forward to throw my arms around Barret's waist. He stiffens in surprise, his muscles locking tight, before awkwardly patting me on the back.

"There, there," he soothes in a distracted voice.

"Barret! It's so fucking good to see you. Are you okay? What happened?" Pulling away, I'm stunned to see hundreds of tiny bite marks littering his body, marring the perfection of his dark skin. Without the combative, cantankerous glint in his eyes, he appears lost and confused. Dazed, almost… which isn't that unusual for Barret, let's be real.

"Goblins," he confesses in a rush of air, pushing me away as if I smell or something. That stings more than I'll admit. He shuffles a few steps backward and awkwardly crosses his arms over his chest. "A whole bunch of them."

Fear washes over me in a torrent, painful in its intensity.

"Where's Jack? Hux?" My chest gives a rattling heave as my breaths saw in and out, in and out, the repetitive nature doing nothing to soothe me.

Guilt clouds Barret's face as he lowers his head, his chin touching his chest. "I'm sorry," he murmurs brokenly.

"What the fuck happened? What did you do?" I demand, the accusation slipping free before I can stop myself. He flinches as if I slapped him, and I instantly feel like a load of shit. And not just any shit either, but one that's so goddamn stinky you need to spray Febreze all over the bathroom for days afterward.

"He...well... One second it was Hux beside me, and the next..." He shakes his head from side to side, still not glancing up. "The next, it was a man with an accented voice and—"

"Balor," I interrupt as something dark claws at my insides. "Are you saying Balor is in control of their body right now?"

"I'm so sorry, Cheese Curd," he says in a tiny voice, refusing to meet my eyes. "I didn't—"

"Hey." I step forward to take his cheeks between both of my hands, lifting his head up. His body rebels at first, his hands curling into fists, before he relents with a sigh and meets my gaze. "This is not your fault, you hear me? I'm sorry for snapping at you earlier. I was just scared and worried and—"

"Because they're your mates. And you love them," he responds softly, a familiar flicker of pain flashing across his face.

"Yes," I whisper, and he nods once, as if he expected that answer.

"I understand. When you love someone, you'll do just about anything for that person." He offers me a tentative smile, one that doesn't quite reach his eyes.

"I didn't mean to snap—"

"Don't apologize, Cheese Curd. I understand." He entangles his hand with my own and gives it a soft, reassuring squeeze. When he releases it, his eyes shift to Cal. He takes a step toward the other man, pauses, glances at me over his shoulder, and then steps backward.

"Barret, you can go to him if you—" I begin, hating the hesitancy in his expression and the despondency in Cal's.

"It's fine," Barret tells me, though his tone makes it sound as if it's anything *but* fine. Guilt fills me like a collection of bees being unleashed. I know Cal told me that they talked about this, that they were okay, but I can't help but feel as if I'm missing something important.

Cal glances at me helplessly, and when I open my mouth to ask for more information, he shakes his head subtly. He waits until Barret meanders toward the other males before sidling to my side.

"I thought you said Barret was okay with the two of us together?" I ask anxiously, my stomach muscles tightening until I fear I'll vomit.

"He is," Cal assures me, though there's a frown on his face that hasn't been there before. "I don't think his attitude has anything to do with that."

"Then what's going on with him?" I demand softly.

Cal narrows his eyes, almost as if he's attempting to calculate a difficult math equation in his head, before heaving out a breath.

"I have some ideas…"

"Care to share them with the class?"

Before he can answer, Vin waves us forward. "Come on, guys. We don't have a lot of time. We need to get out of this maze as soon as possible if we're going to win."

"Come on." Cal grabs my hand and pulls me forward. "Let's get out of this hell hole. We can talk about it later."

CHAPTER 33

DIMITRI

I've never been a worrying type of man before, but every second that passes has my heart growing larger in a steadily shrinking iron claw until blood pools around my feet. The audience waits with bated breath for the first monster to escape the maze, but…no one does.

I soon become so distressed and agitated that I can't remain still. Politely excusing myself, I make a beeline toward my office and begin to pace across the soft carpeting.

I told Violet how to get out of the maze, so what the fuck is taking her so long? I even allowed Frankie to sneak his tracking device into the maze in order to find her.

So where the fuck are they?

Why aren't they here?

Scrubbing a hand through my white-blond hair, and disrupting my immaculate ponytail, I resume my pacing. My feet leave shallow prints in the carpeting, but I don't stop. I *can't* stop. Fear for Violet and the others overrides just about everything else.

They'll be okay.

They have to.

I refuse, absolutely refuse, to accept any other alternative. Maybe it took Violet longer than I intended to decipher my clue. After all, I couldn't risk telling her in simple terms how to escape, so I needed to speak in code.

But perhaps I overestimated the golden-haired beauty…

A knock on my door has my head snapping up to see Charles the Third, a descendant of the Yeti, glaring up at me. He's significantly shorter than my impressive six-foot, four-inch height, so he's forced to stand on his tiptoes in a pathetic attempt to look intimidating. When I continue to regard him with the cold impassiveness I perfected over the years, he sighs and lowers his eyes like a good, submissive pup.

"Someone wishes to speak with you, Headmaster Gray," he tells me, his words muffled from where his chin is resting against his chest.

I tap my fingers against my thigh, just out of his eyesight if he were to lift his head up and stare at me. I can't allow him to see even a moment of weakness, a weakness I hadn't felt only months earlier.

Before *she* came into my life.

Before she disrupted everything I thought I knew.

Before she shattered my defenses with one fatal swoop of her fucking lashes.

"A visitor?" I tsk my tongue, moving to claim the high-backed chair behind my desk. "Can't this wait until after the games are done?" I keep my tone bored and aloof, teetering that precarious edge between impassiveness and violence, and Charles the Third flinches almost imperceptibly.

I lift my bourbon glass up to my lips to hide my smirk.

"He demands that he speak with you now," he presses, and I blow out a breath. The life of a headmaster at a pretentious academy is tedious at best, a soul drainer at worst. Monsters from all across the world believe they can wave their pocketbooks at me and I'll be falling at their feet, begging to do whatever they ask of me. Maybe the old headmaster behaved that way, but not me. Never me. I'll beg for nothing and no one, and I'll only fall to my knees for a queen. For *my* queen.

"Fine." My smile is sharp enough to cut through skin, unveiling the muscles and bones beneath. "Let me speak to him."

Charles the Third whimpers, repeatedly bowing his head in submission, before leading me out of the office, down the hallway, and into a conference room we don't normally use.

I fix the sleeves of my cufflinks before stalking inside, intent on giving this pathetic, insufferable man a piece of my mind.

His back is toward me with his hands clasped, allowing me to see nothing but a snow-white suit and dirty brown hair. Everything about his posture screams relaxed and comfortable, something that instantly puts me on guard. Most monsters know who I am and what I'm capable of, hence the fear I evoke in all of them.

But this man…

He doesn't appear fazed.

"I was told you would like to speak to me," I say curtly, not bothering with pleasantries. I much prefer to get the conversation over with instead of drawing it out.

The man turns, flashing me a smile, and I take a moment to survey him as he does the same to me.

Cold, almost black eyes. A sharp beard and mustache that emphasizes the planes of his face. A lazy smile that tells me everything I need to know—he knows who I am and doesn't consider me a threat.

My hackles rise.

"Ahh! Headmaster Gray! It's so great to see you," the man says, that rictus smile on his face broadening.

I choose not to respond, assessing him as I do with any threat. He appears to be placing more weight on his right leg than his left, letting me know that he's probably right-handed. His posture is immaculate, his back perfectly straight and shoulders bent, but he's not centered. One strong push will send him toppling over. I also note a scar peeking through the collar of his white suit. That probably means that there are more injuries in that immediate vicinity, injuries I can exploit if the need arises.

I keep my expression calm and placid as I meet his chilling stare. "I do not appreciate being dragged out of my office like a damn whipping boy," I tell him curtly. "I'm a very busy man, Mr…" I trail off with a quirked brow, waiting for him to fill in the blanks.

That enigmatic smile remains on his face as he steps forward with one of his hands raised. "Morningstar. You can call me Lucifer, though."

A chill sweeps through my entire body, freezing my internal organs even as my expression remains aloof. No one would be able to see the way his words slash at me. I'm a master at crafting a mask out of nothing, at hiding my true emotions.

"Lucifer Morningstar," I say flippantly, giving his hand a firm shake before releasing it. "I believe I've heard of you."

A genuine laugh escapes him as he grabs at his stomach. "I imagine you did, boy." My eyes twitch at the name, but I don't comment. "Hell only knows that I've heard of you. Dimitri Gray, son of the famous Dorian Gray. The best assassin in the entire monster community. You still have your painting, boy?"

I don't answer, refusing to divulge something so personal with a monster like him.

Violet's biological father.

What the fuck is he doing here?

"Is there something you want, Mr. Morningstar?" I say pleasantly, claiming a seat at the table and reclining backward. I refuse to allow him to see how much he has shaken me.

He grins at my obvious refusal to follow his instructions and takes the seat opposite me. He has an accent—Southern, perhaps—but it's faded, nothing but a lilt of vowels now.

"I heard that this year's games are some of the best yet," he tells me, slapping his palm down on the table. If he expects me to flinch or cower away, he has another think coming—and yes, it's think. Humans damned the saying over time.

"It's been interesting, that's for sure," I say dispassionately. "Is that why you're here?" I lean forward, clasping my hands together and placing them on the table. "For the games?"

"For the winner of the games, actually," he responds, shooting me another jovial grin that only serves to unnerve me further. Which is what he wants, I suspect.

This man…

He's the definition of evil.

He created a fleet of monsters simply because he was bored with the humans. I have no doubt he can get rid of us just as easily.

"I would like to congratulate them and offer them an all-expenses-paid trip to Hell to celebrate." Another disarming smile. Another palm slapping against the wooden table. Another chuckle that reminds me of a hammer being thrown against metal.

"That is…mighty generous of you," I tell him, praying that he can't hear the hammering of my heart in my chest.

Why is he doing this?

Does he know about Violet?

I've spent my entire life keeping her existence a secret

from him and others like him. For all the world knows, she's Dracula's daughter.

And that's the way it has to remain.

"Well, I'm in a generous mood," Lucifer tells me. "I thought the winner of this year's Roaring deserved a little something extra, don't you think?"

"I'm sure your generous donation will be much appreciated."

Get out of there, Dimitri.

Get out of there.

"If you'll excuse me," I begin, pushing out of the seat, "I have something I need to do before the final game of the Roaring ends."

Lucifer waves me away with a cheeky smile. "Of course. I imagine you're a busy man. I'll show myself to my rooms for tonight." He nods once, a single dip of his head, but doesn't make a move to exit until I do myself.

Lucifer? Staying here? On campus?

Fuck.

I keep my pace even as I move down the hall and back toward my office. I don't see Charles the Third anywhere, but I imagine the miserable twat is putting a suite together for the great Lucifer Morningstar, the creator of all monsters.

Fuck. Fuck. Fuck.

What am I going to do now?

I've just entered my office, breathing deeply through my nose, when a flash of golden hair captures my attention.

"Vi—" I stop abruptly when the woman stands, and I realize that it isn't Violet in my office with me, but her mother. A woman I haven't seen since I was a young boy.

She absently brushes at a blonde curl as she stands, turning around to face me.

"Hera," I say stoically.

A frown mars her face—a face so eerily similar to that of the woman I love—as she whispers, "We need to talk."

CHAPTER 34

VIOLET

Well, I suppose Dimitri is good for something besides mind-blowing orgasms. Not that I'll ever admit to his face that he excels at them…

After left turn after left turn after left turn, we arrive at a portal glimmering like gossamer spiderwebs and freshly spun starlight. I swear that the longer I stare into the swirling chasm, the more I notice new things, like streaks of pink and purple, a splatter of gold, and freckles of neon green.

"Is this it?" I don't dare speak above a whisper, unwilling to disrupt the tranquility that has blanketed the maze.

"I don't know what else it'll be," Cal grunts out, his face creased with concentration and pain from holding all of Alex's weight on his shoulders. He's been alternating holding the necromancer with the other guys, but in a true Cal fashion, he needs to prove that he's the strongest of them all. And now that we've had sex? I can shamelessly admit I've been admiring his tightly corded biceps as they flex.

"So do we just meander our way through?" I query, taking a tentative step toward the swirling abyss. "Skip? Shake our booties? Belly flop? Dive?" I slowly shake my head and pause a few feet away as warning alarms blare in my head. "This seems too easy."

"Do you really think the gamemakers will *Harry Potter* this joint and send us to a field of death?" Mason demands, and my lady parts do a little jig at the fact he knows *Harry Potter*. A man after my own heart. He is totally a Hufflepuff. Me? I'm a Slytherin girl, who really, really likes taking Hufflepuff men to bed and making them my bitch—

"We need to go through. Before any monsters catch up with us," Vin asserts with a scowl. He glances surreptitiously in both directions. "That is, if we're even the first group of monsters to arrive here."

"We have to think positive," I tell him firmly. Clearing my throat, I add, "I actually have an entire musical number written specifically for—"

"Dear God, no."

"Please no."

"Violet, I love you, but if you sing, I'll stab you."

"I don't have any earplugs."

"For heaven's sake, no. Just no. Fuck no."

The guys' voices rush together in adamant refusal of my gift to mankind—my singing voice. It only killed, like, two mice, so I call that a win.

My mates can be such shits.

I fold my arms over my chest and scowl. "I hate you all. No orgasms for you." I stare pointedly at Vin, who glowers back at me. "No orgasms for you." This is directed at Mason, who grins at me without remorse. "And no orgasms for you and you." I turn to Frankie and Cal respectively.

I can't help but notice the hurt that flashes in Barret's eyes as he ducks his head, but before I can question his strange behavior, he says, "We all need to go together if we want to win together."

"But…" Something occurs to me, and a penis-sized hairball gets stuck in my throat like toilet paper clogging a toilet. I turn toward Barret, my lips slanting downward. "But Hux and Jack aren't here. And if you guys don't exit the maze together…"

"You don't win," Frankie finishes. A tiny crease emerges between his eyebrows, and I just know he's thinking of ways to get us out of this mess.

"But it's not Hux or Jack in control right now," Vin points out with a scowl. "It's Balor."

"*Fucking* Balor," I correct.

Fucking Balor.

Frankie's hand begins to tap against his thigh, and I can practically hear the grinding of gears in his head as he thinks. Metaphorical smoke blows from his ears. "I still think there's a way to separate all of their consciousness and put them in—"

"As if I'm ever going to allow you to separate me from my brothers," an unfamiliar voice declares languidly. Or…a familiar voice, but also an unfamiliar voice. The husky tone is the same, but neither of my men has a heavy Irish accent.

Balor.

In the flesh.

Well, in the flesh of *my* guys.

I spin around to glare at the smug asshole, spewing fire at him with my eyes. I hate that he wears the face of the men I love, but I also can't deny that he looks significantly different than both Hux and Jack. Hux chooses to wear his dark hair down and behind his ears, revealing a wicked scar that curves down his cheek. Jack, on the other hand, always has his hair in front of his face and a pair of glasses on.

But Balor…

Balor's black hair is haphazardly thrown into a bun at the top of his head, a few inky strands escaping its binding to frame his face. He has a lazy smile stretching across his lips, a smile I've never seen on Hux or Jack before. Cocky, almost, with an undercurrent of danger and violence that warns me away. He exhibits none of the warmth and kindness of Jack or the protective intensity and insanity of Hux.

Balor will never be the man Hux and Jack are. He's just a piss-poor imitation.

"It's great to officially meet you, dear," Balor says with a cheeky grin directed at me. I return his infuriating smirk with a growl, allowing my fangs to slip out.

"I can't say the same for you, asshole." My hands curl into fists by my sides, and only Mason's placating hand on the small of my back stops me from lunging forward and killing him. But I don't yet know the mechanics of their situation and I don't want to risk harming Jack and Hux in the process. "Give me back my men."

"You mean sweet little Jack and mean old Hux?" Balor asks with a mocking pout. When I continue to glare at him, too angry to speak, he releases a bark of laughter. "You know, I was told you were funny, but I didn't think you were an idiot."

"Name calling is rude," I retort before I can stop myself, because apparently, I turn into a five-year-old on the playground when I'm pissed off.

"If you don't give us back Hux and Jack—" Vin barks out, but Balor interrupts him with another lilting laugh.

"What will you do?" He chuckles good-naturedly, grabbing a tiny bone he must've sharpened into a dagger from the waistband of his pants. "Kill me?" He brings the bone to his wrist and begins to slice.

"No!" I scream in horror, lurching forward before anyone can stop me. A maniacal glint enters his eyes—eyes that I've come to love—as I tear the bone from his hands with my vampiric—demonic?—strength and speed and toss it aside.

His smile turns taunting, cruel, reminiscent of a frosted over sword. "You won't hurt me, demon spawn, because you love the men inside of me."

Before I can think of something witty to say—because I definitely can't deny his assessment of the situation—he lunges forward and presses his lips to mine. For a millimeter of a second, I freeze, relishing in the familiar feel of Hux and Jack's lips. But while Hux always tastes like peppermint and Jack has a distinct spearmint flavor, Balor's kiss reminds me of slimy scales on a fish.

I shove him away so hard that he stumbles onto his ass, laughing enigmatically.

"Fucking prick!" I bellow as my men storm forward with murder on their minds. Vin grabs at the bone on the ground and holds it against Balor's neck.

"I want to fucking kill you," he hisses, his expression pained as his hunter blood battles for dominance against his empathy. "I want to kill you so fucking bad."

"But alas, you can't. And you won't. Boohoo." Balor pantomimes wiping at his eyes before leisurely climbing to his feet and brushing off his pants. "But that was a good kiss, huh, Vi?" He winks at me, and disgust curdles in my stomach like rotten milk.

"I'd rather kiss a frog," I snap.

Anger momentarily darkens his features, features that somehow look both similar and eerily different from Hux and Jack's, before he adopts his customary smile once more.

"Such a shame. Such a shame." He tsks, shaking his head sadly. "At least your rude reaction assuages the guilt I once felt over giving your venom to Diedre Stevens."

"Giving my venom…?" Horror manifests as a fist inside of

my stomach, pounding against my rib cage with every consecutive breath.

Diedre Stevens, Dracula's biological daughter, was my teacher and a vampire. When vampire hatred became more and more prominent in the monster community, she sought to make a martyr out of me. As such, she murdered a bunch of students and planted my venom in their wounds, framing me for their deaths. When I confronted her about it, before she passed away, she confessed that she received my venom from one of my lovers.

I hadn't overly thought about it since then, assuming they were nothing but the ramblings of a dying, crazy woman, but now...

"It was you," I breathe in shock.

Balor gives an elaborate bow, chuckling under his breath. "Of course it was. Did you really think one of your men would've truly betrayed you?" Disgust twists his features until he no longer looks even remotely similar to Hux or Jack. It makes it easier to stare directly at him. "They're all sickeningly in love with you."

"Why would you work with Ms. Stevens?" Frankie demands, his fingers once again tapping a staccato against his thigh.

"Let's just say that our interests momentarily aligned back then," Balor confesses with a dismissive wave of his hand, apparently not ready or willing to give his evil villain monologue just yet.

"You fucking asshole!" I scream, anger bursting out of me like a raging fire.

Balor, as flippant as always, sighs heavily.

"Are we going to continue to stand around here with our dicks in our hands or are we going through the portal?" he asks, leaning against the closest wall and crossing his arms over his chest.

"We're not letting you leave here," I blurt.

That sickening grin from before reappears on his face, though he doesn't make a move in my direction. "No? So you're willing to lose Hux, Jack, and Barret? How heartless of you."

"Fuck you."

Anger clouds his eyes as he pushes away from the wall and stomps forward. "Listen here, you little bitch—"

Vin, Cal, and Mason step forward, barring Balor from getting to me, while Barret and Frankie close in on either side.

Over Cal's ruffling red wings, I see Balor freeze, a myriad of expressions flickering across his face. Anger, hatred, and then finally, that flippancy that drives me goddamn insane even though I just met the guy.

He takes a deep breath, his shoulders touching his ears before dropping, and regards us all with a cocky, carefree smile. "I apologize for losing my temper. I just felt the need to remind Violet over there," he turns toward me, causing all of my men to tense and snarl, "that if I don't come with you guys, Barret won't be eligible to win. And as such, he'll be forced back into detention. Is that what you want?" He sidles a step closer, looking like the cat who ate the cream—but I'll die before I allow him to put his tongue anywhere near my cream. "I know Barret isn't one of your boy toys, but do you really want to see him locked away?"

"Shut the hell up," Cal interjects.

Barret turns toward me helplessly, his green hair moving like crazy on top of his head. "Violet, you don't have to do this for me. I accepted my place in this world many, many years ago. Balor needs to be contained—"

"And we can contain him once we escape the maze," I interrupt, turning to face Barret completely and trusting my men to hold off Balor if he decides to attack. Not that he'll be stupid enough to, considering he's severely outnumbered. We might not be able to kill him, but I'm sure Jack and Hux will forgive us for a little light maiming.

"Cheese Curd…"

"Barret…" I mimic his tone, capturing his hands with both of mine. "All of us are getting out of here. Together." I twist to address the other men as well. Vin still looks irritated, though he always looks like someone pissed in his Cheerios, and Frankie appears distressed by something. Mason flashes me a soft smile, and Cal gives me a nod of solidarity. And Balor…

The smug asshole is staring at his goddamn nails as if he's thinking about getting a manicure or some shit after this is all over.

"Together," Barret whispers, squeezing my hands before instantly releasing them.

"Everybody hold on to each other," Vin cautions, already wrapping his hand around Balor's bicep and yanking him forward. "We need to go through at the exact same time in order to be declared winners. Do you guys understand?"

"Ohhh. Keep manhandling me. I like it," Balor singsongs, and Vin growls at him to shut up.

"Who has Alex?" I demand, realizing that Cal must've dropped him during the standoff against Balor.

"I do," Mason says. He kneels down, swings Alex's body over his shoulders, and shakily rises to his feet. "Fuck, he's a heavy asshole."

"Let's do this," I say seriously, reaching my hands out to capture Cal's with one and Frankie's with the other. I wait until we're all chained up before turning my attention toward the silver portal of light. "On the count of three. One—"

"Three!" Balor calls cheerfully.

And as one, we step through the portal.

The first thing that greets me is the roar of the monsters, the cheer of the crowd.

At least, they're cheering until they see who steps out.

Shocked gasps ripple through the assembled masses before silence descends.

I glance down the line of men surrounding me, reassuring myself that they're all here and okay, before focusing on Mummy, who parts the crowd with a wave of his hand. I can't see his expression with the bandages wrapped around his face, but his eyes are bright. Smiling, even.

"Ladies and gentlemen, monsters and ghouls!" he bellows, though he doesn't need to. The crowd is utterly silent. I swear I could hear a pin drop. "I present to you, the winners of this year's Roaring!"

Silence.

Cloying, oppressive silence.

And then…

Raucous cheers and yells surround us. Some of the audience members get to their feet and clap. Others boo and scream and holler that we must've cheated.

Their opinions don't even matter. They slide through one ear and out the other.

We…

We won.

We actually fucking won.

We're the winners of this year's Roaring. Cal, Barret, Hux, and Jack have their freedom.

I'm distantly aware of some healers rushing forward to take Alex from Cal, of Stefan Van Helsing stalking forward to congratulate his son, of Vanessa cheering our names enthusiastically, of—

Wait. Where's Dimitri?

I scan the crowd, searching for the stoic headmaster, but can't catch a glimpse of his white hair anywhere. Something dark claws at my throat as my heart thumps unevenly.

Why isn't he here?

I glance toward the men on either side of me, and my panic intensifies when I notice that Balor is no longer with us. I'm one hundred percent positive he was there a mere second earlier, to the right of Vin.

"Where the fuck is Balor?" I have to raise my voice to be heard over the roar of the crowd, but it captures Vin's attention. He turns away from his father and focuses on me.

"I don't know," he grunts out. "He was right here one fucking second ago—"

"Violet!" Dimitri materializes in front of me, and a torrent of relief washes over me. That relief turns into trepidation when I take in his frazzled appearance. His eyes land on my shoulder, my forehead, my collarbone…anywhere and everywhere but my inquisitive eyes.

"What's going on?" I demand.

He shakes his head, seemingly at a loss for words, before gritting out, "We need to go."

"Go?" My brows furrow, the rushing of blood in my head drowning out the cheers of the crowd. Everything seems to be happening in slow motion, almost as if my brain can't quite compute what my eyes and ears are seeing and hearing.

Dimitri turns to address the audience while I struggle to get my bearings, struggle to orient myself to a rapidly spinning world. He says something I can't hear, something that exacerbates my migraine and amplifies the cheers of the crowd, before putting a hand on the small of my back and guiding me off the tiny stage and toward the academic building. I can hear the footsteps of my men behind me, but they're a distant sound, barely audible over the rapid pounding of my heart.

All I know with unwavering certainty is that something happened, something bad, and if we don't get out of here soon, all of this work will be for nothing.

We'll die before we get even a chance to enjoy this precious freedom we fought so hard to receive.

VIOLET

"Dimitri, where are we going? What's going on?" I fire off as I follow him through the twining halls of the academic building and toward his office. His pace is brisk, forcing me to run in order to keep up with him. And after all the running, fighting, and diving I did inside the maze a few minutes earlier? Your homegirl here needs a break. "Dimitri!" I snap, my thin patience splintering with every second of silence.

He whirls around to face me, his eyes frantic and his already pale skin translucent with fear. That terror—the likes of which I've never seen on his face before—tightens his features, crinkles his nose, and causes his white brows to dip low over ice-cold eyes. "Not here."

"I don't like this," Frankie murmurs to me, moving to stand on my other side. I interlock my fingers with his, seeking comfort in his apathetic neutrality, before continuing on down the hall.

"We need to get a portal open and Violet through it.

Now," Dimitri tells us, pushing open the door to his office and gesturing for us to enter. It's cramped with all of us in one location, and I find myself sandwiched between Cal and Frankie. Not the worst position for a girl to be in…

"What's going on, Gray?" Vin snaps, his fingers twitching by his sides as if he's imagining wrapping them around the hilts of his blades. "What's the meaning of this?"

"I'll explain later." Dimitri stands in front of a mirror on the wall and begins to chant under his breath. And for the first time…I see his reflection.

The legend of Dimitri and Dorian Gray describes a painting that is tied to their souls. Apparently over time, the painting becomes even more hideous and grotesques with every sin they commit. What a lot of people don't know, however, is that you're able to see their souls through mirrors as well.

As his long lashes flutter shut, caressing his high cheek-bones, I study him uninterrupted.

He really is a beautiful man, all chiseled features and hard planes. The softness of his lips is juxtaposed by his cleft chin and those icy blue eyes which seem to see into my very soul.

In the mirror, he appears…different. I don't quite know how to articulate it with words. He still looks like the Dimitri Gray I've come to know and lust over, but there's a heady smoke that seems to hover around him. A gray smoke—not necessarily black but also not pure white. A few scars mar his perfect skin, but they're not as numerous as I would've expected from an esteemed monster serial killer and assassin. It's almost as if his soul isn't tarnished by hate and vengeance, as if there's still hope for him.

My thoughts cut off when he steps backward, revealing a mirror that is now a swirling abyss of bright pink stars.

A portal.

"Hurry up," he barks, gesturing for us to move in front of him. "You need to get—"

"Headmaster Gray." Charles Thethird, as he likes to be addressed by, steps into the room with a subservient dip of his head. I still think Thethird is a strange last name, but who am I to judge rich, pretentious assholes? "Our special guest would like to see the victors now."

Special guest? Why don't I like the sound of that?

"What's the meaning of this, Gray?" Mason murmurs under his breath, closing in behind me until his chest is flush against my back. His arms band around my waist, holding me protectively against his front.

Dimitri releases a heavy sigh, something akin to resignation flaring in his eyes before he conceals it. He ignores Mason's question and focuses on the gamemaker.

"Yes, yes," he says to Charles Thethird before turning toward us. "Come with me." He takes a few steps toward the door before pausing, his hand clenching the frame tight enough to turn his knuckles white. "Violet? Why don't you grab the thing out of your room before you join us?"

The thing?

What crack is Dimitri smoking, and where can I get it?

"Vin, go with her," Dimitri adds with a dismissive wave of his hand, already stalking forward.

Charles Thethird clears his throat. "Our special guest specifically requested that all of the victors attend." As an afterthought, he hastily adds, "Sir."

Dimitri's jaw clenches, visible even with half of his back facing me.

"Very well," he manages to grit out. "Come along."

We move down the halls of the academic building and to a section of the school that houses conference rooms. Leaning toward Frankie, I whisper, "I don't like this."

"I don't like it either." His nose wrinkles as if he's gotten a waft of something particularly repugnant. "But what else can we do?"

"Pretend to be possums and play dead?" I suggest.

"Don't know if that'll work, Pinkie," Mason says from behind me, but not like he's completely dismissing my idea. Even he can admit it holds some merit.

"Sure it will," I protest immediately. "You just have to—" I dramatically open my eyes as wide as they will go and allow my tongue to dart out before falling backward like a plank of wood. Mason catches me before I can go splat on the ground, as I knew he would.

He stares at me for a long moment before he heaves out a breath. "If you want to play dead, Pinkie, you have to remember not to blink."

My voice is muffled from how far out my tongue is. "I'm not blinking," I say…as my lashes flutter rapidly against my cheeks. Dammit.

"Sure you're not." His lips twitch in amusement as he sets me back down on my feet. He reaches for my hand before he's pushed to the side by Cal.

"My turn," he huffs out, annoyance tinging those two words. "We all know I'm the superior hand holder here."

"Cal, we talked about this. You need to tone it down a couple dozen notches." I bite down on my lip to conceal the giddy grin that wants to unfurl across my face, pressing closer against his side. "But I'm really happy you're here."

Warmth invades his eyes, replacing the cockiness from mere seconds ago, and he leans forward to press a chaste kiss against my forehead. "Me too, baby. Me too."

"Violet," Dimitri's voice is low as to not be overheard by Charles Thethird, "stay near the back of the group."

"I really don't understand what the fuck is—"

We step inside the conference room, and the room spins. Stops. Tilts on its axis, throwing me about like a rag doll.

A tall, arresting man stands on the other side of the room, his hands clasped behind his back as he studies the books on the bookshelf. When he turns toward us, an enigmatic grin pulling up his lips, I feel as if my head has been cracked open with a sledgehammer and brain goo is cascading down around me. The hard angles of his face are accentuated by a dark beard and mustache that are a shade darker than his mop of hair. His features are cold and alert despite the friendly smile adorning his face. A white suit clings to his tall, muscular figure as he regards us.

But it's his smile that makes me pause, makes my entire body tense up as if a puppeteer is tugging on my strings.

Because it's *my* smile.

I can see the exact moment my mates come to the same conclusion I just did. All of them move to conceal me from his view, subtly rearranging their positions until I'm near the back of the crowd, short enough not to be seen. For once, I'm praising my bio mom's tiny genes. Not that her genes are tiny, per se, but she's a rather short woman for a goddess, so she must—

"Gentleman!" The stranger's voice booms through the conference room as he spreads his arms out wide. I peek around Cal's wings to see him better. "My name is Lucifer Morningstar—"

Hundreds and hundreds of poisonous spiders begin to crawl through my stomach.

"—and I wanted to congratulate you personally for winning the Roaring."

Mason recovers first, flashing a charming smile in the man's direction. Not just any man—but my birth father. And the creator of all monsters. And the ruler of Hell. And the supreme overlord of evil. And—

"It's a pleasure to meet you. Heard good things about your work. Impressive Yelp reviews in Hell," Mase rambles. "I've been thinking about taking a trip down there myself one of these days."

Dimitri makes a noncommittal noise in the back of his throat, a combination of a grunt and a growl, before smoothing over his expression. Charles Thethird, who still stands beside Dimitri, cowers slightly.

"It's funny you should mention that…" Lucifer's grin widens like the vampire who ate the asshole. "Because I want to offer you guys an all-expense-paid trip to Hell."

Cue—five bodies suddenly tensing in alarm. Only Dimitri remains calm, though I suspect it's because he already knew what Lucifer was going to offer.

"Ohhh…" Mason trails off when he realizes how badly he fucked up by saying he wanted to visit Hell. "That's mighty generous of you," he finishes at last.

Lucifer throws his head back in laughter. "Yes. I've been hearing about how generous I am all day." His eyes shift to Dimitri, who keeps his expression cold and impassive. When Lucifer glances back toward our group, his gaze seems to fixate on where I'm hidden behind Cal's red wings. "Who is the little one in the back? Step forward, child. Let me see you."

"Ummm…"

Think fast, Violet. Think fast.

"No thanks!" I holler, masking my voice by making it incredibly high-pitched. And then I remember that he never met me before so I'm allowed to keep my normal voice. Clearing my throat, I add, in a much lower and masculine tone, "No thanks."

Dammit.

Lucifer's eyes flare, his power pulsating through the room and causing the tiny blonde hairs on my arms to stand at attention. "No thanks?" A note of warning leaks from those two words in tangible waves.

"I'm…just…" Scrambling to come up with an excuse, I blurt the first thing I can think of, "I'm ugly. I'm so, so ugly that I don't dare be in your presence, your excellency. I make babies cry all the time. Like, I step outside, and women faint and men run after me with pitchforks. When I was born, the doctor took one look at my ass and one look at my face and announced to my mom that she was having twins. Funny story—I once stopped traffic because I was walking down the sidewalk and the paper bag I always keep over my head blew off. Twenty people died…and only five of them were because of the car accident. The rest passed away simply because they stared too long at my ugliness."

Silence descends over us all as I shift awkwardly from foot to foot, peeking at Lucifer around Cal's shoulder.

Nobody speaks—nobody dares to—until Lucifer releases an elongated sigh and raises a single finger in the air, crooking it in the universal 'come-hither' gesture.

"Come here."

It's not a suggestion.

Bracing myself, I step around my men's muscular bodies and come face to face with the man who spermed me.

Wait. That sounds wrong. Ignore that.

Lucifer lazily glances up from where he was focusing on a smudge on the wooden table. And then…

It's a gradual procession—one thing after another as time stands still. First, his eyes go comically wide and he stumbles over his own two feet, something I never thought I would see the great and powerful Lucifer Morningstar do. Next, his mouth drops open as pure and unbridled shock splays across his features. Finally, his arms lift into the air, reaching toward me.

"It can't be," he murmurs, recognition sparking in his eyes.

Before I can respond—though I have no idea what the

fuck I even want to say—the door to the conference room opens behind us. We all turn to look, but dark, cloying gray smoke obscures my vision, enters my nostrils, burns my throat. Darkness blankets my vision as I try to ward off the growing dizziness.

Attack.

We're under attack.

And then darkness pulls me under.

CHAPTER 36

VIOLET

"**B**loody anus tits," I murmur, my head lolling against my chest.

What...?

Where...?

My head jerks upright so fast, I feel a little lightheaded.

What the fuckity fuck of all the fucks?

I appear to be in a tiny room, the white walls and white flooring giving it a stark, unwelcoming feel. Aside from the chair I'm sitting in—read as, aside from the chair I'm tied to —there's nothing else in the room with me. At least, nothing I can see, though I suspect there might be something or someone behind me. A drain rests in the very center of the room, where the floor caves downward.

Yup. I don't like this.

Nope. Not today, Satan. Not today.

Is Lucifer behind this?

He must be. How else would someone have gotten the drop on us? Obviously, he discovered the truth about who I am and sent some of his minions to kidnap and kill me. But then why did he look so surprised when he saw me? Was it because he thought I died in the maze? Was he shocked that I found my way out and won the Roaring like the badass bitch I know myself to be?

But when the door to the bright white room opens a few minutes later, it's not Lucifer who steps inside.

It's Stefan Van Helsing.

My lips pull away from my teeth before I can stop them, my fangs popping downward and breaking the skin of my lower lip.

"You…" I hiss as anger thrums through me, a large ball of electrical energy. "You did this."

Ugh. He'll definitely not earn any father-in-law of the year awards.

Darkness descends across his face, his lips twisting into a hideous scowl. He steps forward, out of sight, and I hear the distinct sound of metal clanking against metal.

I was right in my initial assessment.

There *is* something in the room behind me.

Fuck.

When he returns, crowding my vision with his sneering face, a god-blessed dagger rests in his hand, the copper handle an extension of his body. The metal blade glints ominously in the artificial lighting.

"You need to pay for all that you've done," Stefan hisses.

"What exactly do you think I did that I need to pay for?" I try to keep the fear out of my voice, the panic, but it creeps in unbidden.

He brandishes the weapon in front of my face, his body taut and ready to spring. "You murdered Christopher."

"I didn't—"

"No," he interrupts scathingly. "I know that you technically didn't." Sharp eyes land on my face, stabbing at my skin repeatedly. "But you know who did."

"I don't know jack shit," I spit out. I'll die before I give up the truth about Cal.

And if the manic gleam in his eyes is any indication? He knows that. It's what he wants.

"Christopher was a good man," Stefan continues, pacing. "A strong warrior for our cause."

"Your cause?" A bark of dry, bitter laughter escapes me. "You mean hating vampires because you're weak, pathetic creatures who—"

"Shut the fuck up!" Spit flies out of Stefan's mouth with the force of his yell. "You guys are cockroaches, plagues to humanity—"

"You can keep telling yourself that all you want to make yourself feel better about your pointless, worthless cause—" The slap forces my head to the side, pain reverberating through my cheek.

"I said shut up," Stefan tells me darkly, lowering his hand back to his side and caressing the edge of his blade. That *goddamn* blade—literally.

The only thing in the world that can kill me.

I doubt a wooden stake will do much, now that I know I'm not truly a vampire, but a weapon forged from the gods themselves? Yeah, I can see that doing some major damage.

"Is this really about your hatred for the vampires?" I ask, ignoring the throbbing in my cheek and the impending violence in his eyes—the type of violence that will leave me a mess of bruises and scars that will never heal properly, even after centuries of rehabilitation. There are some things that can't be fixed, can't be bandaged or stitched back together with thread. Torture is one of them. "Or is this about my friendship with Vanessa and Vin—"

"You filthy whore!" Another slap has my head snapping to

the side, red stars erupting across my vision. "I don't know what my children see in you, and honestly? I don't care. If Vin wants to get his dick wet, then so be it. At the end of the day, he'll come back to me. He'll always come back to me." He sounds so sure of himself, so smug, that I want to laugh.

This fucker is completely delusional if he thinks Vin will *ever* choose him over me.

"Or is this about Christopher?" I continue, unable to resist poking the metaphorical bear. "You and I both know that he wasn't the outstanding citizen you made him out to be. He abused his wife and kids—"

"Shut the fuck up!" he bellows in my face, his own turning red and then purple with anger.

And then…

Realization settles in my stomach like a bloody bowling ball.

"Christopher wasn't just a friend, was he?" I whisper as I stare at the broken, angry man standing before me. That hurt… It only stems from someone who lost the person they loved more than life itself. "He was your mate, wasn't he?"

I don't need him to confirm or deny my theory, but I can see in his eyes that what I'm saying is the truth. That's why Christopher's death hurt him so badly, that's why he wants retribution and vengeance.

They weren't just friends and colleagues. They were lovers.

Stefan's hand is around my throat before I can even blink, squeezing, squeezing, squeezing, and squeezing until I fear I'll pass out again.

"Don't you dare speak of things you know nothing about," he hisses in my ear, his voice a lethal bark.

A strangled gasp escapes my throat in lieu of an answer, and he releases me with a disgusted growl.

My breathing is shallow, erratic spurts of air, and I

desperately want to rub at my throat where his hands just were. Instead, I manage to choke out, "How did you do it, anyway? How did you kidnap me? What was the gas you threw into the room?"

"God-blessed daggers crumbled up and made into a gas by Frankenstein himself," Stefan answers, flashing me a cunning smile. At my look of disbelief, he adds, "Don't worry. Frankenstein didn't know what I planned to use the gas for or who I planned to use it on…but that doesn't mean he won't kill you if he has the chance. You may be his son's mate, but you're still vampire scum."

Something cold and sinister unravels in my chest like an angry python, squeezing every organ it passes as it travels through my body. "You know about that?"

"I know a lot of things, Violet Dracula." He lowers himself to his knees and places his hands on both of my thighs. The blade of his god-blessed dagger nicks my skin, but I keep my expression aloof, not allowing him to see even a glimpse of the pain I feel. "Like, I know all of those men are your mates, including my good-for-nothing son." His lips curl into a distasteful sneer. "One of the reasons I need to eliminate you once and for all—before you can ruin him."

"I love him—Ahhh!" Pain blossoms in my thigh, and I lower my tear-filled eyes to the dagger protruding from my skin, blood soaking my shorts.

"Vampires don't love," Stefan whispers, brutally ripping the dagger out of my skin and wiping it on my shirt.

"Motherfucker!" I scream, trying to ignore the agony racing through my bloodstream, setting my insides on fire. "Fuck."

"Did you know," Stefan begins conversationally, his eyes intent on the bloody knife in his hand, "that you can use god-blessed daggers on all-powerful entities as well? It won't kill them, but it does hurt like a fucker." His eyes snap to mine.

"That was the only way we could keep Lucifer down, you know. The gas didn't take him out, so we were forced to fight him head-on. Thirty to one. We lost good men in that battle before we were finally able to stab the father of all monsters in the heart." He once again bends at the waist until we're eye to eye. "Why is that? Why is he fighting for you, Violet Dracula? Are you fucking him as well?"

"Eww! No! Just let me go!" Tears rush down my cheeks before I can stop them, but fuck, this hurts like a bitch.

"I've killed a lot of vampires over the years. Crystal, Sherry, Bebe, Ali…but none of them are going to be as satisfying to me as it will be to stab my knife into your chest and pluck your black heart out." He brings the dagger down to my untouched thigh and stabs me with it.

A scream rips free of my throat before I can contain it, before I can bite it down. "Fuck you!"

Murmurs behind the closed door to the torture room capture both of our attentions. Stefan's grin widens on his face, his features suddenly bearing a striking resemblance to Vin, before he stifles it.

"Ahh. My playmates have arrived." Stefan stands, uncaring that he still has blood on his hands, and moves to open the door to let his friends enter. I vaguely recognize the first man as one of Vin's relatives—perhaps a cousin?—but the second man gives me a pause. He has bright blue skin, darker blue hair, and gills that cover his entire muscular body.

The Loch Ness Monster.

And behind him, her head lowered and orange hair cascading around her face, is Cheryl fucking Ness.

"You!" I seethe, and her head snaps up, her eyes widening in alarm. Genuine shock splays across her face when she sees me, and she glances at her father in surprise.

"Boys, are you ready to have your fun with the little

vampire bitch?" Stefan asks, stepping aside to let Loch and Van Helsing Douche come forward.

"She's not bleeding enough," Loch says. At least, I think that's what he says. His voice is a strange combination of dolphin screeches and English. Bubbles pour from his mouth as he grabs the proffered dagger from Stefan.

"We can change that," Van Helsing Douche murmurs with a malicious grin. Before I can even think of a witty come-back, he punches me in the face, forcing my head to jerk to the side.

Cheryl gasps out loud behind them, but I don't pay her any mind.

"Fuck you all. Fuck you and your tiny dicks and your unsatisfied wives—"

Agony explodes in my stomach, and I cry out. Only my eyes move to glance down at the dagger inside of my abdomen, Loch's fingers still wrapped around the hilt.

"I would think a prisoner like you would have some manners," he hisses, and I would've found his high-pitched, dolphin voice almost comical if I wasn't in such agonizing pain.

Unable to stop being a badass—I refuse to die cowering —I bite out, "And I would think you would take some medi-cine to help you get an erection, but we can't—FUCK!" Strangled sobs rip free of my lips as I stare at the second dagger in my arm. Blood. Blood everywhere. I'm covered in it.

"Cheryl, darling, grab a weapon and come help your father!" Loch calls, barely sparing his child a glance. There's a beat of silence, and then I hear the thump of footsteps as she races toward the table of tools and torture devices just out of my line of sight. I hate that more than anything else. If I were able to see the collection of weapons, I would know what to expect. Instead, the objects on the table are nothing but a mystery, one that's impossible for me to decipher until it's too late.

"We're going to make you scream, Violet Dracula," Stefan promises. "And then we're going to kill you."

"Good luck with that, assholes." I spit out the blood that has formed inside of my mouth and grant them a rare, malevolent grin. "If you know the truth about my mates, then you know that they'll never stop coming for you. That they'll feast on your blood and your guts—fucking hell!" My head drops forward, darkness blanketing my vision, as pain splinters from my other arm where yet another dagger embeds itself inside of my skin.

These men…

They're the worst kind of monsters. They don't care about anything except the need to see me bleed, the need to make me suffer. I know with unwavering certainty that I'm not going to make it out of this room alive.

They're going to kill me, and they'll do so with matching smiles.

Something slices at my hands tied behind my back, and at first, I think it's one of the assholes intending to cause me more harm. But when the rope restraining me falls to the ground, I realize it's not any of them.

It's Cheryl.

What the fuck?

Van Helsing Douche moves to stand in front of me, his dagger pointed at my eye.

"I always wondered how a vampire would look with no eyes…" He lowers the hand holding the dagger in a swooping arc, and I don't even have time to raise my arms and defend myself.

I don't need to.

One second, his arm is lowering, and the next, he's halfway across the room, Cheryl on top of him.

"Stop!" she begs tearfully as she grapples with the knife. Loch screams her name, but not as if he's fearful for her life. More as if he's angry at her for daring to intervene.

Cheryl dies in a span of seconds.

One moment, she's on top of Van Helsing Douche, attempting to get the knife from him, and the next, she's on her back, that very dagger in her forehead.

It's quick and sudden and not at all the dramatic death I would've expected. But that's the way death truly is. You don't get a warning or a dramatic goodbye. You just…die.

She's dead.

Cheryl Ness is dead.

And she died protecting me.

Something twists and tightens inside of me, almost like a padlock falling to the ground and freeing the monster within. I suppose you can say that I get unleashed, a fierce anger and indignation I never felt before surging through me in almost palpable waves.

I can't tell you what happens next.

I want to describe it as a blackout, though I'm not sure if that's an adequate description. Maybe I just get so focused on the bloodlust and rage that I lose a tiny piece of my mind, if only for a second. Or maybe…

Maybe the monster that Lucifer and Hera created finally gets set free.

All I know for certain is that when I open my eyes, I'm standing in a pool of thick red blood. Bloody parts are strewn in every direction—hands, fingers, arms, intestines, hearts, heads, and even a wayward penis. Their bodies are unrecognizable, nothing but bloody slabs of meat.

Only Cheryl remains untouched, as if my monster moved her to a corner of the room to give her some semblance of peace and dignity. Her hands are clasped together on top of her stomach, and I must've shut her eyes at one point.

But it doesn't change the fact that blood covers every inch of the room.

Oh god...

My stomach tightens, bile creeping up my mouth, and it takes every ounce of willpower I possess not to vomit.

Blood.

Bodies

Death.

Oh god.

Oh god.

Oh god.

The door to the torture room is thrown open, and I turn in alarm to see Dimitri Gray and some of the other professors stomping inside, their features stone-cold and determined. All of them freeze when they take in the death and destruction visible throughout the room.

"I can explain," I whisper brokenly, my eyes flicking from the blood staining every inch of me to Dimitri's horrified stare.

"Did you kill these monsters, Violet?" Mummy asks, stepping forward, his tone laced with horror and sympathy.

My mouth opens, closes, and then opens again, the copper tang of blood staining my tongue.

"I can explain," I repeat.

Another of my professors—Mr. Pumpkin, no relation to the man Cal killed in the maze or Cynthia's mate—steps forward.

"Violet Dracula, you know the rules about killing monsters outside of the games." Sympathy clouds his eyes before they harden, turning to stone. "You are under arrest for the murder of—"

"Wait!" I beg, stepping backward instinctively. I turn pleading eyes onto Dimitri, but he doesn't meet my gaze.

"—Stefan Van Helsing, Loch Ness, Christopher—"

"Please wait," I beg, tremors rumbling through my body.

Blood.

So much blood.

So much death.

You did this, Violet. You killed them.

"—detention for the next one thousand years," Mr. Pumpkin finishes, slapping a pair of magic-infused handcuffs around my wrists.

Oh god.

No.

I don't know if it's exhaustion, pain, or fear of what's to come, but I find myself tilting precariously to the side as dark butterflies flit across my vision. Dimitri rushes forward, just barely catching me before I fall, fall, fall.

And for the second time that day, I'm aware of nothing.

CHAPTER 37

BALOR

Today's the day.

Today, I'll bring my people home.

My monsters.

The old gods and goddesses that have been warped by time, becoming beasts that are barely recognizable.

My hands are slick with sweat, with heady anticipation, as I storm into the conference room I know Lucifer to be in. According to my sources, he's been distraught all day, though they haven't been able to uncover why.

No matter. The more distressed he is, the easier it'll be for me to make my case.

He doesn't glance up when I enter, his back arched over the wooden table and his hands clenched into tight fists. I can tell he senses my presence, but he doesn't speak, not at first.

After a moment, he growls out, "Balor."

"Lucifer." I nod cordially, but everything inside of me

wants to leap across the table and rip his head clear from his body.

We don't waste time with pleasantries. Slowly, Lucifer lifts his head and pierces me with a dark glare. "I know why you're here."

"Then you know I'll do just about anything to get my people back," I respond without preamble, allowing a healthy dose of the hatred I feel for him to seep into my voice.

"You know I can't allow that to happen." He suddenly appears tired, bone-weary, something I never thought I would see on the great Lucifer Morningstar. His eyes fall to a stain marring the smooth mahogany table.

"No?" I flash him a cocky smile and move to claim the seat opposite him at the table. "Then let's talk about something else, shall we?" I tap my chin, pretending to contemplate it, before dropping all pretenses and glaring at him with all the hatred and fury I possess. "Take...your daughter, perhaps?"

He stiffens, the move almost imperceptible, before sliding his hard eyes back to me.

"I'm listening."

A cold grin cuts my face in two as I recline in the seat. "Perfect."

To be continued...

ACKNOWLEDGMENTS

Thank you so much to my team of alpha and beta readers! Without your input, this book wouldn't be what it is today.

A special thank you to my incredible family for sticking with and supporting me.

Thank you to Jennifer, for being able to edit my book at the last second! And I would also like to thank Logan for making such an incredible cover.

And finally, I would like to thank you, the reader, for joining me on Violet's journey. I know it's been a while, but I appreciate you guys sticking with me. I hope to have Prodigium Academy 4 out very soon!

Prodigium Academy (Horror Comedy Academy Reverse Harem)

1. Monsters

2. Roaring

3. Venom

Tory's School for the Trouble (Bully Horror Academy Reverse Harem)

1. Between

2. Beyond

3. Beneath

Kings of Grove Academy (Contemporary Academy Reverse Harem)

1. Mania

2. Psychotic

Supernaturalette (Interactive Reverse Harem)

1. Introductions

2. First Dates

3. Group Outing

4. Game Night

5. Exes

6. Truth or Dare

CO-WRITES

Afterworld Academy with Loxley Savage (Academy Fantasy Reverse Harem, COMPLETED)

1. Dearly Departed

2. Darkness Deceives

3. Defying Destiny

Darkest Flames with Ann Denton (Paranormal Reverse Harem,
COMPLETED)

1. Demon Kissed

1.5. Demon Stalked

2. Demon Loved

3. Demon Sworn

STAND-ALONES

Toxicity (Contemporary Reverse Harem)

Not All Heroes Wear Capes (Just Dresses) (Short Comedic Reverse
Harem)

Charming Devils (Bully/Revenge Reverse Harem)

Goddess of Pain (Fantasy Reverse Harem)

Demon's Joy (Holiday Reverse Harem)